return ticket
traffic warden mysteries

Michelle Diener

about return ticket

It's autumn, 1963, and there's a dark cloud hanging over London. Literally.

The thick, impenetrable smog is the perfect cover for a killer who's stalking the streets, not that traffic warden, Gabriella Farnsworth, knows that when she's approached by three young boys who say they've found a body.

When her boyfriend, Detective Sergeant James Archer, gets assigned the case, he begins to build a picture of the killer's patterns and becomes increasingly nervous every time the smog settles over the city.

Especially when bodies are found once the mist clears.

Gabriella's diverse contacts on the street provide vital information that help James understand that these murders are not the start of a killing spree, they are a continuation of one that came before.

They'll have to go back to what happened during the Blitz, to another time when London was shrouded in darkness, to find the clues to catch the man who's returned to kill again.

James and Gabriella know that they have to solve the mystery before the next fog descends, because when it does, the killer will strike again.

chapter
one

BASTARD INCOMING.

That's what Gabriella's colleague and friend Liz called what was about to happen.

Gabriella had to admit, it was a perfect description.

She wrote out the ticket on Kings Road in Chelsea, listening to the sound of shouting and swearing drawing closer.

She refused to scrawl and run, which every nerve in her body was urging her to do, as a man moved toward her like a storm, spewing thunder and lightning. Instead, she held her ground, carefully filling in the details as he got louder and closer.

When he was a few car-lengths away, she could finally make out what he was screaming.

"Hands off my car!" He slammed a fist into a parked vehicle he passed as he moved toward her, and she heard the meaty smack of it and tried not to flinch.

She slipped the fixed penalty notice into its plastic sleeve and had just begun to tape it to the windscreen of the Land Rover when Shouty Man arrived.

"Give that to me." He ripped the plastic sleeve off the window, and tried to tear it, but the plastic was too robust and he struggled with it for a few moments, his face red, his massive hands twisting as he tried to rend it down the middle.

Eventually, humiliated, he worked out he had to pull the ticket out, and he did, throwing it on the ground and jumping up and down on it a few times.

Gabriella had taken a step back, and as she watched the tantrum, a well of laughter bubbled up inside her. Nerves, she admitted, but also, it was funny to see a middle-aged man act like a baby.

Passersby began to stop and look and he seemed to come to himself, aware that he had a growing audience. He raised his arm and shook his fist. "What are you staring at?"

"A grown man acting like a toddler," a woman with the clear, crystal-cut accent of the upper west end, opined, lifted her nose and walked off, her little dog trotting by her side.

"Bitch," the man muttered under his breath, but her comment seemed to have taken the wind out of his sails.

Gabriella saw he was dressed in rough trousers and jacket, and the smell of cow manure coming from the tires that she had caught a few whiffs of while she had filled out the penalty notice suddenly made sense.

She had herself a farmer, on a foray into the Big Smoke.

"Jumping up and down on it won't help," she said, keeping her tone crisp and even. "If you can't afford to pay, you can contact the city and work out a payment plan." She gave a nod and hitched her satchel up on her shoulder as she began to walk her route again.

"Can't afford . . ." The farmer spluttered. "I'll have you know, girlie, I have twenty trucks coming into the city every market day. And every single one of them seems to have a fine by the end of the day. It's daylight robbery!"

Gabriella shook her head and kept walking, not willing to engage any further.

The thunder of boots behind her made her heart leap in her chest as a heavy hand came down on her shoulder, and she was spun around.

"Now see here . . ." His face was right up in hers, skin flushed, mustache quivering. The stink of stale tobacco wafted off him.

"Sir." She tried to shrug his hand off. "I don't make the rules. My job is to follow the law. If you have a problem with it, take it up with the lawmakers." She wanted to knock his arm away with her own, but she was afraid to provoke him any more than he was already provoked.

"You need some help there, miss?" One of the men who had been watching the incident from the start, having just gotten out of his Plymouth a few parking spots down, asked.

"Do I need some help, sir?" Gabriella asked him.

The farmer looked at his hand, lifted it, and took a step back. Shook his head, and stomped off, muttering under his breath.

Gabriella gave the Plymouth driver a nod of thanks, and swung back to her route.

There wasn't a day that went by without some excitement, but this one pushed the limits.

She turned down a smaller street, just to have a bit of time to get herself back together, and saw three boys up ahead.

From their furtive behavior, they looked up to no good. Her stomach sank, because she did not feel like another argument, but rather than run away, they ran toward her, faces a little pale under the dirt and smudges on their cheeks.

"Miss, miss!" The one in front's eyes went to her uniform. "Youse the police?"

"Traffic warden," Gabriella said. "But I can get the police. What's wrong?"

"We found a body, miss." The second boy nearly ran into the back of his friend. "In the rubble."

"In the rubble," the third boy echoed, pointing back the way they'd come.

Gabriella knew which rubble they meant. One of the final half blocks destroyed during the war that had yet to be cleared and rebuilt.

Something to do with an argument over who owned it, she'd heard.

"What kind of body?" she asked. She didn't think they were lying, they looked too shocked, but she didn't want to call the police and then find it was a cat or something.

"Maybe a lady?" the first boy said. "The shoe is a lady's shoe."

"Can you tell me where?" Gabriella asked, walking in the direction they'd come. "You don't have to show me."

"Protecting evidence," Boy Two said, sagely, but she thought she caught an undercurrent of relief in his voice.

"That's right," she agreed.

"Where'd you learn that, Billie?" Boy Three asked.

"Me bruvver's detective magazines. Gets 'em from America, he does."

They had reached the rubble, and Billie pointed to the top of the pile. "Up there, miss, over the top of the bricks. Just out of sight over the other side."

Hidden from the street, Gabriella thought. "Thank you, boys. You wait here, I'll just do a quick check."

She was wearing her sturdy shoes, but still the going was treacherous. Some of the bricks had been crushed into small, sharp pieces, others balanced on each other precariously. By the time she reached the top of the pile she was sweating, despite the cool autumn weather. She had begun to smell the decomposition long before then, though.

She had to breathe through her mouth to stop herself from retching by the time she could see over the side.

A woman lay, half-buried under debris, one stockinged foot outstretched, the shoe a little distance away. A hand reached out to the side, with a delicate watch on the wrist, although her skin was purpling and swollen with decomposition. Her jacket was a neat houndstooth.

Gabriella carefully reversed as the ground shifted beneath her feet. She was relieved to have something to focus on that wasn't the death and desecration behind her.

When she reached the road again, the boys were still there.

"It's real, isn't it?" Boy One asked.

They had been hoping she would tell them they were wrong, she realized.

She gave a grim nod. "It's real."

She looked around, saw there were no shops down this road, only a few narrow entrances that she guessed were to the flats in the low buildings that lined the road.

This was a pricey area, but the flats opposite would be affordable housing while a pile of rubble lay across from them as the only view.

She headed back toward the Kings Road, where there would be a telephone box, or perhaps a friendly shopkeeper.

"Where ya going?" Billie asked, as he and his two friends followed behind her.

"To find a phone." She reached the Kings Road, and then, to her deep relief, saw a bobby walking along on the other side of the road.

She knew him. His beat was the same as her own, and they crossed paths regularly.

"Constable Evans!" She gave a wave, and he turned to her in surprise. "I need help."

He was young. Maybe even younger than she was, but he had a ponderous, deliberate way about him.

He more than hit the height requirement for the police force, standing at least six foot four, and she wondered whether his size led to the careful way he had, although James, her boyfriend, was almost as tall and muscular, and he moved with a kind of fluid grace.

Evans checked for traffic and then crossed over to her, his eyes going to the boys. "Trouble?" he asked.

"We found a body," Boy One said. Then he glanced at Billie and Boy Three, as if suddenly wondering if he should have spoken up.

"These boys were playing in the rubble down the alley and

they found a body. I've checked. They aren't mistaken." She grimaced at the thought of what she'd found.

"Bad?" Constable Evans asked.

"Bad," she agreed. "She's been there for a while."

Evans thought about it. "I should stay at the scene. Can you go to the station, let the station commander know?" he asked.

She gave a nod. "The boys can show you where she is."

Her words seemed to both thrill and horrify the boys, but they danced away, impatient for Evans to follow them.

It was the shoe, Gabriella thought with a shiver as she walked toward the Chelsea nick. That's why she felt as if she was floating a little bit above herself.

She had found the body of a young woman just a few months ago, and in a macabre mirror of the scene, Patty's shoe had come off and lain a little way from her foot, just like the woman in the rubble.

She had never wanted to see anything like that again, but now she had.

She gritted her teeth, and walked a little faster.

chapter
two

JAMES WAS WAITING for her when she got back to the Metropolitan traffic warden center.

He was leaning against the wall, head turned her way to watch her approach.

Her heart did a little leap in her chest.

She hadn't seen him for two weeks, although he'd told her he was coming back from his trip to Cardiff yesterday, which was a Sunday.

He looked tired.

She came to a stop in front of him and wished they weren't out on the street, in front of her work, or she would have stepped into his arms and laid her head on his shoulder.

He studied her face. "Go get out of your uniform, and we can go somewhere for tea."

His Welsh accent was a little stronger than usual, the two weeks in Wales giving back what he'd lost after a year in London.

"Give me ten minutes," she said, biting back what she really wanted to say, and slipped past him, up the steps. She pushed open the heavy wooden door and stepped into the cool, slightly musty smelling entrance.

The passage echoed to the sound of her hard-soled shoes on the linoleum as she made her way to her boss's office. Mr. Greenberg would want to know that one of his wardens had encountered a dead body on the beat.

He probably already knew, but she had a feeling he would expect her to tell him herself.

He was in his office, with the door open. "Miss Farnsworth." He looked up as she knocked lightly, and gestured her in.

"Afternoon, Mr. Greenberg. Did the Chelsea nick tell you about the body?"

Mr. Greenberg got to his feet. "The body?"

They obviously hadn't had time yet. Or Mr. Greenberg didn't have a friend there.

"Some boys found a dead woman and approached me, because of the uniform," she said.

"Where?" He turned to the massive map hanging on the wall behind him.

She stepped around his desk and pointed.

"The old Billick building? The bomb site?" He sounded astonished.

"She was half hidden under the rubble." Gabrielle realized she was gripping her satchel extra tight.

"What did you do?" Greenberg asked.

"Fortunately Constable Evans was walking his beat and I hailed him. He stood guard and I went to get help from the nick. Then I carried on with my route." She had been relieved that they didn't think she needed to go back. Almost embarrassingly relieved.

"Well, I'm sorry for that. Did you see the body?" Mr. Greenberg tapped the spot on the map, and then picked up a red pin from the little shelf below the map, and stuck it in.

"Briefly, just to check the boys weren't mistaken." She tucked a strand of hair behind her ear and began to reverse out of the room. "I just thought I'd let you know, sir."

"Appreciate it, Miss Farnsworth." Mr. Greenberg was still studying the map.

She left him to it, going back to the change rooms and getting out of her uniform.

She was pulling on her boots when Liz came in.

"I see Mr. Detective is out there waiting for you," she said as she flopped down on the bench. "Haven't seen him for a while."

"He went home to see his parents. His mother is ill." She hoped Mrs. Archer was better. She knew it worried James that he was so far away.

"And now he's here, waiting for you straight after work." Liz grinned. Then she gave Gabriella's outfit a good once over. "It'll do," she said with a nod.

It forced a laugh out of Gabriella. Liz had a knack of doing that. "Ta very much." She mimicked Liz's favorite saying.

"You have a good evening." There was no subtlety in Liz's eyebrow waggle.

There was no subtlety in Liz, full stop. Gabriella liked her all the more for it.

She gave a wave and left out the front for a change.

James was still leaning against the wall, eyes closed, one foot up against the bricks.

He opened his eyes as she ran down the steps.

"You look tired," she said, hooking her arm through his. "Take me to a grocer's and I'll make you dinner."

His eyes lit up at that. "You're sure?"

"I never joke about food."

Mr. Rodney was at the Calypso Club, Gabriella guessed as they arrived at her building. All the lights were out in his ground floor flat.

She led the way up the stairs, with James carrying the bag of groceries. Jerome's flat was silent, too, and Gabriella guessed he'd probably walked Mr. Rodney over to the club.

"How's your mother?" she asked when they were through the

door. James set the groceries down on her little table and she began to lay out the ingredients she needed for the meal. She had wanted to ask him earlier, but something had made her wait until they had some privacy.

"She seems to be better," James said. "It wasn't as bad as I imagined, although she could have been putting on a good front for me so I wouldn't worry."

He stood beside the table, looking a little unsure of himself.

"Do you think she was doing that?" Gabriella asked, pulling out her chopping board.

He flexed his hands as he lifted his shoulders. "I hope not."

She didn't understand why, but she had the sense he was standing on the edge of a precipice, looking down, and pushed her own shyness and vulnerabilities to the side.

She moved to stand right in front of him, lifted her arms around his neck and lifted up on her toes to kiss him. "It's nice to have you back," she murmured.

He sighed, as if relieving himself of a heavy weight, and drew her closer, kissed her like a man who'd been thinking of kissing her for a while.

"Nice to be back." He held her close to him, his hand running up and down her back as if to convince himself she was really there.

They were stepping out together, as Liz would say, but this felt more. More serious.

They had kept things light, or tried to, after the intensity of the investigation Gabriella had gotten swept up in a few months ago, but she had really missed him when he'd gone up to his parents, and she guessed, from the way he held her now, that he had missed her, too.

"Something's wrong," she said, tipping her head back to look at him.

He hesitated. "My boss. Whetford. Coming back from a break made me realize how difficult he really is."

Gabriella had had the misfortune of being questioned by

Whetford in the past, and she thought he was more than just difficult, but she gave a nod. "I met him, remember?"

James frowned down at her. "I'd forgotten that."

"What's he done?" she asked, stepping back reluctantly to put water on to boil.

James didn't answer right away, and Gabriella looked over her shoulder, curious about his silence.

Eventually he shook his head. "He's lazy, and he's never available."

She had a feeling he was leaving a lot out, but she didn't press.

He joined her at the tiny kitchen counter. "Can I help?"

She decided he needed something to do, so she gave him parmesan to grate at the kitchen table, and busied herself with the rest of the meal.

"Do you have a whole lot of work piled up after your trip?" she asked as she chopped tomatoes.

"Yes." He stretched out on the narrow, wooden chair. "But it's mainly paperwork. How are things going with you?"

She considered not telling him about the body, because discussing it was the last thing she felt like doing, and then realized that was just silly.

She added the spaghetti to the water and turned to lean back against the counter. "Some boys found a woman's body today. They saw my uniform and called me to help."

James pushed up from the table, and she knew he was thinking about what had happened a couple of months ago. Of how much that had affected her. "Where?"

"In Chelsea. Just off the Kings Road. That backstreet with the old bombed building they haven't rebuilt yet." She turned back to the stove and scraped the tomatoes into the saucepan, threw in a pinch of salt.

"Gabriella." He came up behind her, gently turned her to face him. "Are you all right?"

She thought of the mannequin-like arm, thrown out as if reaching for something. The shoe. She shook her head.

"I'm surprised I didn't hear about it," James murmured as he let her turn back to the stove. "Could you see how she was killed?"

"She was half-buried under the rubble, I didn't even see her face." Gabriella took a breath and tossed in some herbs. "She had been there for a bit. Her skin . . ." She shook her head. She shouldn't have brought this up while she was cooking. She felt less and less like eating the meal.

James seemed to realize it, and began to tell her about his trip, about walks in the hills with his father, and his surprise at how differently he saw things since he'd been working in the Big Smoke.

She let him distract her, and neither of them mentioned the woman again.

chapter
three

DETECTIVE CONSTABLE HARTRIDGE looked very relieved to see James.

If James had wondered how things had been in his absence from New Scotland Yard, he thought he could tell by the enthusiastic greeting.

"I'm sorry I didn't see you yesterday, sir," Hartridge said. "DI Whetford had me checking into something for him, and it took me out of the office."

As he explained, the enthusiasm died, replaced by a nervous demeanor. Hartridge seemed worried about what he'd been asked to do.

James realized he and Hartridge would need to talk at some point about Whetford, and how dirty he was, but here in the office, a floor down from Whetford himself, was not the place.

The feeling he'd had yesterday when he'd come into the office after his break had been telling. He had felt depressed. Had wondered what he was doing here, with a boss as bent as Whetford directing him.

He'd left early, gone straight to find Gabriella, and had been on the verge of telling her he wanted to pack up his life in London and go back to Cardiff.

He hadn't, though.

Seeing her, spending time with her, had given him pause. It was way more complicated now that he'd met her.

He would have to think through his options carefully.

"Anything I need to be read in on?" he asked to fill in the silence.

Hartridge hesitated, then seemed to shake off his mood. "No, sir."

"What do we have pending, then?" James had come back to the Yard after his dinner with Gabriella, hot and restless, and had finished up all the paperwork he'd found on his desk.

"No active cases," Hartridge said.

"What about the body found in Chelsea yesterday?" he asked. "Who's been assigned to that?"

Hartridge frowned. "Body? I didn't hear anything about it."

"Some boys found a woman in the rubble of that old building that was bombed in the war. Chelsea is Miss Farnsworth's route, and the boys approached her to help."

"Miss Farnsworth?" Hartridge's eyes widened momentarily. "That's how you know about it?"

James nodded. "She saw the body. Says it was half buried under the rubble."

"Like that woman a month or so ago," Hartridge saw the connection right away. "The one the pathologist said he couldn't determine cause of death, because the bulldozer that uncovered her had inflicted too much damage."

James was glad Hartridge was on the same page. "Yes, at least on the surface, it seems similar. I'd like to have a look at the body, see if there are any other reasons to link the two deaths."

"Dr. Jandicott was never happy about that death. Couldn't prove suspicious death, but I got the impression he *was* suspicious." Hartridge moved to the filing cabinet, pulled out the file. "He insisted on keeping her in cold storage until someone claimed her."

"Well, let's go see if he's had a chance to look at the new

body." James had a strong need to get out, far away from Whetford.

Hartridge grabbed his coat and tucked the file under his arm.

It was a bad sign, how eager they were to escape, James thought as they took the stairs down. That wasn't what he'd thought his working life would be like when he joined the Met.

But at least they had a puzzle to solve.

That helped.

"How did you know about this?" Dr. Jandicott pulled the sheet back on the woman lying between them, face somber. "There were no detectives called to the scene."

"I know the traffic warden who was there when the body was found. The way it was described to me, it sounded similar to the other one we got last month. The woman found under the rubble of that building site near Hyde Park." James stared down at the body. The skin looked like one big bruise, and the woman's face was swollen.

The smell was indescribable.

Hartridge made a sound beside him, and then ran from the room, and both he and Jandicott turned to watch the constable push through the doors before they turned back to the victim.

Jandicott flicked him a look. "It was the first thing I thought about, too." He gently turned the woman's head. "See here, she received a killing blow to the back of the skull."

"Could she have fallen backward and hit her head accidentally?" James asked.

"Not unless she fell back precisely onto the head of a hammer," Jandicott said, tone grim. "See here? That circular indentation is a hammer head, or I'm a monkey's uncle."

"But that wasn't the case with the other death?" James remembered there was damage to the body, but he couldn't remember all the details.

"A ruddy great digger scooped her up, and then the bucket came down on her skull. Crushed it to bits. I couldn't tell what happened to her from what we were able to salvage from that scene." Jandicott sounded disgusted. "But the whole thing was suspicious. We couldn't identify the body, but we found a missing person's report that seems to match the height and hair color of the victim, as well as the fact that she lives near where the body was found. The family of Sara Parker says she went missing coming home from work on a night with a particularly bad fog. They're desperate to find her, and they don't want to believe the body we've got is Sara. I can't say, either way, because of the state of the remains. We could have identified her on her dental records, if the skull hadn't been crushed."

"How long from when Sara Parker went missing to the body being found?" James asked.

"Three weeks. And the body had been lying there about that long," Jandicott said. "She was probably killed that same night, if it's Sara Parker."

"So he sneaks up on them in the dark, and hits them in the back of the head with a hammer?" James wondered out loud.

"Again, if the cases are linked." Jandicott gently pulled the sheet up again.

"You think they are," James said.

"I have a suspicion. Suspicions are not facts."

"True." James felt a hard-edged determination rise up in him. "I'll have to go find some then."

"Well, this woman here was definitely murdered, about a week ago by the state of the body, and the case is as yet unassigned."

James gave a slow nod. "Put me down on the paperwork—if there's a problem with it, I'll let you know."

"Good." Jandicott looked satisfied. "First piece of business, you need to find out who she is. There was no handbag found at the scene. No identification at all."

"At least we have an intact body this time. It'll make it much easier." James looked down at the shroud. "I'll see who's been reported missing, so you don't have to send the dental records out to all and sundry."

"You said you know the traffic warden who discovered the body. I saw her name on the report. She's the one who was caught up in that ugly case a few months ago?" Jandicott eyed him with interest as he made for the door. "The Australian girl?"

"Yes, she told me about it. That's how I made the connection with the other case." James paused at the door. "She said the body was half-buried under the rubble, just on the other side of the heap."

"It would have been difficult for someone to carry a body up that heap of broken bricks and timber," Jandicott said. "They probably got to the top and dropped her over the other side, rather than risk falling on the downward slope. Then they probably unbalanced some of the rubbish on the top and let it fall on her. Basically as minimum an effort as possible."

"Still, you'd need some strength to carry a body up shifting rubble, wouldn't you?" He hadn't thought of that angle until now, but they weren't looking for a small man.

"You'd need muscle," Jandicott agreed. "And there's no way he could have used a wheelbarrow or anything like that up that steep slope of debris. The only way would have been to carry her, either in his arms or over his shoulder."

"I need to go look at the scene," James said. He gave a farewell nod to Jandicott and went out to look for Hartridge.

Whetford wouldn't care if James assigned this case to himself, James decided. Whetford only cared if he was inconvenienced. He was so divorced from the day to day functions of the office, he probably wouldn't notice the assignment hadn't gone through the usual channels.

As James reached the door and saw Hartridge outside, sitting on a bench across the road, he wondered what Whetford had got Hartridge to do.

Whatever it was, it had taken some of the shine off his constable, and James didn't like that.

He didn't like it at all.

chapter
four

GABRIELLA STARED at the familiar Land Rover, then looked down the street to see if the shouty man was going to come at her again.

There was no sign of him.

The mud-sprayed car was parked on double yellows and partially blocking the entrance to a delivery zone behind a row of shops. There was no question a ticket was warranted.

She filled out the form with quick, efficient strokes of her pen, and slid the fixed penalty notice into its plastic sleeve. The wind had come up, chill, with a hint of bite, and she looked up at the dull gray sky and thought it looked like rain.

"Miss Farnsworth."

The hail came from her left, and she turned and smiled when she saw Detective Constable Hartridge coming toward her.

"Nice to see you," Hartridge said as he came to a stop beside her. His gaze went to the Land Rover, then flicked to her clipboard and pen.

"Nice to see you, too," she said. She tilted her head. "You've been assigned the case of the woman in the rubble?"

He gave a nod. "It's just been officially declared a suspicious death."

Gabriella stepped up to the Land Rover and leaned over to stick the plastic sleeve on the windscreen. She put her hand down on the metal bonnet for balance.

Her whole arm seemed to fly upward, pushed by an invisible force, and suddenly she was lying on the pavement, icy pins and needles prickling her arm, as if she had shoved it into freezing water.

She lay, looking up at the darkening sky, and wondered what had happened.

She heard Hartridge give a shout, and he staggered briefly into view before collapsing beside her.

Voices were rising around them, and Hartridge got up on one knee, and looked down at her.

He looked pale, and he was sweating, but she couldn't understand what was going on.

Suddenly James was on her other side, his hand on her arm, his head turned as he shouted over his shoulder.

The first words she could understand were from an older gentleman, with white, flyaway hair, wearing a tweed suit complete with waistcoat, who pushed James aside.

"Let me through, then." A stethoscope was produced and shoved beneath her jacket, over her heart.

She blinked, and drew in what felt like her first proper breath since she'd gone flying, although that couldn't be right.

"Did the same to me, Doctor," Hartridge was saying over her. "But I'm a lot bigger."

"Her heart rate is stabilizing," the doctor said, then focused on her. "Can you sit up?"

She struggled weakly to comply, and then felt James's hand on her back, easing her up.

"What . . . ?"

"That Land Rover has been electrified," the doctor said. He tut-tutted. "Nasty business." His nicotine-stained fingers came to rest at the pulse at her throat, and he checked his watch. The pungent smell of tobacco enveloped her as he leaned closer. "You need to go home and rest. I don't think the electric current was strong enough to do lasting harm," he said. "But if you start to feel dizzy or lightheaded, go to the hospital immediately." He stood up and hefted his bag. "I'm in a hurry, I'm afraid, but she seems to be recovering." He walked away, and was swallowed by what Gabriella realized was a sizable crowd.

"The car was electrified?" She was still sitting down, and being at ground level, so to speak, she realized she could hear a faint hum coming from the vehicle. Mr. Shouty Man had set a trap.

"I've taken down the number plate," Hartridge said. "We'll find out who he is."

"Are you all right?" she asked, suddenly remembering that he flew backward, too.

"Better than you." He grinned. "Got a bit more heft to me."

James's grip on her hand tightened, and she realized he'd been holding it for a while. She turned to him and lifted her other hand, and guessing what she wanted, he pulled her to her feet.

For a brief moment she wondered if her legs would hold her, and then she found her footing. She straightened up.

"Bastard." She glared at the car.

James gave a grim nod. "Bastard indeed. I'll give you the address associated with this car, so you can send the fine to him in the post."

"I'd like to give it to him personally." She looked up and down the street. The crowds were slowly drifting away, now the drama was over, and there was no sign of him.

"You know him?" James sounded surprised.

"Had a set-to with him yesterday. Just before the boys who found the body came to call me for help. He was thoroughly unpleasant." She brushed at her skirt and flexed her hand again, but it was already feeling much better. "Are you here to see where she was found?"

James nodded. "Do you think you can show me?"

She knew he didn't need her to, there would be markers, but she had the feeling he was reluctant to let her out of his sight.

"Yes." She paused, watching as Constable Evans approached from up the street.

His gaze went to her, then to James and Hartridge. "Problem?" he asked.

"That car is electrified," Gabriella said, pointing. "It gave me and DC Hartridge a nasty shock."

"Do you know who it belongs to?" James asked Evans.

The big man shook his head. "No, but I've seen it recently. Comes around maybe twice a week."

"I'll see what charges can be laid," James said. "Both Miss Farnsworth and DC Hartridge could have been seriously hurt."

Evans promised to keep an eye out for the owner, and they walked away, keeping a slow pace, mainly, she suspected, for her, but also for Hartridge to get his balance again, too.

She still couldn't believe Shouty Man had electrified his car. It was clearly meant to stop him from getting a ticket. The craziness of the lengths he had gone to to save himself a fine gave her pause.

This was not a well individual.

When they reached the heap of rubble, she saw the tape the police had put around it had been broken or ripped, and it flapped in the stiff breeze with a snap, snap, snap.

"She was over on the other side of the slope?" James asked.

Gabriella nodded. "If you're going to go up and look, watch your footing. It's hard going."

"And yet he carried her up." James said it softly, as if to himself, and Gabriella realized that was true.

"Someone strong, then." She looked up and down the street. "Someone could have seen him. Those windows there are for the flats, I think. And this is a shortcut from the Kings Road. Someone could have come along."

"Strong and brazen," Hartridge confirmed. "Or so caught up in what he was doing, he didn't even think about witnesses."

"That's the best case scenario," James said. "Because that means there's more chance we'll catch him when he does it again."

"Again?" Gabriella frowned.

"We think this is the second time," James told her. "I'm pretty sure there'll be a third."

chapter
five

JAMES WATCHED the police car he'd had come by to pick up Gabriella disappear around the corner. He would not hear of her going back to headquarters under her own steam.

"She seemed all right," Hartridge said.

James glanced at him. "How are you? You were thrown to the ground as well."

Hartridge shrugged. "I felt like I was going to throw up at first, but it passed quickly. The tingles in my arm took a bit longer to fade, but I'm honestly right as rain now."

Gabriella had lost consciousness for a few seconds, which worried James. But she had also assured him she was fine. "What kind of idiot electrifies their car?" he wondered.

"She said he had a go at her yesterday, ranting about his ticket. He obviously knew he was parking illegally today, and she would likely come along." Hartridge shook his head. "He knew he would hurt her."

James felt a cold, hard anger spark inside him. "We're going to track down his address," he said. He didn't say any more, but he knew he would not let it go.

"And what if a child had touched the car?" Hartridge wondered. "If it threw Gabriella back, a child would have been seriously hurt."

There had to be a law against it, although James knew the car was theoretically the owner's to do with as he liked. But it was reckless endangerment of some kind.

"Sir?" A thin, reedy voice asked from behind him. "You the police?"

James turned. A boy, about eight or nine, stood in shorts and a jumper, his legs mottled red with the cold, his knees filthy. He hopped a little from side to side to keep warm in the bitter wind.

"You one of the boys who found the body yesterday?" James asked.

The boy shook his head. "No, they're older'n me, and they don't let me play with 'em, but I saw something, sir."

James nodded, walking carefully down the rubble to stand beside him on the pavement. "What did you see?"

"How come you don't wear a uniform?" the boy asked.

"We're detectives, and sometimes we have to look like normal people, so we don't wear uniforms," James said.

The boy eyed him for a moment, as if looking for any sign of deception. "To fool the crooks, like?"

"Yes," James agreed.

The boy jerked his head in a nod. "I saw a man with a wheelbarrow," he said.

That would be one way to get the victim here without a vehicle, James guessed. But a wheelbarrow wouldn't easily go up the rubble pile, so he probably still had to carry her up.

"When was this?"

"That night there was all that fog," the boy said. "The pea souper, me gran calls it."

James had been away, although he'd heard there had been a serious fog for a few nights in London. That would explain the murderer's brazen behavior. The fog would have kept most people off the streets, and given him perfect cover as he went about his business.

He would need to find out from the pathologist if the time of death matched up to the fog. He would bet that it did.

"What did the man look like?" James wondered what this child had been doing wandering around on a foggy night by himself.

"I never saw his face," the boy admitted. "I live up there." He pointed to one of the windows overlooking the street. "He had a hat on and a coat. But he had something bundled in the wheelbarrow."

"Did you see where he went?" James asked.

The boy shook his head. "Me mam found me out o' bed and I had to get back in."

At least he hadn't been wandering the streets, James thought with relief. The man who had killed two women would not hesitate to kill a child to keep his secrets.

"I'm Detective Sergeant Archer," James said, holding out his hand. "What's your name, then?"

"Percy," the boy tentatively extended his own hand, as if he had never shaken a hand before. "Percy Bellows."

"Well, Percy, here's my number. If you ever see a man with a wheelbarrow in the night again, please ask your mother to call me at Scotland Yard." He pulled a card from his inner jacket pocket and handed it over.

Percy took it reverently, then shoved it in his back pocket. "I helped?"

"You did, thank you."

Hartridge had been watching the exchange from halfway up the rubble pile, and suddenly some of the bricks gave way and he slid down a little.

"Cheers," the boy said, turned and ran into the alleyway between two of the buildings opposite.

"You think you can trust that?" Hartridge asked. "He might just be trying to keep up with the boys who found the body."

"Maybe," James agreed, but he didn't think so. "Even if he is, it's an interesting thing to invent, isn't it? He didn't say he saw the body, or the murder, just a man pushing a wheelbarrow through a pea souper."

Hartridge gave a grunt, widening his stance a little to keep his balance. "Good point."

"Let's go look over the other side. See if there is anything the pathologist missed." James carefully climbed the rubble pile again, and stepped over the top.

There was plenty of rubbish caught amongst the debris and smashed bricks. The wind would have blown plenty here over the years since the site had been tidied up by a bulldozer, pushing all the rubble up into a pile in the center of the lot to keep it out of the way.

The sun had managed to struggle out from behind the heavy clouds about ten minutes ago, and a glint caught his eye. He bent closer, and hunkered down, trying to extract whatever it was from between the bricks.

"What is it?" Hartridge, who was looking around to his right, asked.

"Not sure." James carefully lifted smashed rubble and stone to one side, and eventually got his fingers around it. He drew it out carefully. "A change purse," he said.

It was cheap—the metal clasp mostly rubbed bare of its original gold plating, but the fabric that formed the pouch of the purse was colorful and pretty. He hefted it. There was change inside it.

He felt the wind ruffle his hair, and decided not to open it here. He rose and slid it into an inner pocket.

"Let's get out of the wind and start looking into missing persons reports lodged since the pea souper," James said.

Hartridge nodded, and they made their way carefully back to the road.

When they came back out onto the Kings Road, James was just in time to see the Land Rover roaring off, turning left at the end of the street.

He'd had to park relatively far down the street, and there was no way he could get to his car and follow the Land Rover. It would be long gone by the time they reached the Wolseley.

"Do you think he knew he was in trouble?" Hartridge asked. "He was going pretty fast."

"Maybe." James scanned the buildings on both sides of the street. "Evans said he sees the vehicle parked around here a couple of times a week. So he's probably visiting someone nearby."

There were mainly shops and a few nice townhouses in this part of the Kings Road. He thought he caught the twitch of a curtain above a homewares boutique, but that didn't signify anything.

Still, it was worth making a note of it.

"What are you going to do about it?" Hartridge asked.

"First I need to find out what we can charge him with," James said. What he'd done should be a crime, but when it came to personal property, James knew things got sticky.

"You think he didn't break the law?" Hartridge sounded amazed.

"I hope he has," James said. He really did. But he had a sinking feeling it wasn't going to be that easy.

chapter
six

GABRIELLA ALMOST DIDN'T TELL Mr. Greenberg about the electrocution.

She'd been involved in a lot of trouble so far in this job, and while it hadn't been her fault, she had a feeling it reflected badly on her. It made her worried Mr. Greenberg might consider letting her go.

She didn't want to lose her position—it paid better than secretarial work, and helped fund her search for her father. Every week that went by that she couldn't find the bastard, dead or alive, was another week her mother and Gino couldn't get married.

So it was with hesitant steps that she approached the boss.

"Miss Farnsworth?" Mr. Greenberg was coming from the staff kitchen, walking back to his office, and she waited outside his door for him.

He ushered her in, a cup of tea in hand, and waved her into his visitor's chair.

"What brings you to headquarters early?" He set his mug down on a spot which, judging from the number of water stains in the wood, was its habitual place, and leaned against the desk.

"The police insisted, sir. They put me in a car and dropped me here." She hadn't been able to argue with James without making a fuss. "There was a run-in with a driver." She worried her lip.

"Tell me." He steepled his fingers and tapped them against his salt and pepper mustache.

She cleared her throat. "I fined him yesterday, and then today he was parked even worse, on double yellows, partially blocking an entrance, but when I touched his car I got a shock and landed on the pavement. A detective constable was there, investigating that body I told you about yesterday, and he also got a shock."

"A shock, as in an electrical shock?" Mr. Greenberg asked, voice sharp.

She nodded.

"This is not the first time I've heard of this. Someone at the fruit and veg market at Covent Garden said something about trucks . . ." He frowned, trying to remember.

"Yesterday, when I gave him his fine, the man did say something about twenty trucks coming in on market day. I think he's a farmer." Gabriella relaxed a little. Not that she was glad someone else had been electrocuted, but that this wasn't a 'her' problem.

"You landed on the pavement, you say?" Mr. Greenberg studied her. "Are you all right?"

She nodded. "There was a doctor in the crowd that gathered around. He told me to seek medical help if I feel faint or my heart starts beating too fast, but that I should be fine. Detective Constable Hartridge is also fine, but he and Detective Sergeant Archer want to press charges."

"Press charges?" Greenberg shook his head. "My counterpart in Covent Garden says they've tried that. There isn't a law against it. The bounder electrifies his car and then backs it into his trucks, all parked touching each other in a long row. No one can put a notice on any of them without being shocked. And because they're all his private property, he gets away with it."

"Detective Constable Hartridge made the point that if a child had touched it, they could have been very seriously hurt." Gabriella was angry all over again just at the thought of it.

"I agree." Mr. Greenberg turned and faced his map. He'd put it up after the murders she had been involved in a few months before and had begun tracking incidents on it. He picked up a yellow pin and tapped the borough of Chelsea with a finger. "Where did this happen?"

Gabriella got up and pointed to the spot.

Mr. Greenberg put the pin in.

"The yellows are attacks on wardens?" she asked, noticing other yellow pins dotted through the map for the first time. Most of them were in Kensington and Chelsea, but that made sense, because that was Mr. Greenberg's own area of responsibility. Any other incidents would have to be told to him by the heads of the other traffic warden stations.

"I've gone through all the reports, starting from three weeks ago," Mr. Greenberg said. "I'm also tracking all deaths that involve my wardens, either as a witness or called on as an authority figure."

The body she'd found the day before was on the map, she'd been here when he'd added it, but now she saw there were two others.

"A homeless man," Mr. Greenberg said, tapping the red pin that was in Kensington Gardens, and Gabriella remembered hearing about a body being found under the bushes in the park.

"And this one?" She hadn't heard about another death, and this one looked very close to her own route.

"The body was found in Hammersmith and Fulham," Mr. Greenberg said. "I only got word of it when I had dinner with some other head wardens last night."

Hammersmith and Fulham was the borough to the west of Kensington and Chelsea, so that explained why she hadn't heard anything about this, but as the crow flew, it was close. "Another homeless person?" Gabriella asked.

Mr. Greenberg's shoulders lifted. "Not sure. The body was found in an allotment garden, half-buried in a trench the gardeners were digging to deal with a flooding issue. I don't know if the coroner has issued a finding yet."

She would ask James when she saw him tonight. He had said he would be round to check on her.

She took a step away from the map. "It's only halfway through my shift, sir, I better get on."

He looked at her from under bushy gray eyebrows. "You're going home, Miss Farnsworth."

She shook her head, holding her hands tight together. "I really am fine. My arm felt strange for a while, and I felt a little dizzy, but honestly, that's all gone now."

Mr. Greenberg looked at her. "You're an adult, and know yourself. If you think you can go on, that's fine, but if you feel any effects at any time, you come in, is that clear?"

She nodded meekly and left, relieved that he trusted her to know what she could and couldn't do.

She stepped back out onto the street, and stopped short. A dark green Jaguar was parked a little way down the road. The station was on a street that ran parallel to the main road and ended in a cul-de-sac. While a footpath allowed pedestrian access to the main road from both ends, cars had no through way.

The car had obviously gone down the street, turned at the tight circle at the bottom, and come back up.

She tried to make out who was sitting in the driver's seat.

She had had a nasty run-in with a man who drove a green Jaguar some months ago, and she had thought a few times that he'd been following her.

That worry had faded over the last month, she realized. She hadn't thought of him in a while, but here was a Jag, parked near the station, and there was definitely someone sitting in the driver's seat.

She would never be safer than now, she decided. She was right outside the station. There were people about, and it was midday.

She stepped off the pavement, making straight for the car,

determined to pass in front of it and see who was behind the wheel.

As she got halfway across the road, the car's engine revved, and began to edge out of its parking space.

Gabriella changed her trajectory, not wanting to put herself right in front of a moving car. Instead, she headed for the driver's door. Forget politeness, she wanted to peer right in.

With a squeal of tires, the car lurched out, clipped the bumper of the old Morris Minor parked in front of it, and roared off.

Gabriella stood in the road, her focus on the Jaguar as it drove away. She had gotten the look she needed.

The man behind the wheel was definitely the man who'd tried to assault her a few months back.

He had refused to look at her or meet her gaze as he pulled out and drove off, but she recalled his jowly face and red cheeks, his blonde mustache, all too well.

She hadn't been mistaken. He *had* been following her.

The question was, why?

She lifted her shoulders high, then relaxed them down, trying to shake the tension off, and then turned and walked back into the station, going straight through and out the back entrance.

It was how she went home every afternoon, and if she took this way, she could cut across further down the road and end up on her usual route. It was a roundabout way of doing it, and it would take her longer, but she was deeply disturbed by Mr. Jaguar's interest in her, months after their clash.

She thought about their interaction as she walked, her head on a swivel, although he would not have had time to get from the main road to her current position if he was still in his car.

She kept close to the railings of the large townhouses she passed, moving at a fast pace.

When she saw a flash of dark green up ahead, she ducked down a set of basement stairs. She stood halfway down, on the slick stone of the steps, grabbed the metal railings above her head and rose up on tiptoe, her face pressed between the metal bars so she could see onto the street.

A dark green Mini Cooper drove past, and feeling a little foolish, but still with heart thumping, she walked back up onto the street and went on her way.

She felt a constant fizz of adrenalin in her blood for the rest of the afternoon, although she didn't see a green Jaguar again.

Either the man didn't know her current route—and that might have been why he had parked outside the station, so he could follow her— or he had somewhere else to be this afternoon.

She was exhausted by the time she made it back to her flat. Mr. Rodney was not in his garden, and given that it looked like it would start raining any moment, she didn't need to guess why.

She loved talking to him, but today, she just wanted to get home, curl up under a blanket, and close her eyes for a little bit.

As she stepped inside, Solomon was coming down the passage from the direction of Mr. Rodney's flat, heading out.

"Gabby," he said.

She smiled back. "Hey, Solomon. How're things?"

His gaze sharpened on her face. "What's wrong?"

She shook her head. "A long day. I got electrocuted, and then someone who I fined a while back was waiting for me outside the station." She lifted her shoulders, surprised at herself for telling him.

"Electrocuted? On the rail?" He tilted his head.

Solomon worked for British Rail, at least some of the time, and she guessed his mind had gone straight to the trains.

She shook her head. "Some farmer electrified his car so no one can attach a fine to it."

Solomon laughed, eyes widening, and then they narrowed. "It's funny, because fines aren't fun, but it hurt you?"

"It did." She didn't have to put up a front here. Solomon was a friend, as well as Mr. Rodney's nephew.

"Then it's not funny. You're just doing your job." He straightened the sleeves of his dark green jacket, and she noticed a pale green neck scarf knotted around his neck. He was the best dressed person she knew, even beating out Liz. But then, she had a very strong suspicion he had plenty of lucrative sidelines, and some of them were not strictly legal.

"No. It wasn't funny. But it looks like it isn't actually illegal, so there's nothing we can do about it." She turned toward the stairs. "I'm just going to get an early night."

"What about the creeper waiting for you outside the station?" Solomon asked. "Who is he?"

She lifted her shoulders again. "Some uppity Hooray Henry. He drives a dark green Jag and has a temper."

"I'll tell the boys to look out for a dark green Jag. Got the number plate?" he asked.

She gave it to him, and he nodded.

"If we see him, we'll let you know." He walked to the door and gave a final wave as he went out.

She didn't believe him.

The boys wouldn't just let her know. They would probably have words with Mr. Jaguar.

And as long as they were able to do it without getting themselves into trouble with the police, she was happy for them to have at it.

chapter
seven

"IT'S time to go home, Ian," James said, rubbing at his temple as he rose stiffly from his desk. Ian Hartridge looked up from the smaller desk they'd set up adjacent to James's larger one and yawned.

"Yeah, we likely won't get any more done tonight," Hartridge conceded from behind the hand he held over his mouth. "Ten missing women in the last three months. That seems like a lot."

"It does." James stretched and tidied the piles of files he'd been working on. He hoped some of the missing women had already turned up, and the files just hadn't been updated. "We'll have to ask the dentists of all ten for their records and compare the dental impressions from our second victim, see what we come up with." He wouldn't approach any of the family members of the missing women until there was more evidence.

But the dentists would likely take their time, and he had a feeling that time wasn't something they had in abundance. If the two deaths were connected, the man responsible would strike again, of that, he was sure.

Hartridge scraped his chair back and yawned again, then froze, his gaze on someone in the passageway outside James's office.

They'd left the door open, and James moved around his desk to see who had had such an effect on his constable.

He'd been expecting to see his boss, DI Whetford, lurking outside, but it was DS Galbraith leaning against the wall opposite his door, lighting a cigarette, as if he was waiting for them to come out.

"You looking for me, Galbraith?" James asked, shrugging into his coat and looping a scarf over his head.

He saw Galbraith's gaze flick to Hartridge and then he straightened and looked directly at James. "Just lighting my fag," he said, blowing out a stream of smoke. "You were away, weren't you?"

"For a couple of weeks," James acknowledged. Galbraith had never said so many words in a row to James since he'd started at the Met eight months ago.

"Well, see you around." Galbraith directed another quick look at Hartridge, then ambled to the stairs and disappeared through the stairwell doors.

"What's going on, Ian?" James asked, when the door swung shut with a snick.

Hartridge shook his head. "Nothing. I don't know what's up with him."

He was lying, but James thought it was out of fear and a wish to shield James from whatever it was that Whetford had sucked Hartridge into. Galbraith was obviously part of it, and that was a new and interesting fact. He'd known Whetford was bent for a while, but he hadn't got a handle on who above or below him was also dodgy.

"When you decide something *is* going on, come to me any time," James said. He saw Hartridge look down at his now-cleared desk, cheeks flushed, and when he reached the door, he turned. "Go out the back entrance. Galbraith looked like he expected you to follow him out." He turned and walked away. His anger at Whetford for drawing Hartridge into what was likely a compromising situation burned in his gut, and he ran down the stairs a little faster than normal, nearly barreling into Galbraith on the last landing before the ground floor.

"Easy." Galbraith twisted away just in time, and James stopped, forcing himself to keep his face neutral.

He didn't know what was going on, and until he did, it was better to act oblivious.

"Sorry, thought you were further ahead of me," he said, easily. He nodded and kept going, feeling Galbraith's cold eyes on him until he was through the door and out into reception.

He hoped Hartridge had taken his advice and gone the back way, because no doubt the moment the door closed behind him, Galbraith had jogged back up to his office to speak to his constable.

On a sudden whim, he wrapped his scarf a bit higher up his face as he turned through the arches to the back courtyard, and instead of going to where his car was parked, he headed for the building's rear entrance, keeping close to the wall, deep in the shadows.

Hartridge came out, bundled up in his coat against the light rain that had started falling late this afternoon, head down, shoulders hunched.

"Hartridge." Galbraith's shout cut through, and James saw Hartridge flinch, then slowly turn back to face the detective sergeant.

He said nothing, and shrugging off the lack of response, Galbraith waved a hand to motion him under the narrow overhang, out of the weather.

Hartridge took a few steps toward him, but didn't join him under cover.

"What did you find out?" Galbraith asked.

"Nothing." Hartridge lifted a shoulder and took a step back. "No one was there."

"Well keep going back until someone is there." Galbraith's tone was short. "Got it?"

"Yes, sir." Hartridge dipped his chin.

"Good." Galbraith turned on his heel and went back inside.

James stayed still in the shadows as he watched Hartridge stare for a few moments at the door, and then turn on his heel and hurry out of the Yard.

James was still wet and still wondering what Hartridge had gotten mixed up in when he drew his car up outside Gabriella's run-down Victorian row house in Notting Hill.

She had a tiny bedsit at the top of two steep flights of stairs, but somehow her place seemed nicer than his own. His two bedroom flat in a much nicer part of town seemed stale and empty, a depressing place to go to at the end of the day.

He and Hartridge had gotten a takeaway of fish and chips while they worked, and he hadn't realized how late it was until just before he'd left the office. It was with relief that he saw Gabriella's lights were still on.

"Mr. Detective."

The voice came from the shadows as he closed his car door.

He thought for a moment it was Solomon, but then Jerome appeared, standing beside the gate that led down the narrow path to the front door.

"Hello, Jerome. How're things?" James nodded to Gabriella's neighbor. He was skinny and long-limbed, his shirt and pants both wildly patterned in a way James would have thought couldn't work together, but somehow, on Jerome, they did. "You going up?"

"I am." Jerome opened the gate, waved him in. "What's this I hear about Gabriella getting shocked?"

"Some crazy farmer," James said. "Doesn't like getting fines, so he electrified his car."

"How'd he do that, then?" Jerome asked. "How does he get into the car, if it's buzzing?"

"Good questions," James said. He hadn't had time to think much about it. "He must have a switch under the chassis some-where so he can turn it off when he wants to get back inside."

That was something to look out for next time. If there was a next time.

He and Jerome parted ways at the top of the stairs, Jerome going into his flat, and James knocking softly on Gabriella's door.

She opened it, standing sleepy-eyed in her bathrobe and slippers. "Come in," she said on a yawn, and stepped back.

A sweet scent enveloped him as he stepped through and he guessed she'd just come out of the bath because when she leaned past him to close the door, he felt the heat of her skin.

He reached out for her as she turned, and pulled her close.

He'd undone his coat as he'd walked up the stairs with Jerome, and she slid her arms underneath it, her head coming just under his chin.

He tightened his hold, astonished at his luck at having this beautiful, extraordinary woman in his arms.

"Hmm. You're cold," she said, rubbing her cheek against him. "And working late, by the looks of it."

A wave of desire hit him, and he suppressed a shudder as he stood holding her, all warm, and sweet-smelling, and sleepy.

She lifted her head and looked up at him. "What is it?"

He kissed her upturned face, a gentle brush of his lips on her forehead, her cheeks and then, finally, her mouth.

She kissed him back, lifting a hand and cupping the back of his neck. It made the fires burn hotter.

Last night he'd been so restless, he'd gone back to the office. Tonight . . . he forced himself to pull away.

She looked up at him, cheeks flushed, eyes languorous.

"You're beautiful," he whispered against her temple. Then he set her away from him.

She blinked in surprise, tucked a strand of hair behind her ear, and seemed to get herself together. "Do you want some tea?" she asked, voice a little husky.

He wanted to have sex with her, but because he wasn't going to do that, at least not tonight, sitting shoulder to shoulder with her on her narrow window seat, sipping tea, would be better than nothing.

He nodded, helping her with the task until they each had a hot mug in hand.

"Did you feel better after you left us?" he asked.

She nodded. "I told Mr. Greenberg what happened, then felt well enough to continue my round." She took a sip of tea and eyed him over the rim of her cup. "He says the Land Rover is well known around Covent Garden Market. More than just DC Hartridge and I have been shocked. And apparently there's no law against it."

James lifted his brows. "I'll contact the Covent Garden lot, find out what they've tried to do against him." But he'd been worried about the same thing. That there was no law against electrifying your own car.

She yawned, and he put down his mug reluctantly.

"You need to get a good night," he said.

He got to his feet, and she followed suit, trailing after him to the front door.

"Sorry to bring up work," she said as he shrugged into his coat, "but Mr. Greenberg said there was another body found—in Hammersmith and Fulham. It's a different borough, but the place where the body was found is actually really close to the border with Kensington and Chelsea. I wondered if you knew about it?"

James felt the hair rise on his arms. "Was it found at another vacant lot?"

"No, an allotment." She pulled her bathrobe tighter. "In a ditch some of the gardeners who own lots there were digging to solve a drainage issue. The body was half-buried, and that reminded me of the one I found. That's what made me wonder if there was a connection."

"Did Greenberg say how they died? Who they were?"

She shook her head. "He only learned of it last night. He has a map on his wall now, after what happened in the summer, and he marked it with a red pin. He doesn't know any of the details, just that a traffic warden was called to the scene first, about two days ago now. They were walking by, and the uniform makes people think we're coppers."

"Thank you. If you hear anything else, about this body, or any others, let me know straight away." He tied his coat, wound his scarf on. He would get nothing out of anyone tonight, but tomorrow, first thing, he'd go to Hammersmith and Fulham.

"You think they are connected, don't you?" Gabriella was looking at him with big, dark eyes.

He forced himself to shrug. "It's possible," he said.

But as he ran down the stairs and out into the rain, he was afraid they were.

chapter
eight

GABRIELLA FELT LIKE A COWARD, but before she left work she took the staircase at headquarters to the floor above, and looked down on the road outside from the upstairs ladies' loo—the only room on that floor that she had access to.

There was no green Jaguar parked there, but she decided to go out the back anyway.

As she ran down the steps, Liz was waiting for her at the bottom.

"What's up?" she asked.

"I wanted to see if someone was lurking outside." Gabriella waved toward the back exit and lifted her brows, and Liz gave a nod of acknowledgement that she was going that way, too.

"You avoiding your copper?" Liz asked, buttoning up her shiny, bright red vinyl coat as they headed for the exit.

Gabriella admired the color, but wondered if the coat would be warm enough. She had on a tweed wool one she'd found in a charity shop, and while it had a few moth holes—hopefully where no one would notice them—it was wonderfully cozy.

The weather looked like it was going to chuck down at any minute, and the sky was so dark and low, it gave her a sense of impending doom.

"I think I've got someone following me. I fined him a while

back, and he was waiting outside yesterday. When I tried to approach the car, just to check it was him, he raced off." She felt a quick surge of satisfaction at how quickly he'd sped off. Like he was scared of her.

It made her feel better about the situation.

But what she actually needed was a look at James's notes from the incident. She had meant to mention it to him last night, but it had slipped her mind. She thought he might have written down the address of the row house Mr. Jaguar had come out of, and she could no longer be sure which one it was. Too much time had passed.

She wanted that information, just in case.

She had made a note of the registration number on the car yesterday as it drove away, and this morning she'd checked it against the one she'd written down in her ticket book from all those months ago. They weren't the same, although the driver definitely was.

He had changed the plates.

"Did you tell me about him at the time?" Liz asked, pulling the back door open for them both.

"It was so long ago, I can't remember." She waited on the back porch for Liz to step out, and they both headed for the bus stop a few streets over. "I was working in Chelsea, and a green Jag was parked on double yellows near a corner. This toff comes boiling out of a townhouse, shouting, red-faced. He must have seen me sticking the fine on the windscreen from inside, and when I started walking away, he really went for me."

They shared a quick look, because while there was often a lot of shouting, it rarely ever got to the point where they were afraid of physical harm.

"How'd you get away?" Liz asked.

"I started to run, I'm afraid to say. I really thought he was going to hurt me, but James was driving past and he switched on his siren and pulled up."

"Let me guess," Liz said, voice dry. "It was suddenly all a misunderstanding, mainly on your part."

Gabriella laughed. "You must have been there."

"In a way." Liz tucked a hand through Gabriella's arm. "Let's go get some tea somewhere. I could murder a cuppa that isn't that strange, iron-flavored stuff they have at HQ."

Gabriella usually never treated herself, because money was always so tight, but she felt like sitting somewhere warm and cozy for a bit, in a brightly lit place to ward off the encroaching darkness. She ran across the road with Liz, laughing and joking until they found a teashop with fresh-looking buns, and settled into a table in the back corner.

"You haven't been over to Dance-A-Go-Go for a while," Liz said, rubbing her hands together to warm them, and then taking a sip from her mug of tea. She let out a sigh of satisfaction.

"I'm trying to save money," Gabriella said. "And after what happened there . . ."

Liz nodded. "I understand. You're friends with Melvin, right? The bouncer? I've gotten to know him a bit, these last few months."

She knew Melvin through Solomon, but not well. "I see him at the Calypso Club when I take Mr. Rodney there for dinner." She eyed her friend. "You're interested in him?"

"Maybe." Liz sent her a quick, saucy smile. "Maybe I think he looks fine the way he stretches out those jackets with those big shoulders."

Gabriella grinned back. "Next time you see him, tell him I say hello."

Liz winked. "Thank you. That's as good a conversation opener as any."

They ate sticky buns and drank tea, and then parted ways at the bus stop. Gabriella's bus came first, and she waved at Liz from the top deck as it shuddered off into the afternoon traffic, the rain just beginning to spit against the roof of the bus and the windows.

The bus route home stopped close by Ruby Everett's house, and the thought of going back to her tiny, dark flat in the gloom suddenly didn't appeal. The warm lights of Ruby's neighborhood sparkled through the rain on the window, and on a whim she got off and ran down the street, jacket pulled up over her head.

She reached the little porch over Ruby's front door moments before the rain started in earnest, and realized with a sudden drop of her stomach that there were no lights on in the house.

Ruby wasn't here.

She would have to go back to the bus stop and wait for the next bus to get home.

It was aggravating.

Except . . .

She ran down the steps, then stuck close to the eaves of the house to avoid the worst of the rain as she headed around the side, to the back garden.

There was a light coming from what had once been the shed, and was now the home of Teddy Roe, Ruby's gardener.

The lawn mower and other garden equipment, which had once resided in Teddy Roe's home, were now housed in a neat little lean-to on the side, and she saw that they had put in a little path from the shed to the kitchen door since she was last here.

She made a dash for the shed door, and gave a quick, light knock.

"Who is it?" Teddy Roe's voice trembled with suspicion.

"It's me, Mr. Roe. Gabriella."

"Gabriella!" The exclamation fortunately sounded enthusiastic, and with a rattle of keys, the door swung open.

"Sorry to barge in on you," Gabriella said, leaning in a little way to get out of the rain. "I thought I'd look in on Ruby, but it doesn't seem like she's here."

"She's gone to pick up a parcel at the post office, is all," Teddy Roe said. "She'll be back for tea, and I'm having it with her. You can join us."

"Thank you. Is it all right if I wait here with you? It's coming down cats and dogs." She eyed the little room he and Ruby had worked on to turn it into a livable space.

"Come in, of course. Come in." He beamed, stepping back and waving an arm. "Looking good, eh?"

"It's looking fantastic, Mr. Roe." She wasn't just saying that, either. Ruby had made curtains for the windows, and they'd painted the interior as well as the exterior. The old wooden floor boards had obviously been sanded and sealed, and there were a few rugs on the floor.

They and the furniture were the only things that looked dodgy.

"Mrs. Everett paid for the paint and to have it all sanded and cleaned," Teddy Roe said, patting the wall. "But I found the rugs and furniture myself." He pointed to a moth-eaten old Turkish rug lying just inside the door. "Found it. Out on someone's bins. Amazing what people'll throw out. Amazing."

She grinned at him. She couldn't talk, what with the moth holes in the coat she was wearing that very moment. "Takes all kinds, Mr. Roe. I love the colors in it." They were a rust red and a dusty blue, and she actually did love them.

"Got me a kettle, to make myself tea whenever I like," he said, showing her. "And a bit o' bread and fruit in a bowl." He lifted the bowl up. "Mrs. Everett gave it to me as a housewarming present."

"It looks so good." She remembered how he'd been sleeping in an old, broken-down car when she'd met him. And when she and Ruby had been in serious trouble, Teddy Roe had come through for them.

"Hello?" A call came from outside, and Gabriella turned to the house and saw the kitchen door was open, and Ruby was silhouetted against the light.

"Hello," she called back.

"It's Gabriella, come to visit us." Teddy Roe had to shout over the rain.

"I'll come and fetch you both with an umbrella," Ruby called back, and then she ran across, a huge umbrella over her, and handed a second one to Teddy Roe. "Gabriella can fit under this one with me."

They made it back to the kitchen with wet shoes but otherwise dry, and Gabriella made toast while Ruby heated the soup she'd made earlier and Teddy Roe fried up some eggs.

Teddy Roe fell on the food like he was never going to see another meal, and Gabriella guessed that might have once been true.

"Heard there were a body," he said, after he'd cleaned his plate and was leaning back in his chair, hands folded over his stomach. "On your patch somewhere, wasn't it?"

He was very connected to what happened on the street. It shouldn't surprise her, it had been his home for years.

"Some boys found a woman in the rubble in that lane off the Kings Road," she said.

"The old Billick building?" Ruby asked.

"I think that's what Mr. Greenberg called it." Gabriella lifted her shoulders. "It was bombed in the war, and they haven't cleared the site yet."

"The old Billick building," Teddy Roe confirmed. "I had to clear it out of people. When it fell."

She'd forgotten he had worked the night crew during the war, pulling bodies out of bombed buildings during the Blitz.

"Was it bad?" she asked, and then felt a fool, because of course it had been bad.

He looked up at her, eyes rheumy but bright blue under his white, bushy eyebrows. "I found a murdered woman in there. Weren't the Germans what got her. Someone much more local."

"That's shocking," Ruby said, leaning forward. "What did the authorities do?"

Teddy Roe gave a snort of derision. "Had their hands full, didn't they? No one wanted to hear me say it weren't from the bomb. Not a soul wanted to listen. So they told me I was mistaken. And when I found another one, they told me I was doolally."

"You found another?" Gabriella asked. "Where?"

He shrugged. "Don't matter. No one believed me." He stood, carefully pushing his chair back in place. "Thanks for the tea, Mrs. E. I'm off to bed." He gave them both a sort of bow, and took the umbrella with him to run back to the shed.

"You made a strange face when he said that." Ruby rose and began to stack the plates, and Gabriella got to her feet to help her, running the hot water into the sink to wash up.

"There's another body been found close to the one I got involved in. It's probably coincidence, but I don't like it." Gabriella shrugged.

"It's been more than twenty years since Teddy worked with the night crew. The chances of a connection are slim," Ruby pointed out.

"True." Gabriella began scraping egg off the plates.

"I was going to leave you a note tomorrow, as it happens." Ruby picked up the drying cloth. "I've found something for you about your father."

Gabriella stopped, turned to her. "Something concrete?" Because she had been looking for months, and every single lead, no matter how promising, had evaporated like mist.

"Something concrete." Ruby didn't look particularly excited or happy.

Which meant the news was bad and she didn't think Gabriella would like hearing it.

"Just tell me," she said, and realized with surprise she felt the need to brace herself. She thought she didn't care about the outcome.

"If my source is right, your father did arrive back in England on the ship your mother says he boarded," Ruby said.

"What's the bad news?" Gabriella asked.

"He wasn't using a fake name." Ruby's lips gave a twist. "Either in Australia, or on the ship."

Gabriella blinked. At first, she'd thought he'd used a fake name to book his fare, because no one named Jonathan Farnsworth had been on that ship. Then she'd considered that the fake name was the one he'd used when he was living with her mother. The one on her birth certificate. "What do you mean?"

"I mean there was someone on that ship, a viscount called Lord Granger, and it turns out his surname is Farnsworth. And his first name is Jonathan." Ruby paused. "You said your father received word that his own father was dead. That he returned to England to deal with his father's estate. That means that when he signed on to the ship's manifest, he quite correctly gave his new title. He'd just become Lord Granger, and that's who he identified himself as."

Gabriella stared at Ruby, aware her mouth was open. "A viscount?" she almost squeaked the words. She'd seen that entry. Had simply let her eye pass over it.

"Gabriella, if this is correct, your father is Lord Granger, and he's living on his family's estate in West Sussex, near Chichester. He appears to be married."

Gabriella had expected that if she found her father alive that he would be married. That he would be a bigamist. He'd done enough to hide his whereabouts, after all. But she had never suspected he had a title. Never suspected he came from wealth.

She had been very young when he'd left, and couldn't remember if he'd ever said anything about his upbringing, but her mother had worked long, hard hours every day in the bakery, and she couldn't really recall what her father had done.

He must have worked somewhere. She would write to her mother and ask her.

"You're shocked," Ruby said.

Gabriella nodded. "Can we somehow confirm this Lord Granger is my father? Find out if he lived in Melbourne during the war?"

"I've already asked my contact at the Home Office to do that." Ruby patted her arm gently. "But we know for sure he spent some time there, as he got on the ship in Melbourne and got off in Southhampton."

"Ruby." Gabriella grabbed her friend's hands and squeezed. "I don't know how to thank you. I've been here six months, and I hadn't gotten anywhere in my search. You've helped me so much."

Ruby smiled. "It's been my pleasure. It feels a bit like the old days."

Gabriella knew Ruby would never reveal what she'd done during the war, but she suspected it involved the intelligence services.

Hence her very good connections in the Home Office.

As she used Ruby's umbrella to make a run for the bus stop, she had to give it to her father. It had taken an old WWII operative to find him.

He thought he was safe and untouchable.

And she was about to reach out and rip back the curtain.

She didn't fool herself that it wouldn't be painful. For them both.

chapter
nine

"WE FOUND THE BODY THERE." Mr. Stanhope, a thickly-accented northerner, pointed to a rough-dug trench running through the middle of an allotment, and James saw a few pieces of crime scene tape were still tied around some of the trellises.

He stepped closer, and then turned as DC Hartridge pushed through the squeaky gate into the urban garden, and came to stand, stiff and uncomfortable, at his side. He'd been that way since the night Galbraith had hunted him down.

"Good morning, sir."

James nodded to him, then focused back on the ditch. "You found her face down, I heard?" He glanced at Stanhope.

"Face down, and partially buried," Mr. Stanhope said. "Like they tried to fill the trench back up, as if we wouldn't notice after we'd just spent all day digging it for drainage. Bloody idiot."

"So they started to bury the body, and then abandoned the effort?" James crouched down, but there was nothing in the trench now but mud, probably because it had rained through the night. He hadn't been able to come yesterday or the day before, when he'd wanted to, and five days was a long time for a crime scene.

He'd had to dance around the bureaucracy all day yesterday and the day before, and still didn't have permission to take this case on as his own. But he had eventually been granted access to the files and permission to interview witnesses.

"Did you know the victim?" James asked. She was still listed as unknown, but what he'd seen of the investigation so far was so haphazard, he didn't take it for granted that the officer in charge had done his job and asked if any of the people who'd found the body recognized her.

Mr. Stanhope shook his head. "Nah, poor lass. I thought at first she'd wandered in by mistake and fallen in, you see. But then I saw the soil over her, and she'd hardly have tried to cover her own body up, now would she?"

"No." James pushed back to his feet. "You see anyone lurking about recently?"

"Looking it over, like? As a good place to dump a body?" Mr. Stanhope's eyes were hard as he spoke. Then he gave a quick shake of his head. "Not that I saw. Wish I had. Wish I knew who did this. They've ruined this place for some of the old timers."

"Old timers?" DC Hartridge asked, and Mr. Stanhope gave a chuckle.

"You're thinking, aren't you an old timer, old man," he said, then his laughter turned into a hacking cough.

Hartridge blushed. "No, sir."

Mr. Stanhope thumped his chest and took a breath. "I'm old enough," he said. "But I'm talking about those who lived here during the war. I'm a relative newcomer to the allotment. This place was an old factory during the Blitz. Went up in flames and they found someone dead inside once the fire was out. Some of the current gardeners live in houses overlooking this place and were there when she was found, so this is bringing it all back."

"How many people have access to the allotment?" James asked. "How does it work?"

"There's twenty plots," Mr. Stanhope said. "See the markers? That's how we divide it up. But it keeps flooding with all these storms we've been having, so we dug this trench through the middle, so all of us only give up a little land, you see?"

"And no one knows who the victim could be?" James asked.

Mr. Stanhope lifted his shoulders. "Not everyone saw her. Only me, Mrs. Henderson, Jimmy and Patrick. The others weren't here until after the ambulance took her away."

He would have to come back with a picture of her, show it around. But first, they could check her against the list of eight names they had on their missing list.

The last two days had been frustrating, but at least they'd been able to take two names off the list they'd compiled.

"Thank you for your time," James said.

"You're all right," Mr. Stanhope said. "Better than the other copper who came. You at least look like you want to find out who she was. T'other one didn't care, either way."

That was the impression James had got, as well, but he didn't say it. He thanked the gardener again, and then led the way out of the gate.

"We don't have the case officially," he said to Hartridge as they walked toward the local station, "but Officer Wilcox is so disinterested, we'll have free rein."

"Where are we going now?" Hartridge asked.

"To find out where the body was taken, and who performed the autopsy." James wished it could have been Dr. Jandicott, but he was the lead pathologist for the Met, and this case had not been assigned to New Scotland Yard headquarters. It was being handled by the local station.

The walk to the Hammersmith nick was short and relatively pleasant. The weather had cleared, and although the air was cold, the wind had dropped and the sun was shining. It was as good as it was going to get on a London morning in autumn.

Once inside the station, James got the same sense of grievance and hostility in person as he'd gotten over the phone the day before from Constable Wilcox.

The man didn't want to stir himself to actively investigate the case, but he didn't want James to have it, either.

"Do you think it will look bad on your file if I take this over?" James asked him.

"Why would you say that?" Wilcox stood in a sudden movement, like a fox scenting the hounds.

"Because I've read your report so far, and you don't appear to have much curiosity about the victim or her death, but you seem very focused on stopping me from looking into it. I can't think of any other reason." James usually took the diplomatic route where he could, but he was tired of the hoops Wilcox had forced him to jump through since yesterday.

"A slapper took the wrong customer into a dark corner, and got herself dead. It happens." Wilcox shrugged.

Beside him, James sensed Hartridge stiffen.

"A slapper? So you know her as a local prostitute, do you?" James took out his notebook and got his pencil ready. "What's her name, because it isn't in your report?"

Wilcox drew in a whistling breath through his nose. "I've never seen her before, but how else did she get there?"

"So she's not a known prostitute?" James kept the pencil hovering over the page.

"I just said I didn't know." Wilcox made a face. "But if you're so keen, fine, take the case." He scooped up a thin file on his desk, shoved it at James. "Knock yourself out, laddie."

"Thanks." James ignored the disrespect and tucked the file under his arm. "Where's the body? When did you attend the post mortem?"

Now Wilcox looked a little nervous. "Eh?"

"Who's the pathologist, and where's the victim now?"

Wilcox glanced at the door, and then back.

"You don't know, do you?" James could scarcely believe it.

"I've got other work, you know." Wilcox pushed off from his desk and walked out to the station's front desk. Leaned in close to the sergeant on duty and then came back. "She was taken to Royal Masonic in Ravenscourt."

"Thank you for your help, Constable." James gave a polite nod and he and Hartridge made for the door.

As soon as they were outside, he blew out a breath.

"What a tosser," Hartridge said as they walked away.

James chuckled. "A tosser who eventually gave us what we wanted."

"Are you joking?" Hartridge asked. "He was happy as Larry to hand it over. It was eating into his tea time."

Hartridge sounded a little more like himself.

It made something tight and worried inside James unclench a little.

"Let's get to the Royal Masonic," he said. "But let's have some breakfast, first."

IT FELT SOMEHOW decadent to be out and about on a weekday morning, not at work.

Gabriella took the bus to Victoria Embankment and eyed the people traveling with her. Mostly young women with small children or retirees, with their wicker shopping baskets and umbrellas.

She had a half day off because she'd worked last Saturday morning, and fortunately the half day she'd been allocated on the schedule happened to land on a Friday. Her friend Ben had told her once it was his slow day. He was a junior in the Inner Temple Chambers, and the solicitor he worked for took long pre-weekend lunches and sometimes didn't appear at all, unless he was due in court.

The bus rumbled past Westminster Bridge, and she watched New Scotland Yard pass by on her left. She hadn't seen James for the last two nights, and wondered how he was going with his investigation.

Just the thought of him caused a little lift to her spirits. She didn't know what to make of her feelings and where they were leading. They were definitely going somewhere, though. And not to a place her mother would approve of.

She wouldn't approve of anything about their relationship,

including the dinners Gabriella served James in her flat, and including the fact that he wasn't Catholic. Or Italian.

The only other country she would take as acceptable for her daughter was an Irishman, because the Catholic bishop of Melbourne was Irish, and her mother was a devotee to the man.

She probably didn't even know where Wales was.

But her mother wasn't here, and Gabriella didn't have even the slightest care about things that seemed to weigh her mother down.

New Scotland Yard disappeared behind her, and the bus stopped a few more times until it rumbled to a halt near Black-friars Bridge and Gabriella disembarked.

She headed down a street and had to wander around for a bit until she found the right building.

She stepped into the gloomy cool and quiet of Inner Temple and found it deserted, or, nearly.

Someone was typing behind a door somewhere—she could just make out the clack, clack, ping—and there was a low murmur of voices further down the passage. Ben had told her he was on the first floor, so she headed up the stairs and when she reached the landing she stopped to study the plaques on the wall, looking for a clue as to where to go next.

A young man in drainpipe pants and a jacket and tie came running down the stairs from the floor above, hand out to swing around the balustrade and take the next flight down, when he caught sight of her.

He nearly pitched down the stairs in his effort to stop his forward momentum.

"Hello," he said, trying to straighten up.

"Hello." Gabriella could see the bright interest in his eyes. "I'm looking for Ben Cohen. Can you tell me where to find him?"

"Ben?" The man blinked. "Sure, I can." He walked past her, down the passage she was standing in. "Just down here."

"Thank you, you can just tell me which door, I don't want to keep you."

She followed behind him, but he turned back with a smile. "No trouble. Happy to help." He began to walk backwards so he could face her. "You sound Australian, like Ben."

"We're friends from Melbourne," she said, and he gave a nod, stopped, and knocked on a door.

"Cohen. You've got a visitor."

Ben opened up, frowned, then frowned even more deeply at the sight of Gabriella. "Gabby." Then he smiled his sweet smile. "Come in."

She had to sidle around the young man who'd shown her the way. "Thanks for the help."

He nodded, eyes still bright with interest. "Well, cheers."

Ben closed the door and shook his head. "I'll have a thousand questions now."

Gabriella grinned. "Don't get a lot of visitors?"

"Don't get a lot of visitors," Ben agreed. "But particularly not beautiful young women visitors."

Gabriella laughed at that, and still shaking her head, sat down in his visitor's chair.

Ben went to a little side desk, switched on the kettle there and found two mugs and some tea bags. "No coffee, sorry. And no milk. We've run out."

"Don't worry about it, I'm fine." She hated black tea.

He switched off the kettle and sat down. "Why are you here? You'll be seeing me tomorrow night with the rest of the group, won't you?"

"Of course, I never miss." At the start of her move to London, Ben, Dominique and Trevor, the three Australians who'd been her cabin mates on the ship over, were the only people she'd known. None of them had ever missed the catch-up they organized every two weeks.

"But this couldn't wait?" Ben asked.

"I want to hire you," she said. "And I didn't want to necessarily discuss it tomorrow at our usual meetup."

"Hire me?" He almost swallowed the words. "You know I'm only a junior?"

"I know. Does that mean you can't look into something for me?"

"No." He steepled his fingers. "I usually get the grunt work from my senior. Looking up case law, drafting submissions, that sort of thing. I'm not expected to get my own work yet. But I can look into something for you. Of course I can."

"All right." She set her handbag on the desk and pulled out the sheet of paper she'd worked on this morning before coming in. "I think I might have found my father, but I need to check this is correct before I approach him. As you'll see, it's a lot more complicated now."

She pushed the paper across to him and he looked down at it for so long, she started to fidget.

"Gabriella." He looked up, eyes wide. "If this is right . . ."

"I'm the Honorable Someone-or-another, I know." She grimaced.

"Not just that . . ." He shook his head. "Your father's son from the result of his bigamy is *not* the Honorable So-and-So, as he no doubt thinks he is. And that will be a very bitter pill to swallow." He got up and took a massive tome off his shelf.

She read the title as he set it down on the desk. "Who's Who?" she asked.

He shrugged. "Gives a list of all the nobs and their offspring, so you can keep track of who to doff your cap to."

"I don't know if he has any other children, although obviously it's possible." She hadn't really run the thread of her father's betrayal all the way through to its logical conclusion. But if he'd married her mother and then someone else, his offspring other than her were illegitimate in the eyes of British law. And had no claim to the ancestral estate.

That would hurt.

"This is explosive." Ben flipped to a page, and his finger stopped at an entry. "One son, two daughters."

Gabriella leaned back.

"How sure of this are you?" Ben asked. "Because this will cause a massive stir, and I'll tell you now, if it comes down to what they'd rather be true, the snobs here would prefer you to be lying, and would love it if you were the illegitimate one."

"I'm pretty sure." She pulled out the documents that Ruby had sourced for her, and then placed her parents' marriage certificate and her birth certificate on top of them.

Ben looked them over, making notes on a pad beside him as he worked through them, noting all the details. Eventually he lifted his head. "This looks rock solid." He tipped back in his chair, gazing up at the ceiling. "This is something that I'll have to run past my senior, because it will draw attention. I can't do anything under the radar." His chair landed back on the floor with a clatter.

She didn't ask what he would do if his senior refused to allow him to work on this. They'd cross that bridge when they came to it. "What's the next step, after you've spoken to him?" she asked.

He shook his head. "I don't know. I'll research it if he gives me the green light but isn't interested in advising me. If he is interested, he'll know the tricks better than me."

She nodded, scooped up the papers, and carefully replaced them in her bag. "Thanks, Ben. You know everything I make that I don't need to live on gets put aside to pay for this search, so please bill me for your time."

He rose as she did, and studied her. "If I have expenses, I'll pass them on, but this is for friendship, Gabs. Don't insult me by insisting."

She hesitated. Gave a nod. "All your expenses," she said.

He put out his hand, and she shook. "Thank you."

He walked her out, not just off his floor, but all the way out of the building.

"How did you get those reports? They're from the Home Office," he said.

"You know the friend I made during that business in the

summer?" She glanced at him. "She did something hush hush in the war."

Ben's eyes widened. "She has contacts?"

"It seems like she has a lot of favors owing, and she wasn't shy calling them in to help me." She still couldn't believe how much Ruby had done for her.

"Well, she got you iron-clad proof." Ben suddenly grinned. "This is going to raise my profile, that's for sure."

She gave him a quick hug. "Hope that's a good thing. I'll see you on Saturday."

She walked back toward the embankment and got onto the bus. As she sat down near the back she tried to identify the hot, tight feeling in her chest.

Anxiety, she decided. And fear. And trepidation.

No one was going to be happy with her once this was set in motion. Other than Gino, who wanted to marry her mother.

Now that she'd discovered her father wasn't dead, just a bigamist, she didn't think her mother would be happy at all. She didn't believe in divorce, although surely the Church would give her an annulment for the bigamy?

She shrugged.

She had set out to find her father and she had.

But she didn't fool herself that there wouldn't be a lot of drama in her future.

And once it was all done, what would be her next step?

She had originally thought she would find him, or find out what had happened to him, and return to Melbourne.

That wasn't so clear, any more.

The bus passed New Scotland Yard on its way back.

Not clear at all.

chapter
eleven

THE MORGUE at the hospital was deserted.

James sent Hartridge back up the stairs to enquire where the pathologist could be, while he paged through the book at an empty reception desk for any sign of when the body he was looking for had been admitted.

The victim had been found just under a week before, so he only had to go back one page, and he found her, logged in at 11 am the morning the allotment farmers had called the police.

They had brought her to this hospital, declared her dead, and sent her straight down here.

The signature of the doctor was indecipherable.

A door opened behind him and he turned to find a man a little way down a dimly-lit passageway, rubbing his head like he'd just woken up.

The man staggered toward him and then came to a stop, swaying slightly in surprise at the sight of him.

"What time is it?" he asked.

James checked his watch. "Nine thirty."

The man rubbed his head again, then belched. Thumped his chest.

James studied him. He couldn't work out if he was over-worked, or drunk.

Then he shuffled closer, and the smell of him hit James.

The mystery was solved.

"Are you drunk?" he asked, politely. It was a rhetorical question.

"No." The man managed half-hearted affront. "Worked all night, is all."

An orderly or a doctor, James wondered. Given the lack of concern he seemed to have at being found in the state he was, James guessed he was a doctor.

He looked down at the book he was still holding. "I would like to be shown a body that was brought in five days ago. And your post mortem report, please."

"Who're you, then?" The man dragged a white coat off a hook on the wall, and struggled to put it on.

"Detective Sergeant Archer, of the Metropolitan Police." He pulled out his warrant card, but the man waved it away without even looking at it. "And you are?"

The man flashed him a look, thumped his chest again. "Dr. Venables. Who're you looking for again?"

James turned the book around to face him, pointed to the entry.

Venables squinted at the page, then shrugged. "This way."

He shuffled over to a door, unlocked it with the key that was already in the lock, and then entered. James followed, and found himself in a cold room with four stretchers, although only two were in use.

"This one," Venables said, and pulled back the covering sheet.

James looked down. "No. The victim in this case is a woman."

"Oh." He shuffled to the second body, and pulled the sheet back a little too hard, so the victim's upper body was exposed.

James pulled the sheet up again, so it lay across her collarbone. "What was cause of death?" he asked.

Venables walked to the end of the stretcher, lifted the clipboard that hung from the back. Stared at it for a long time. "Haven't got 'round to this one, yet."

James studied him for a beat, then turned on his heel and walked out of the room. He knew some of the fury he felt was a result of what had happened with Wilcox, but he no longer had patience for incompetence or disinterest.

He had seen a telephone on the reception desk and he lifted it and put a call through to Dr. Jandicott. While he was arranging for the body to be transferred into Jandicott's care, Venables had come out after him, and was now leaning against the wall, arms and legs crossed.

"So I don't have to do the post mortem?" he asked when James replaced the receiver.

"No, the body will be transferred to Dr. Jandicott."

"That's good." Venables pushed away from the wall, then turned as the door to the stairs opened and Hartridge stepped out.

"Eh?" Venables asked, looking between them.

"We're going, Hartridge." James noted down the time the body had been admitted to the hospital from the book, and then turned back to Venables. "You can go back to bed now."

Venables looked at him, unsure, and then muttered something as he stumbled back down the passage, into the room he'd originally emerged from.

"What is that *smell*?" Hartridge waved a hand in front of his nose. "Whisky?"

"I think so." James led the way up the stairs.

"What did he say was the cause of death?" Hartridge asked.

"Fortunately for us, he hadn't started the post mortem, because given the state of him, you couldn't rely on a single finding." Which wasn't right.

James asked the way to the superintendent's office, and made a formal complaint.

"That'll cost him his job," Hartridge said as they got back into the Wolseley. "The staff I asked when I went to look for him said he's often absent and has a drinking problem."

"Then *they* should have told the superintendent. If this

becomes part of a criminal case, and it came out in court what kind of state he's in while on the job, there'd be no justice for the victim." James was aware he sounded strident, and softened his tone. "If he'd called it an accidental death, and we weren't looking into it, then whoever's responsible would have gotten away with killing her, and that's not right."

Hartridge was silent as they drove away, and James didn't try to draw him into conversation.

He headed over the Thames to speak to a Mrs. Jenkins, who'd reported her daughter missing.

Of the eight missing reports, Mrs. Jenkins had made hers ten days ago. That would coincide with the death of victim two almost exactly.

They pulled up outside a home in East London, a tiny three story row house, sitting at the end of a long stretch of red brick houses, all with doors opening straight onto the street.

Mrs. Jenkins' door was black and nicely painted.

James knocked and waited, aware of eyes on him and Hartridge from up and down the street.

A few curtains twitched across the road, and passers-by slowed, watching them with eyes that held more than a little hostility.

The door opened a little and he saw a sliver of a woman's face. "Yes?"

"Mrs. Jenkins? I'm Detective Sergeant Archer, here to follow up on a missing person's report you made over a week ago?" He held out his warrant card.

She made a sound of surprise and pulled the door open. She was standing in house slippers and had obviously just taken off her house coat at the sound of the knock, as her jumper was on a little skew, and the coat itself swayed on the coat stand.

"You have news?" she asked, breathless. "News about my Beth?"

"No," James said, and he didn't hide his regret. "We're just getting more information, if you don't mind?"

She looked suddenly deflated, but shuffled back a little more. "Come in."

"This is Detective Constable Hartridge," James said, as he stepped in. "We don't want to take up too much of your time."

"If it would get me my Beth back, I'd stand around on one leg and chat until hell froze over." Mrs. Jenkins straightened her jumper, and her eyes snapped. "Would you like tea?"

"No, thank you." James could see she was far too upset to make them some, anyway. Best to get this done.

She led them through to the sitting room, and he sat carefully on the edge of a sofa, while Hartridge wisely chose to stand against the wall.

"Can you tell me the circumstances of Beth's disappearance?" James had the report, but he detected a distinct lack of detail in the wording.

"You have the report the police took from me?" Mrs. Jenkins asked, looking at the folder he held in his hands.

"I do, but I'd prefer to hear it from you. DC Hartridge will take notes while you talk, if that's all right?"

She looked over at Hartridge, gave a nod, and settled down in the armchair she'd chosen. "She was coming home from work at the hospital. She's on the late shift, and it was one of those nights we had the bad fog." She waved her hand at the window. "Dark and gloomy all day, it was."

James felt something in him stir. Percy, the little boy who lived opposite the site where the woman was left by the killer, had said it was foggy the night he saw the man with the wheelbarrow.

And Mr. Stanhope said there'd been a storm the night before they found the body in the ditch.

This killer used the weather to give himself cover. James made a mental note to check when the next fog or storm was predicted.

"And as far as you know, she left at the usual time and was coming straight home?" James asked.

Mrs. Jenkins gave a tight nod, her lips pinching under her teeth. "Spoke to the nursing sister myself, I did. She told me my

Beth left at the usual time. Said she was looking forward to getting home out of the pea soup."

"Can you tell us her usual route?" Hartridge asked, and James looked over at him with approval.

It was a good question.

Mrs. Jenkins told them the bus she took, and her usual route from the final stop to home.

"Does Beth have a dentist?" James asked.

Mrs. Jenkins made a sound, standing quickly, arms tight around her middle. "You've found someone? Someone dead?"

"We investigate suspicious deaths all the time," James soothed her. "We'd just like to have her dentist's name for the report in case we do think we've found her and need a method of identification."

Suspicious, but unwilling to go down the road she'd started on any further, Mrs. Jenkins gave them the name of a local dentist. She let them look around Beth's neat, spotless room and then saw them off from her doorstep, arms still tightly crossed, as if she might unravel if she let go.

"You think one of the bodies is Beth?" Hartridge asked as they walked toward the Wolseley.

"She didn't run away. She has no reason to leave her mother to worry like that. Her room, the way her mother talks about her . . . they were close. And when we talk to the hospital where she worked, my guess is they'll tell us Beth was never so much as late, let alone one to miss nearly two weeks of work."

If she'd taken a few days to go off with a man she'd met, or off on a holiday she hadn't told anyone about, she'd be back by now.

"If she's not one of the three bodies we've already got," James said, "then it's because we haven't found her yet."

chapter
twelve

GABRIELLA SLID the second sourdough loaf in the oven, and
dusted off her hands.

She started cleaning up Mr. Rodney's kitchen, wiping down
the kitchen table where she'd been kneading the dough. She
always baked when she needed to calm her thoughts, and since
she'd seen Ben that morning, her mind had been racing.

The front door opened on the murmur of voices, and she
called out a greeting.

"Gabriella." Solomon walked in, looking sharp enough to cut
through steak.

"Hey there." She smiled as she walked over to the the sink and
rinsed out the cloth she'd been using.

"Smells good." Mr. Rodney appeared in the doorway, head
lifted a little as he breathed in the scent of the loaf cooling on a
rack on the counter top. "You've spoiled me now. I can't stand the
mass produced supermarket rubbish anymore."

Gabriella lifted her brows. "I should hope so. My bread bears
no relationship to that dreck."

"Smells like a good bakery in here." George was the last one
into the kitchen.

Gabriella's smile widened. She liked George a lot, although
she didn't see him often. He was Solomon's right hand man in

whatever they did together, and she wasn't talking about their jobs for British Rail. "Hi George. How're things?"

They had all been out to dinner at the Calypso Club, and Gabriella could smell the scent of spices on them.

"Good, good." He turned at the sound of a knock on the door and went off to answer it.

"You expecting someone?" Solomon asked his uncle.

Mr. Rodney shook his head. "Maybe it's Jerome?"

George stuck his head in. "Jerome says there's a man here for you, Gabriella. Just been up to knock on your door. Not the copper."

She wiped her hands dry and walked to the front entrance. Just Jerome stood in the hallway.

"I let him go. Wasn't sure if you wanted him to know you were in." Jerome shrugged.

"He left?" Gabriella hurried to the main entrance to the old Victorian that had been divided into small apartments. She was curious as to who it could be.

As she opened the door, she was just in time to see Ben closing the garden gate in the weak light of the street lamp.

"Ben!"

He turned, smiled in relief, and came back up the path toward her.

"I was visiting my neighbor. Come in." She stepped back, giving him room to enter, and then saw George, Solomon, Jerome and Mr. Rodney all watching from the hallway.

She cleared her throat. "Ben, these are my friends and neighbors." She introduced them, and Mr. Rodney insisted on inviting Ben in for tea.

"You came over on the ship with Gabriella from Australia?" Mr. Rodney sounded intrigued. "You're one of the friends she meets with every now and then?"

"Yes." Ben glanced at her, as if surprised at how much Mr. Rodney knew. "Trevor, Dominique, Gabriella and I traveled over to London together from Melbourne. We like to keep in touch."

"Mr. Rodney used to live opposite me on the second floor," Gabriella explained. "We walked to the bus stop together a few times when I went out to meet you and the others."

"Now I have this lovely flat," Mr. Rodney said, waving his hand around. "And it came with an oven that Gabriella can make her bread in."

"She made the bread for the passengers on the ship over," Ben said. "We all worked in the kitchen, but Gabriella was the only one who had actual skills." He sniffed the air. "I'd forgotten how good it smelled."

They indulged in small talk for a while, and finally Gabriella realized she couldn't stand it any more. "What couldn't wait until tomorrow?" she asked Ben. "Have you been told you can't help me?"

There was sudden silence.

"What's this about?" Mr. Rodney asked. "Help you with what?"

She clasped her hands, trying to contain her nerves. "Ruby Everett has found my father for me. Or, we think she has." She had no qualms talking to Mr. Rodney about it. She had long ago told him her reason for coming to London and he had given her help in her early efforts to find birth and death certificates. "Ben is a lawyer and I asked him to look into what my next steps should be."

"Gabriella, this sounds very promising." Mr. Rodney set his mug of tea down.

"I know." She lifted her shoulders to get rid of tension. "I wanted Ben to make sure the information was right before I approached the man Ruby thinks is my father."

"You make it sound as if there might be trouble," Solomon said.

She looked over at him, gave a nod. "Big trouble."

"How so?" George asked.

"Because of who he is. Did your senior tell you you can't do it?" she asked again, her gaze fixed on Ben.

"No." He looked like he was uncomfortable talking about it, and she realized he didn't want to say anything in the company of people he didn't know.

"You can speak freely." She had been through a lot with every person in this room. She trusted them, and knew they might have some interesting insights.

Ben looked around, and then gave a nod. "My senior hired me, an unknown Aussie outsider, because he's pretty anti-establishment. I think he's got a chip on his shoulder against the upper classes. The rumor is that he's the bastard son of a lord or something. Got sent to the right schools and universities by his father, but his old man never acknowledged him openly. It led to him being tormented by his legitimate peers.

"I don't know if that's true, but it is true that he has utter contempt for a lot of his colleagues. He hides it pretty well, but it's there. He hired me mainly because I'm an Australian who has no connections to the law community here."

"So he's fine with you helping me?" Gabriella asked.

"He's positively thrilled." Ben rubbed the back of his neck. "Maybe a little too thrilled."

"Why's that?" Solomon asked.

"Because Gabby's father is a viscount." Ben lifted both hands. "And her case will destroy her father's reputation and cut the children he's had with the woman who thinks she's his wife off from what they think is their inheritance, and put it in Gabby's hands."

There was a moment of stunned silence.

"You're a lady, then?" George's amusement broke the tension.

"Maybe," Gabriella said, sending him a grin. "Could you tell?"

"Of course." He pointed a finger at her.

"You're worried his motives are revenge against the establishment that rejected and hurt him, more than representing Gabriella's interests?" Solomon asked.

Ben gave a nod. "Exactly. But he'll do this pro bono, Gabby. He says it'll be a pleasure."

She had, at most, been expecting some advice from Ben. To have a full silk, a QC, actively involved in her case, was not something to dismiss out of hand. It was more than she'd envisioned, by far.

"You think having him on this will be to my advantage?" she asked Ben.

He gave a nod. "He's brilliant. And when he sets his mind on something, I haven't known him to lose yet. He'll be an attack dog on your behalf, but in this case, it might be on his own behalf, too."

"A balm for slights of the past, not necessarily from those involved in this case, but from others in their group?" Mr. Rodney asked.

Ben nodded. "And once we set out on this path, I don't think there's a way to get off until it's done."

"You still want to go ahead, Gabriella?" Solomon asked.

She thought about it, but not for long. "My father's trapped my mother in limbo for years and years. She can't move on with her life because of him, while he's married and has a whole new family. I'm going ahead."

"All right, then." Ben stood. "I'll let my boss know."

She got up herself, gave him a quick hug. "Still see you tomorrow?"

He nodded. "I'll be there."

Solomon had been leaning against the counter, but now he pushed himself away. "You need a lift, Ben? George and I are off and we could drop you somewhere."

There was something going on behind Solomon's friendly offer, and Gabriella wondered what it could be, but Ben happily agreed and they walked out together.

The oven timer for the second loaf broke the silence that had fallen as the front door closed, and Gabriella realized she had been sitting, hands clasped, almost in a daze.

"I'll take this loaf and be out of your hair, Mr. Rodney." She pulled it out of the oven and wrapped it in a cloth.

"You be careful, Gabriella." Mr. Rodney had gotten to his feet as she'd dealt with the bread. "It sounds as if your father and his new family have a lot to lose if you come into their life. I'll tell Solomon to get the lads to keep a close eye."

"I will," she promised. She could add her father into the same group as the man in the green Jag. And the farmer who'd electrocuted her.

As she and Jerome walked upstairs together to their flats, she pondered on the number of people who seemed to have a reason to wish her harm.

Fortunately, there were more people who consistently helped and supported her. She had friends at her back. She wasn't going to go up against her father alone.

She firmed her resolve. Her father had made his bed. Now he would have to lie in it.

chapter
thirteen

IT WAS past the end of the work day, and it was a Friday.

James knew it was the best time to catch people at home, and he was planning to try and reach every one of the eight people on his list.

They'd already visited a few places where no one was home, and they would be looping back there for another try.

They'd spoken to the hospital where Beth Jenkins worked, and as he'd suspected, all her colleagues were convinced something terrible had happened to her.

Two of the stops they'd made had allowed them to tentatively cross names off their list, as it seemed more likely that one of the women had returned to her home in Scotland without telling anyone, and another had been seriously ill.

He and Hartridge would check those out in the morning, but James's gut feel was that the one was safe and sound with her mother in Glasgow, and the other was perhaps in hospital, perhaps dead, of the asthma that had plagued her her whole life.

The fog had been very bad the day she'd disappeared, which had initially made James fear she was one of their victims, but her landlady, who'd reported her missing, had admitted she had been struggling with the weather conditions, and when they'd gone to her place of work, one of her colleagues had told him and Hartridge as they were leaving that the last time they'd seen her, her lips had been blue.

"This next one has a high likelihood of being one of our victims." James pulled up beside the well-kept home on a typical suburban street. "The report was made by a Mrs. Davies. According to her, her daughter Tamara never came home after a night out."

As he stepped out of the car he looked down the street, unsure if this neighborhood was on the rise or spiraling downward. For every neat garden and well-maintained front porch there was a house with rubbish lying around it, and overgrown grass. This part of the city was near the docks, and conveniently close to the center of town, so he guessed eventually it would be on the rise, no matter what was happening with it now.

Most of the houses were semi-detached, but the Davies home stood in its own little garden, enclosed by a neatly painted white fence.

"Handy for work," Hartridge said, echoing his own thinking as he studied the neighborhood. "Might actually be affordable."

"Not for long," James predicted. "It's got location going for it."

Hartridge gave a nod, and James guessed they'd both be looking into this area when they got a chance.

He was renting, and Hartridge was currently housed in the Met's single quarters barracks.

Getting his own place would be good. If he decided he wanted to stay in London, that was.

His thoughts turned almost automatically to Gabriella, and he realized he missed seeing her, even though this would only be the third evening in a row he hadn't stopped by to visit her.

Hartridge had opened the gate, and he followed him up the stone paving to the front door.

A small dog yapped and barked from within, and Hartridge had just lifted the knocker when the door swung open.

"Yes?" The man who stood in the doorway was beefy, with thick muscle-roped arms, visible because he had turned up his shirt sleeves despite the cold weather.

James took an instant dislike to him.

He had seen the look in the man's eyes before, when he'd worked as a constable, breaking up pub fights. This was someone who'd break a bottle over the back of your head and then kick you in the ribs when you were down.

A stone cold scrapper.

The way he stepped back at the sight of them told James he didn't like that James was as big as he was, and a little taller. He really didn't like it at all.

James sometimes wished he was a less threatening presence, especially when dealing with victims, but he was glad of his height and his build now.

He took his time looking down at his notebook. "Mr. Davies?" He let his Welsh burr out as he asked the question. "You a Welshman?"

Davies blinked, shook his head. "Not that I know." He narrowed his eyes. "Who're you, then?"

"Detective Sergeant Archer." James extended his warrant card. "This is DC Hartridge. We're following up on the missing person's report your wife lodged two weeks ago."

From the sudden frown, James guessed Davies hadn't liked that his wife had filed the report. "Right." Davies took another step back. "Following up how?"

"We're just wondering if your wife had heard from the person she reported missing in the meanwhile?" James asked. "Her daughter?" He looked down at his notebook again.

When he looked back up, a woman was standing just off to the side. She was in a house dress, her hair was tied up in a scarf, and there was a fading, yellow bruise near her hairline, on her left cheek.

"Evening, Mrs. Davies," he said. "Sorry to disturb you. We're just following up on your daughter's disappearance."

"You found her?" Mrs. Davies grabbed the door jamb, clutching it with both hands, as if that's the only way she had of keeping herself on her feet.

She was careful not to touch her husband, James noted.

"No, sorry. We're just wondering if you'd heard from her since she disappeared. This was two weeks ago, is that right?" James's gaze settled back on Davies.

"Didn't come home after she went out drinking with her friends," Davies said. "I told her, you go out on a boozer, you'll come to a bad end." He pursed his lips.

"And that's what you think happened?" Hartridge asked, pencil out to write notes. "That she came to a bad end?"

Mrs. Davies gasped out loud, and then hurried away, and her husband looked after her, absolutely no expression on his face.

"I don't know what happened to her. That's your job, innit?"

"It is," James said, nodding. "And please rest assured, Mr. Davies, we'll leave no stone unturned."

Davies looked up sharply at that, as if sensing the threat. "Well good, because we haven't seen hide nor hair of her since that night."

"And what do her friends say? Have you talked to them?" James asked.

"Don't know who they are, do I?" He narrowed his eyes. "The wife might." He shouted for her, and she scurried back, a handkerchief held to her face.

"Do you know the names of the friends your daughter went out with the night she disappeared?" James asked.

"I only know Yvette, who lives down the road. Yvette Henderson." Mrs. Davies pointed down the street. "Number 12."

"Thank you. And please let us know if you hear anything." James passed his card to her, ignoring the hand Davies put out for it. "We'll let you get on with your evening."

Davies slammed the door in their faces, and they walked silently back to the pavement and got into the Wolseley.

"You didn't like him," Hartridge said. "Was that because he never invited us in?"

James shook his head. "Every other person we visited today immediately assumed we were there because we had some news. That the person they'd reported missing had either been spotted or found."

"Yes." Hartridge gave a slow nod.

"Davies didn't act as if that was even a possibility." James pointed to number 12, and Hartridge started the car and drove the short distance to Yvette Henderson's.

"You're saying he didn't ask questions because he already knows the answers?" Hartridge sounded shocked. "You think he knows what happened to his daughter?"

"I do. I think he's the one who did something to her." James looked out the window at the slightly more run-down house where Mrs. Davies said her daughter's friend lived. "Did you also notice that everyone else used the missing person's name, some quite a few times. Davies didn't say her name once."

"You don't think he's our killer, do you?" Hartridge stared at him, then gave a shake of his head. "No. But you do think he's responsible for this one."

"I do." And it pained him. James could think of no reason why Davies would be surprised and confused at their presence unless he knew his daughter was dead, and that her body wouldn't be found.

They knocked on the door of number 12, and a young woman answered, wearing huge hoop earrings, slim-fit trousers and a soft jumper in a pale pink that matched her lipstick.

"Yeah?" she asked.

"Yvette Henderson?" James held out his warrant card.

"Oh, my God! You found Tammy?" she breathed.

"Sorry, we haven't. We've just come from her parents—"

"That bastard." Yvette's eyes sparked.

"Language, Yvette. And who have you got standing in the

doorway?" A woman who was clearly Yvette's mother came and stood beside her, a cigarette dangling from brightly painted lips. "Yes?"

"Police, Mrs. Henderson." James held out his warrant card again.

"It's about Tammy, Mum." Yvette stared at them, hostility in every line of her body. "They've been listening to that pig, Davies."

Her mother looked appalled, but she also didn't correct her daughter, which James took to mean she agreed with her daughter's assessment, but didn't like her using bad language in public.

"You think Mr. Davies had something to do with Tammy's disappearance?" he asked.

Yvette seemed to deflate. "No. I thought she'd been nabbed walking back from the bus stop."

"Didn't you walk together?" Hartridge asked, and it was a fair question. Their houses were in sight of each other.

"I wish I had, but I came home earlier than she did. I had to open the shop at 8 that week, you see, because we were doing stock take. So I had to call an early night. But Tammy only had to be in the office by 9, so she kept dancing." Yvette closed her eyes, and a tear tracked its way down her cheek.

"Did you see anyone suspicious on your way home?" James asked her, making his voice gentle. "Anyone that gave you a bad feeling?"

Yvette looked at him, and then shrugged. "Plenty. But that's every time I go out. Weren't no different, if that's what you mean. No one stood out more than usual."

"Thank you." He looked down the street, towards the Davies residence. "Would Tammy have told you if there was something wrong at home?"

Yvette took the handkerchief her mother held out to her and dabbed at her eyes. "Like her father backhanding her and her mum, you mean?"

"Yes." James nodded. "That's what I mean."

"He's a brute." Yvette's mother shook her head. "One of those in charge on the docks, he is. Struts around. And has a nasty temper."

"He'd lash out on a whim," Yvette told them. "Tammy was scared of him. And saving up to move out."

The fog had come up while they had been talking to Yvette, and the car was almost invisible when they got back to it. They got in and sat in silence for a moment.

"You think he killed her?" Hartridge asked.

"It's possible. She comes back, maybe a little drunk. Talks back. He's maybe been drinking himself, hits her. Hits her harder than usual, because she dares disrespect him. And suddenly he's looking down at the dead body of his daughter." James could see it all too well.

"That's . . ." Hartridge shook his head. He reached for the ignition with the key, and James shot out a hand, clamped his forearm.

"Shh," he said. Tipped his head to the pavement, to the man walking past, head down, collar pulled up against the cold.

"Davies?" Hartridge breathed.

"Yes." And James wondered where he was going after his chat with the police.

"Where do you think he's put the body, if he did kill her?" Hartridge asked.

"I'm guessing he threw her into the Thames." If he worked the docks, which Yvette's mother seemed to suggest, then he'd know the tides, would know where to put her in that would pull her downriver.

"That's why he knew we weren't there with any update. He doesn't think her body will ever be found." Hartridge swore softly. "Bastard."

"If we're right," James cautioned. "He might just be a cold one. A brute who's loose with his fists but not responsible."

"Sure," Hartridge said. "But you don't believe that."

No. No, he didn't.

But that didn't get him any closer to knowing who'd killed the other three women in London.

Still . . .

He leaned forward, looking for the silhouette of Davies in the fog. "Let's follow him."

chapter
fourteen

THE PUB WAS LOUD.

James and Hartridge stood outside it, and shared a look.

If they went in, Davies might notice them, and given the building's proximity to the docks, he guessed the place was full of Davies' fellow dock workers.

They would be severely outnumbered.

"I think a strategic retreat is in order," James said. "We won't learn anything here, anyway." If they had followed Davies to the dock, or if he'd acted suspiciously in the vicinity of the river, James would have kept eyes on him, but it looked like he was just off to spend the night with his mates.

Hartridge nodded, and James thought he relaxed a little.

"We have two names left on the list." And so far, Mrs. Jenkins had been the only one they'd spoken to whose daughter seemed a viable match. "It's only seven. Let's knock on a few more doors."

The fog was almost impossibly thick now, especially by the river. It caught the back of James's throat and he coughed as he almost walked into the side of the Wolseley.

People walked past, stumbling around a little as they headed for the diffused light of the pub's lit up windows, and he got inside the car with a sense of relief.

"Maybe we should call it a night?" Hartridge said. "Driving in this will be dangerous."

James didn't want to, but as Hartridge started the engine and turned on the headlights, he could barely see the road in front of them. It would be reckless to continue.

"Let's drive to the barracks to get you home," James said, eventually. "I'll continue on to the Yard to pick up my car."

Hartridge nodded, not even trying to protest that he didn't need a lift home.

When they finally reached the tall, austere post-war block that housed the single officers of the Met, Hartridge was leaning forward in his seat, eyes glued to the road.

"Whew, that was dicey." Hartridge dropped his hands from the wheel and shook out his shoulders. "I'm glad that's over."

James still had to drive to New Scotland Yard and get his own car, and he wasn't looking forward to it. He got out of the Wolseley and walked around the front to the driver's side. Hartridge opened the door and stood, his gaze going to the front of the barracks. He froze in place, eyes on someone hovering by the entrance.

"Who is it?" James kept his voice soft, and the thick fog dampened the sound even more.

Hartridge looked at him, then turned back. "I think it's Galbraith," he said on an exhale.

"Come to do what, exactly?" James was tired of guessing.

Hartridge sighed. "It's a long story."

"Then get in the back, keep low, and come home with me tonight." He slid behind the wheel, and after a moment's hesitation, he heard Hartridge quietly open the door behind him and get in.

He drove the five minutes to the Yard, parked in a dark corner, and the two of them got into James's Morris.

Hartridge said nothing as he drove home, swinging by to get fish and chips along the way.

He ate far too much fish and chips he thought as he handed

the wrapped package of their dinner to Hartridge. They drove home with the scent of vinegar filling the car.

When they got up to his flat, he found plates and cutlery, and they ate in silence, both hungry after their long day.

Eventually, though, Hartridge set down his beer and leaned back.

"Thanks," he said, nodding toward the decimated dinner. "Galbraith would have probably given me a hiding."

James lifted his brows. That wouldn't surprise him, knowing what little he did of Galbraith. And if Hartridge fought back, he could be accused of striking a superior.

"What's all this about, Ian?" James pushed his plate aside.

"While you were gone, DI Whetford came into the office, said he had a job for me." Hartridge began to peel the label off his beer.

"A dirty job," James guessed.

Hartridge looked up, eyes bleak. "A dirty job," he agreed. "I'd heard the rumors, but I didn't know for sure."

"What game is he running?" James asked.

"He had me arrest this bloke on what he said was an anonymous tip. A bookie down the White City greyhound track. The charge was insider trading." Hartridge blew out a breath and shook his head. "Then two hours after I had him in custody, Whetford told me to let him go, and me and Galbraith were to drive him home."

"Did Whetford interview him first?" James asked.

Hartridge shook his head. "I thought maybe the person who phoned it in withdrew the accusation, or something." He lifted his shoulders. "But that wasn't it."

He lifted his bottle, took another sip, and eventually slumped a little deeper into his chair. "On the way home, Galbraith pulled in to this little car park and started telling the bookie, Arnie Forks, that we had him bang to rights, but if he wanted it to all go away, he could pass along any tips he heard—anything dodgy going down—and any inside information on which dogs might win which race."

James slumped a little in his chair himself.

"I honestly thought Galbraith might be playing him, you know?" Hartridge shook his head. "Like, setting a trap."

"But he was serious," James guessed.

Hartridge sighed. "When we dropped Forks off, Galbraith told him to remember my face, that when I came around, he better have some good info for me, or he'd be back in interview, with no easy way out next time."

"That's what Galbraith was trying to get out of you? What you'd gotten from Forks?"

Hartridge nodded. "Yes. I waited until I saw Forks leave the two times Galbraith sent me, and then knocked, so I could say he wasn't there."

"And Galbraith isn't happy. Probably getting pressure from Whetford, who wants to keep his hands as clean as possible." James had known Whetford was on the take, but this was more. This wasn't looking the other way, or taking a backhander to lose evidence. This was going out and actively coercing criminals into providing inside information for his own profit.

"What do I do?" Hartridge asked. "How do I get out of this?"

"We'll find a way." James was not standing for it. "For now, sleep on my couch, and we'll head out in the morning for the last four interviews—the two who were out when we came calling, and the two we didn't get to this evening."

"What about Davies?" Hartridge asked.

"I'll talk to the Thames Division," James said. "Ask them to let me know if they find a body in the river."

"You really think he killed her and threw her in the Thames?" Hartridge stood and began clearing up.

"I don't think he meant to kill her, but once he did, he panicked." James could see it all too easily. "What we need to do is go over and interview Mrs. Davies while he's at work. See what she has to say without him there."

"She won't say anything," Hartridge said. "She's too beaten down. Too scared of him."

"Maybe," James conceded. "But she loved her daughter. It was her who reported Tamara missing, and that did not please Davies at all. And she is obviously very worried about her."

He washed the dishes and Hartridge dried.

The fog lifted a little, the wind blowing it seaward, and he stared out the window as the sky cleared.

"What are you thinking?" Hartridge asked.

"I'm thinking our man might be out hunting tonight, given the fog. But now it's lifting, maybe we'll get lucky. Let's hope he didn't find a victim in time."

chapter
fifteen

GABRIELLA MADE a point to get to the pub early.

Ben was always there first because he lived closest, and she wanted a few minutes alone with him before Dominique and Trevor arrived.

She'd spent her Saturday morning shift thinking about what was coming next in her case, and realized she needed to get a timeline out of Ben.

He waved to her when she walked in, and she rubbed her hands together as she made her way to the booth, nose and cheeks stinging in the sudden warmth of the pub.

"You're early," Ben said.

"On purpose," she told him. "I wanted to know what to expect from your boss. I don't even know his name."

"Monty Havelock, QC." Ben said the name with a put-on upper class accent.

"That's how he speaks?" she asked.

"He speaks better English than the queen. All part of what drives him, I think. He won't allow a single chink in his armor." Ben's lips twisted in a wry smile. "He'll be in touch next week some time. He'll be on this quickly, I promise you that."

She gave a nod. "Can you tell me what Solomon's business was with you, when he gave you a lift home?"

He looked up, eyes wide, and then leaned back. "Client privilege, Gabby. I can't say."

"So he's now a client." That was all she needed to know. Solomon had hired Ben for something. She wondered what it could be, but it wasn't surprising. Solomon was getting more organized. She could tell by the number of people he seemed to command, and the fact that he'd had the money to recently buy a car.

Sooner or later, he'd come to the attention of someone in authority. If he hadn't already.

It was wise to get a lawyer on his side ahead of any possible trouble.

She hoped Ben knew what he was getting into, but she also hoped Solomon was able to stay out of trouble. A lot of people depended on him, including Mr. Rodney.

"He's an interesting man," Ben said. "Where does his family hail from?"

"Trinidad and Tobago. And don't you ever confuse that with Jamaica," Gabriella told him, very seriously. "Ever. It's like mistaking Australians for New Zealanders."

"Got you." Ben grinned, then looked toward the door and waved.

Dominique and Trevor walked in, removing hats and coats as the heat inside hit them.

There was the usual laughter as they got drinks and settled in, catching up and exchanging news. Neeky had been working at Terrific Teen magazine for a few months now, and had managed to get off the reception desk and into the main office. She was telling a hilarious story about trying on bright pink and yellow eye shadow for one of the feature writers, putting one shade on each eyelid, and then forgetting it was still on when she took the bus home.

"I brought your cousin some samples," she said, holding out a pretty package to Trevor. "I remember you said she reads Terrific Teen."

"Ta." Trev took it with a grin. "That'll get my points up."

"And you, Gabs?" Dominique leaned forward. "Any news about your dad?"

Gabriella shared a quick look with Ben, then gave a nod.

"What?" Neeky reached out to grip her hand. "What did you find? And Ben knows? How come?"

Gabriella laughed. "Ben knows because I asked him to take on my case. Ruby Everett helped me find my father. And what she found was my father has a title."

There was a moment of silence.

"You're kidding?" Trevor frowned.

"No. I wish I were. My father got on that ship as Lord Granger, and that was exactly who he was." She had sent a letter to her mother yesterday. She had agonized over the wording, and hoped to get some answers from her. "My uncle always said he never liked my father because he always acted like he was better than everyone else. Now I know why."

"Where is he based?" Dominique asked.

"Sussex. Near Chichester. He has a wife and family." Her lips twisted. "Or, not a legal wife, given I have the marriage certificate between him and my mother that predates his second marriage. And he has three kids."

"Three kids who think they're legitimate heirs, but who are not," Ben added.

"Shit." Trevor leaned back and looked over at Ben. "That's where you come in. It'll get ugly."

Ben nodded. "This is going to shock the circles he runs in, and it will likely devastate his family."

"Bloody hell, Gabs." Neeky shook her head. "What a bastard."

"The thought of how long my mother has held off getting into a new relationship, wondering what happened to him, and there he is, married with three kids." Gabriella had known that was likely, if he wasn't dead, but now that she had the actual proof, it was enraging.

"Well, congratulations," Trevor said. "You did it."

She nodded. She should feel elated. She thought she would be, if she ever succeeded. But she wasn't. She felt angry and sad and sick to her stomach.

Careful what you wish for, her aunt had murmured to her when she was saying goodbye to everyone at the Melbourne docks.

Gabriella had understood the warning, but she had thought helping her mother move forward would be worth it.

She still believed that, but it came with a price that was higher than she'd ever imagined.

She wondered if she wanted to see her father in person, and lifted her shandy as Trevor declared a toast to her success. She would put that decision off for another day, she decided as she forced a smile onto her face and took a drink. There would most likely be more than enough time to decide.

They all left together, walking out into a dense fog that had gathered while they'd been in the pub.

Ben coughed. "These pea soupers are happening more and more often," he said when he got his breath back.

"The one a couple of weeks ago was the worst," Neeky said. "I was coming home, and I literally couldn't see my hand in front of my face."

Gabriella had worked an early shift the day it was really bad, so she'd been home before things got too dangerous. Last night, though, it had been bad for quite a while before the wind came up and started to lighten it.

This morning, when she'd worked the early Saturday shift, it had still been hanging in the air, although a wispy and insubstantial shadow of what it had been the night before.

Ben coughed again.

"You going to be all right?" she asked.

"Yes." He waved it off. "But I think it's time for me to get home."

He and Trev needed to go in the same direction, so they

walked her and Dominique to the bus stop and then headed off together.

Gabriella could hear Ben's cough fade into the distance as she and Dominique stood huddled under the bus shelter.

"I'm proud of you, Gabs. You've done what you set out to do." Neeky tucked her hand into the crook of Gabriella's elbow.

"Not quite. But at least I've found him. There's a very small chance everyone has got it wrong, and it's not him, but . . ."

"But you don't think so?" Dominique asked.

"No." There were too many coincidences for him to be anyone else. "But it's going to get ugly, just like Trevor said. I'm going to be upending a family's peaceful life, and even though it's my father's fault, I bet most of them are going to blame me."

"They'd be wrong to, but . . . yes. You're the stranger, and he's their dad or husband. And they're going to lose a lot because you've popped up." Dominique gripped her arm harder as the bus pulled up, hurrying them both up the stairs and out of the fog and cold.

They sat near the front on the lower level, taking the first two seats together they could find on the packed bus. "Everyone's calling an early night, what with this weather," Dominique said, looking around. "It's horrendous, and I heard on the radio at work yesterday that they're afraid there'll be a few more really bad ones before this is over."

It *was* horrendous. Gabriella looked out at the gray smoke that swirled around the window, impenetrable and slightly other-worldly. There was a pall over the city, a choking, polluted cloud, and she wished suddenly for the uncomplicated, blue skies of home.

"Do you miss Melbourne?" she asked Dominique as the bus driver changed gear and jerked her in her seat.

"I miss the weather. God. I really miss the weather. But the independence is gold, Gabs. Priceless." Dominique rested her head on Gabriella's shoulder, her blonde hair tickling Gabriella's nose.

"That's true." She had not liked the pressure to marry a good Italian boy and have babies. Not at all. "They would have fifty fits if I brought James home with me."

"What do you mean? You haven't even brought him home to *us*." Dominique lifted her head and turned, face showing exaggerated outrage. "And best you do, young lady. I demand to meet this person."

Gabriella laughed. "I've meant to so many times, but it's so hard to say when he is and isn't working. Why don't we organize a picnic in Hyde Park on a Sunday afternoon, unless it's raining? If James can make it, all good. If he can't, it will still be fun."

"And what if it is raining?" Dominique asked.

"Then we go down the pub." Gabriella shrugged.

"Deal. I'll send a note to Trev, you send one to Ben, find a date that works. I'm curious as a cat about your man." Dominique had gone out a lot since she'd moved to London, but no one had lasted more than a few dates. They wanted to go too far, too fast, she'd told Gabriella. And some got ugly when she pulled the brakes.

"It's like they think they're entitled to my body in exchange for a meal of fish and chips," Dominique had told Gabriella, outraged. "Like I can't buy my own bloody fish and chips. Like that's all I'm worth. No thank you."

It was a strange new world from the one their parents had grown up in. Boundaries were being pushed, but both Gabriella and Dominique didn't see why they should be forced into anything they didn't like or want.

"Some of the girls don't have enough self-confidence to say no," Dominique told her. "I see it at work. They try to pass it off as being hip, but they look a little lost."

The bus turned a corner, pushing them both up against the window, and Dominique got to her feet. "This is me."

Gabriella often got out with her and walked her home, then walked home herself, but tonight, staying in the bus seemed like the sensible option.

They hugged goodbye and Gabriella watched the fog swallow Dominique up in a single gulp as she stepped out into the night.

"Filthy tonight, it is," the bus driver said to her as he pulled the doors closed. "Where you getting out, love?"

"Notting Hill," she told him. Taking this bus meant she and Dominique could travel most of the way together, but it dropped her off at the far end of Notting Hill. Not her usual route.

Still, the slightly longer walk was worth the extra time with Neeky.

When the bus reached her stop, she stepped out into slightly yellow-tinged smog, and the sulfur smell caught her in the back of her throat. She lifted her scarf around her mouth as she coughed her way across the street and started walking home.

A breeze began to swirl around her as she walked, clearing the way ahead almost perfectly and then sweeping the fog around her to obscure absolutely everything again.

She kept her eyes on the ground and almost walked straight into a light pole, jerking back just in time. She stood still for a moment, getting her heart beat under control, and suddenly the way cleared again, the breeze parting the yellow smoke so that she was looking straight at a dark green Jaguar, parked facing away from her, three houses down from her building.

She could just make out the number plate, and it was the same as the one she'd seen the other day, outside of headquarters.

She stood, rooted to the spot for a moment, fear a tingling, crawling spider on her skin.

She shuddered. He was watching her house.

How had he known where she lived?

She would have to work that out later. Right now, she needed to decide what to do.

Confront him, or slip around the back way and come into the building from the rear courtyard?

She knew if she snuck in, she would be aware of him lurking out here, watching.

The thought of it was unbearable.

So, confront, then.

She gripped her bag strap a little tighter, and tried to bolster herself with the memory of how quickly he'd run away last time. Although, this time he wasn't in front of the traffic warden's headquarters on a work day afternoon. He was on an empty, fog-darkened street, late at night.

He might be braver this time.

Then she'd have to be braver, too.

She walked forward, and as she did, the fog enveloped her again. She reached the passenger window, on the pavement side, and rapped hard against the glass.

She had the sense of him starting within—perhaps he'd been asleep—and then she opened the door, half expecting it to be locked. But it wasn't. It swung open, and she bent a little, staring straight at him.

"What are you doing here?" She was proud her voice wasn't as thin and high as she was afraid it would be. "Why are you watching me?"

He was shocked. She could see it on his face in the weak interior light that had come on when she'd opened the door.

"Well?" She narrowed her eyes.

She saw the moment he decided to bluster—his gaze slid to the side and then back to her, and he sat a little straighter. "I don't know what you're talking about, missy."

She laughed in his face. "You know full well. So let's hear it, why are you following me? And how did you find out where I live?"

He lunged toward her, and she stumbled back, but he was simply going for the door. He pulled it shut, locked it, and started the car.

She stood on the pavement, wondering what she could do, when Solomon suddenly appeared in front of the car's bumper.

Jerome seemed to materialize out of the fog beside her, and George was on the driver's side.

The man had locked the passenger door, but he hadn't locked

the driver's door, and George pulled it open, reached in and switched the engine off.

For a beat there was absolute silence and then Gabriella walked around to stand next to George.

"The lady asked you a question," George said.

Mr. Green Jag seemed to fold in on himself, eyes darting all over the place. "Let me go."

"Not until you answer the question." Solomon rapped his knuckles on the front bumper. "Can't be too hard, now can it?"

"I just wanted to have a word with her," Mr. Jag mumbled. "Warn her not to say anything."

"Looked like you were running away to me," George said.

"I decided it was a mistake to approach her this way," Mr. Jaguar said.

"Say anything about what?" Gabriella asked, pushing aside the fact that he was talking to George, ignoring her standing right there.

"About where I was when you fined me." Mr. Jag snapped out the sentence, finally looking at her.

"To who?" She lifted her hands, baffled.

He was silent for a moment. "My wife," he said eventually.

"How would your wife even know to ask me?" Gabriella asked.

"Not her personally." Mr. Jag sneered as he said it, lifting his nose slightly. "But she's hired someone to look into it. The Jag's in her name, and she got the fine. Well, not at first, I saw it come in and I threw it away. But somehow one got through before I could ditch it. And she suspects I intercepted the others, so now she's suspicious."

"And she told you this?" Gabriella asked, flummoxed. What lives did these people live?

"No." Again, the condescending sneer. "I overhead the conversation she had with the private detective on the phone."

"Picked up the receiver in another room, did you?" Solomon asked, with an amused grin.

Mr. Jaguar gave him a cold look, then turned his head to glare at Gabriella. "Never mind. Just keep your mouth shut, you hear?"

"Or what?" George asked softly.

For a moment, Mr. Jaguar was quiet.

"Man asked you a question," Solomon said. "Or what?"

As if aware of the dangerous ground he was walking, he suddenly shook his head. "Never mind."

"You don't come back here," Solomon said. "And if you do, understand this. You mess with our friend, you mess with us. And, Mr. High and Mighty, you don't want to mess with us."

George stepped back, and Mr. Jaguar closed the door probably harder than he meant to, started the engine, and then, when Solomon stepped onto the pavement, rode off in a screech of tires.

"Thank you. Really. That was so great of you." Gabriella nudged George. "I was really nervous."

"Didn't stop you confronting him," George said.

She shrugged. "I considered creeping in the back way, not speaking to him, but I'd have known he was out here, lurking, and I wanted to find out what was going on."

"Next time, come find us," Solomon said. "But I respect you for fighting your own battles."

She blew out a breath. "And hopefully, thanks to you three, that's one battle won."

chapter
sixteen

JAMES WANTED to spend Sunday with Gabriella.

He didn't care what they did.

He woke early and got dressed, checking his watch as he ate toast, wondering if it was too soon to go round to her flat.

He had no idea if she slept in or not. The two times he'd spent the night with her had been under fraught circumstances, and they didn't really count.

He had spent the whole of Saturday at New Scotland Yard with Hartridge, going through any like crimes, after he'd come to the conclusion their killer was too efficient to be doing this for the first time.

They had gone back five years, and while there had been a few that looked similar, they had not managed to find anything that was close enough to be a sure thing.

He shook his shoulders, trying to put that all aside. He needed a break, and he needed Gabriella.

As he pulled on a jacket and got his wallet and keys, his telephone rang, and he turned to look at it with trepidation.

It could be Gabriella, ringing him up from the phone box on the corner of her street, inviting him to breakfast, or it could be work.

He lifted the receiver.

"Archer." DI Whetford's voice was clipped. "There's a nuclear disarmament march today. Seems like a lot of rank and file have come down with the flu, and uniform are stretched too thin, so the Met is having to offer up our detectives. Sorry if you had plans today, but you'll need to come down and suit up by ten."

James kept his voice steady with some effort. "Ten?" he asked. It was seven thirty now.

"They're marching into the city from Aldermaston. Ten's the earliest they'll get here, by Uniform's estimates." Whetford cleared his throat. "Get hold of DC Hartridge and make sure he comes, too."

That seemed like a very specific request.

"I'll be happy to stop by and let him know, but won't he already have heard, if everyone is being called in?"

"Perhaps." Whetford's tone was sharp. "But as your bagman, he's your responsibility."

James leaned against the wall, wondering what game Whetford was playing. "Sure, I'll swing round, see if I can give him a lift."

"You do that, Archer." Whetford cut the call short.

Whetford was James's immediate superior, but someone senior from uniform branch could just as easily have rung him up. And Whetford never stirred himself to any effort unless there was something in it for him.

This felt like a set up, or a trap, even though James had read the paper that morning, and the march had been mentioned. It was definitely happening today, and they definitely needed all hands on deck.

He went back to his room to change into heavy boots and uniform pants, the only things he had in the flat of any use on a cordon line. He would have to get a thick jacket at headquarters.

He drove to the barracks to find Hartridge, but parked a few streets away. If Galbraith was watching, as he had a suspicion he might be after the strange call from Whetford, he'd rather slip in unnoticed.

He couldn't decide if he was being paranoid or not, but it didn't hurt to be cautious.

He used the side entrance to the building, following behind two officers who turned as he came up behind them. He knew one of them, remembering him from a case earlier in the year, and nodded in greeting.

"Here for Hartridge?" the officer asked.

He recalled the man's name. "Morning, Norris. Yes, we've got a lead on our current case, but I've also had word that they're short staffed for the CND thing. We've been asked to help."

"You and everyone else, mate," Norris said with a grimace. "I'll show you where Hartridge's room is."

But he didn't need to. Hartridge was coming down the stairs when they stepped into the main entrance hall.

He exchanged some banter with Norris and his friend, and then ran lightly down to James, who jerked his head back toward the side entrance, and led Hartridge out.

"Galbraith came knocking," Hartridge said. "Do you know what that's about?"

"That's interesting." James glanced at him. "Did you answer?"

"No. I'm ashamed to say I hid under my bed, but you told me not to interact with him, and I was worried he was going to break the door down. Someone obviously reported his banging, because the barracks manager came up and gave him his marching orders from what I could hear through the door."

"Whetford called me. Made sure to let me know I was expected to help at the CND march, and that I was to make sure you were with me." By the sounds of things, Galbraith was originally supposed to arrange that, but James guessed that when he couldn't get hold of Hartridge, Whetford had to actually stir himself to pick up a phone.

No wonder he sounded so sour.

James led the way to his car, and once they were inside, he tapped his fingers on the steering wheel. "Something is up. I don't believe it's the normal course of things for Whetford to phone me himself to tell me we have to be at the march. I'm guessing if we turn up at headquarters, we'll be assigned somewhere very specific, where we'll get a beating, all conveniently explained away by violent elements participating in the march, if we ever think to bring charges."

Hartridge looked over at him. "A beat down to ensure our cooperation, you mean?"

James nodded. He couldn't see how Whetford's insistence on them being together and at the march made sense any other way.

"What'll we do?" Hartridge sounded defeated.

"I've got an idea." James leaned back. "Do you know where Norris is going to be situated today?"

Hartridge nodded. "He's stationed at the nick near Hyde Park Corner, and the march will go straight past there, through St. James' Park."

"Good enough." James had read in the paper that morning that the marchers were finishing the march at Trafalgar Square, so walking through St. James' Park made sense. Wherever Whetford was going to put them, it wouldn't be in the wide open park, in easy view of multiple witnesses. So that's exactly where he'd make sure to go.

"Go back in, find Norris, and tell him I just realized the interview I mentioned to him will put us close to his nick, and rather than battle the crowds and traffic, we can present ourselves there rather than at New Scotland Yard. Tell him to keep protective gear aside for us and that we'll check in with whoever's in charge of his section."

"Whetford will accept that?" Hartridge asked.

"Whetford never told me where I had to help out, just that both you and I had to. He assumed we'd show up at headquarters, but we won't be disobeying the order to assist by presenting else-where." James glanced over at him. "Go now, before Norris leaves."

Hartridge nodded, getting out of the car and running back down the street. He was back fifteen minutes later, a little out of breath.

"All sorted," he said as he slid back into the car. "Norris will let his sarge know we're going to help in their sector. We're to arrive by nine fifty at the latest." He leaned back against the seat and blew out a breath. "Even if we aren't technically disobeying orders, Whetford won't be happy."

"No." That wasn't a small thing, James knew. Whetford would retaliate. So he would need to find a more permanent solution to whatever this was.

This shakedown by his own boss.

"What do we do now?" Hartridge asked. "We don't actually have a new lead, do we?"

"No." And not much could be done today, James realized. Most of the people on their list would not appreciate a call on Sunday morning. He turned to Hartridge. "Where did you drop off the bookie that Galbraith arrested?"

"Wembley Stadium. He's the go-to man for greyhound racing." Hartridge glanced at his watch.

He had a point.

It was already after 8 in the morning, so they didn't have time to drive out to Wembley and back.

"All right. Let's go sit somewhere and talk about what we're going to do about Whetford," James said. "I've only had one piece of toast for breakfast."

"I didn't have breakfast at all. I was hiding from Galbraith." Hartridge looked like the world was suddenly a better place.

"Let's find somewhere close to Hyde Park Corner. We can walk to Norris's nick when it's time." James merged with the traffic and headed for St. James' Park.

He had thought of a plan, but it had a flaw—he didn't know how high up the corruption went.

If he tapped the wrong shoulder, he could be landing both himself and Hartridge in even more trouble.

So maybe the solution was to assume everyone was bent. Right up to the Police Commissioner himself.

chapter
seventeen

JAMES CALLED Dr. Jandicott first thing on Monday morning.

He relaxed a little when the pathologist told him no body had been found after Saturday night's fog, and he asked if he could come round to discuss the body found in the market garden.

Then he called the Met's river police, Thames Division, and asked for the boat patrols to keep an eye out for the body of a young woman, gone missing near the docks. He didn't give any details, just in case someone there had loose lips and connections to the dock workers, and Thames Division promised they'd let him know if they found anything.

"I think I've found Catherine Lithlow." Hartridge knocked on his door and entered. "She's a patient at St Mary Abbots Hospital on Marloes Rd." He was more cheerful this morning. It was as if a weight had been lifted.

James knew it was because they had discussed a plan to get them out from under Whetford's heel yesterday, before the CND march. He wanted to warn him that they still had to implement it, and there was a chance it wouldn't work, but he let it go.

This wasn't the place to talk about it, anyway.

"Catherine Lithlow," he said instead, trying to remember who that was. "The woman with asthma?"

James recalled the pinched, nervous landlady who'd

submitted the missing persons report, corroborated by Ms. Lithlow's boss, that she would never up and leave, especially not without taking her things or giving notice. "Why hasn't she sent word to her work and landlady?"

"She was hit by a car in the fog. They think she had an asthma attack and stumbled into the road. She was unconscious until yesterday."

James shook his head. "That's a story. Well, send a uniform round to confirm it's her, and then tell them to let her workplace and landlady know." It felt good to cross a name off their list. "Also, get someone to call Glasgow again, see if they can track down Fiona McTavish's mother, and find out if she's seen her."

"Will do." Hartridge disappeared.

James got his things together and walked out to the small office Hartridge had next to his own and poked his head in. "While you set the wheels in motion on those two, I'm going across to see Dr. Jandicott. I'll swing back afterward and we can go interview the last four on our list."

Hartridge almost seemed his old self as he waved in confirmation, the phone tucked under his chin.

James closed his door, and found Whetford bearing down on him.

He arranged his face into a friendly expression. "Morning, sir."

"Archer, I thought I told you it was all hands yesterday. That wasn't a suggestion, it was a direct order." Whetford's eyes were red-rimmed, and James wondered for the first time if he was on the drink. He looked terrible.

"I did help yesterday, sir." James inserted just enough indignation to sound hurt. "I called the front desk to let them know the traffic was too backed up for Hartridge and I to make it to the Yard on time after we followed up on a lead we got on Saturday evening, and so we went to the nearest nick on the march route. Helped out Sergeant Darle in Piccadilly. We were on the line at St. James' Park."

"What?" It was the last thing Whetford had expected to hear. "We were expecting you here, man."

"Sorry, sir, but the march caused so much traffic chaos, we would never have made it back here." He lifted his shoulders. "They needed us just as much at St. James, sir. Sergeant Darle kitted us up, and we were on duty until after 5 in the evening."

"And you called this in, you say?" Whetford was left flat-footed, but James didn't think for a moment that he was appeased. He hadn't wanted James and Hartridge here because they were needed. He had been trying to set them up for something.

James was even more sure of it now that he was looking Whetford in the eye than before.

"I couldn't get anyone in the offices, so I called the front desk. They most likely couldn't get through to anyone to pass it on, either." He had made sure to ring moments before they left for St. James' Park. He wanted to be sure no one could ring back and try to reroute them to wherever Whetford and Galbraith had set their trap.

Whetford gave him an icy stare, turned on his heel, and walked away.

James watched him go.

There was no longer any doubt about it. He would have to set things in motion. Implement the plans he'd been making for a while now.

Because if he didn't, Whetford would get the better of him. And that wasn't happening.

He made his way to the stairs, and kept a friendly smile on his face as he passed his fellow officers, nodding politely. Wondering which of them was neck-deep in graft.

When James found Dr. Jandicott, he was sitting at his desk, sipping tea. He took the chair the pathologist offered him.

"You want to know about the body you sent over on Friday?" the pathologist asked. "The one from the Royal Masonic."

James nodded. "Any similarities to the others?"

Jandicott tipped his head to the side. "Before we get there, why wasn't she touched? She was found four or five days before I got her, wasn't she?" He looked around his desk for the paperwork, and flipped open the file. "They have a run of dead bodies at the Royal Masonic?"

"No. There were only two in there. But the pathologist is an alcoholic." James reached across and tapped the file. "Thank goodness I got to her before he did. If it's murder, the case would have been in jeopardy, given the state of him."

"It was murder," Jandicott said. "You ask if it was similar? It was near identical. Blow to the back of the head, exactly like the victim found in the rubble."

He had known it. James got to his feet, walked to the window to look out. "He half-buried her in a ditch."

"I read the report," Jandicott said. "He also struck her face. It's possible she heard him coming up behind her, turned, and he hit her, spun her around, and then delivered the blow to the head."

"He didn't strike the others?" James turned, thoughtful.

"I can't say for certain with the first body, because it was seriously decomposed by the time the victim was found, not to mention damaged by the digger, but he didn't hit the woman from the bomb site in the face." Jandicott reached for another file, opened it. "Abrasions on her palms. I think he came up behind her, hit her in the head, and she was conscious enough to throw her hands out as she fell. Then he hit her again, and it was more or less over."

"So two strikes?" James sat back down. "And two on the market garden woman, too?"

Jandicot nodded. "With her, as I said, it was a hard strike to the face, spinning her around, then a blow to the head to get her down, and a second blow to finish her off."

"And he's tried to hide all three bodies. Did a lot better of a job with the first one." James leaned back in his chair. "He got lucky there, or he'd scoped it out ahead of time and knew about it. A deep hole in that construction site." He thought back to where they found the body, and realized it would be useful to put up a map and mark where each body had been found, just like Gabriella told him her boss was doing.

He hadn't seen her for almost a week. He knew that wasn't a particularly long time, but he missed her. Really missed her.

"Beth Jenkins might be one of our victims," he told Jandicott. "Her mother provided her dentist's name for us." He got out his notebook and neatly wrote the address on a piece of paper and handed it over.

"Which one of the victims do you think she is?"

"The second one." James hoped for the sake of the fierce-eyed, grieving mother that it wasn't so, but like her, he didn't think Beth Jenkins would have taken herself off without a word.

Jandicott gave a nod. "Something to work on, at least. How're you going with the other two, if Victim One isn't Sara Parker?"

James shook his head. "There may be one possibility, but I think it's more likely the father killed her and dumped her in the Thames."

Jandicott blinked. "Are you being serious?"

James nodded. "If not, the girl ran away because the father's too loose with his fists. But the way he was acting . . ." He realized he had to clamp down on his temper. "I think he hit her in a rage, and she died. He works down the docks, and I think he threw her in the river to cover his tracks."

"Well." Jandicott seemed flummoxed. "If she comes in, I'll let you know."

James got to his feet. "Hartridge and I have four more people to interview today. Things ground to a halt last night, with the pea souper."

"Our killer's ideal conditions." Jandicott stood. "I'll get the wheels turning with checking Victim Two's dental records."

James made his way back to his office, but Hartridge was nowhere to be found. He walked down the back way, considering his options, and as he reached the rear exit, Hartridge cleared his throat and stepped out from behind the back of the staircase.

"Hiding?" James couldn't think of any other reason for his behavior.

"Galbraith was looking for me." Hartridge grimaced. "Again."

James's hand tightened a little on the door handle as he opened up. Whetford had come looking for him. Galbraith had done the same to Hartridge. Neither one of them should be creeping around New Scotland Yard, trying to avoid another detective. He needed to put more thought into his plan, and bring this nonsense to an end.

"Let's go." He headed for the Wolseley, with Hartridge right on his heels.

"What did Dr. Jandicott have to say?" Hartridge asked, dodging past him and getting in on the driver's side.

"That it's the same attacker." James handed over the keys and got in the passenger side. He flicked his gaze over at Hartridge's profile. "Galbraith speak to you?" he asked.

Hartridge shook his head, then shot him a grin. "I hid in your office. Behind the door. Then I took off for the back entrance."

James nodded.

"Galbraith came into your office, by the way." Hartridge cleared his throat as James swung back to look at him, and then kept his eyes on the road as they left through the big iron gates of the Yard.

"And did what?" James asked softly.

"Took a hard look at your desk." Hartridge hunched his shoulders. "I was more concentrating on being invisible, and hoping he didn't close the door for more privacy, because I was tucked up behind it, but someone else came down the passage and he left. He didn't touch anything, just looked at the files you had out."

So Galbraith would have seen the paperwork he'd caught up on since his return from leave, James thought. That was all he'd left out. Slim pickings for Galbraith, if he was looking for something to hang on him.

Whetford might be getting worried about Galbraith's inability to get Hartridge to be his messenger boy. And he might just suspect that Hartridge had told James what was going on. Especially after he was able to avoid whatever Whetford had in store for them on Sunday.

James would need to watch his own back, now, as well. So the sooner he sorted this out, the better.

And all while he and Hartridge were on the hunt for a monster.

chapter
eighteen

THE FOG from the night before was more or less gone in the morning. It held on—a wispy, lacy shawl compared to the thick blanket of the night before—but as Gabriella walked her route, the breeze cleared it, shredding it into nothing and leaving the sky clear and blue.

Even though it was cold, she felt a massive lift at the sight of the sky, and felt better than she had for a while.

Some of that was because Mr. Jaguar had been dealt with on Saturday night. She didn't realize how nervous he'd made her until the threat of him had been neutralized.

She wondered if whoever his wife hired would manage to track her down, and what she would say to them if they did.

She genuinely didn't remember which townhouse the man had come out of, but she did remember the general location on the street. It was possible that would be enough of an answer. If she was inclined to give it.

She turned off the main thoroughfare, walking down a quieter road which had a church halfway down it. All the houses and buildings along the way were new, a clear sign this street had been bombed during the war, and she noticed the church roof looked new on one side, and there was some construction going on in the bell tower, with scaffolding and a skip bin sitting in the small car park.

A workman was halfway up the scaffold, the *ting ting* sound of a chisel striking stone clear in the morning air. He turned, arms full of broken bricks, and tossed them down into the skip below, but as the bricks left his hands he gave a shout of pure shock and fear.

His gaze was fixed on the skip below, and Gabriella stopped in her tracks. He lifted his head, caught sight of her, and waved wildly.

She moved toward him, crossing the street and walking into the car park while he clambered down the scaffold.

"There's a girl in the skip." He shouted it out as soon as he reached the ground. "I threw bricks onto a girl in the skip."

He was frantic, beside himself, and he ran toward the skip, tried to look inside it, and when he couldn't see over the rim, ran back to grab a wooden box which Gabriella guessed the workmen used as a chair when they had a tea break. He set it down and boosted himself up.

"Is she moving?" Gabriella asked.

He was hanging onto the side of the skip, and he turned a white, pinched face toward her. Shook his head.

"Let me see." She didn't want to, but if she was going to call it in, she needed to have seen it for herself.

He looked like he wanted to say no. "You're a lass," he said. "You shouldn't . . ." He noticed her uniform at last, and gave an uncertain nod. Stepped down.

Gabriella stepped up, and still had to go on tip toe to look over the metal edge. A woman lay crumpled and folded up, her stockings torn, facing away. Gabriella knew it was cowardly, but she was very glad for that.

The killer had boosted her over the edge and let her fall willy nilly.

Unlike the body she'd seen at the bomb site, this victim

looked like she was asleep, except for the matted blood in her blonde hair, the rust red shocking against the pale gold.

She stepped back, almost overbalancing, and the workman caught her arm to steady her.

"Did I . . ?" He rubbed a handkerchief over his forehead.

"She was already dead." Gabriella patted his arm. "Someone killed her and left her in the skip."

He blew out a breath, and staggered back, leaning against the wall of the church, shaking his head.

"Is there a church office here?" she asked.

He waved to his left, and she walked around until she found a narrow pathway that led to a small house with two entrances.

The vicarage and the church office, she guessed.

She knocked on the main door, as the office looked closed, and it was opened moments later by a vicar wearing his dog collar, his light blue eyes curious and friendly.

On hearing about the body, he ushered her into the tiny entrance and showed her the phone.

"Should I . . .?" he looked out the door, torn.

"Maybe the workman who found her could do with a strong cuppa?" she suggested.

He bustled off to make it, grateful to have something to do, and Gabriella called the local nick.

She was putting down the receiver when the vicar came out with a steaming mug, and they walked back to the church together.

The workman was still leaning against the wall, and he took the tea gratefully, gulping it down.

The three of them stood awkwardly, waiting for the police, and when Constable Evans arrived, she let out a sigh of relief.

"Miss Farnsworth." Constable Evans nodded. "You called the station?"

"This gentleman was working on the building when he looked down into the skip and saw a body. I was passing by on my rounds and he asked for my help." She nodded toward the workman.

Evans gave a nod, walked to the skip and used the box to look over the edge. He stood for a moment, looking in, then stepped back.

"You've seen the body, Vicar?" he asked.

The vicar shook his head. "You want me to see if I know her?" he asked, voice a little uncertain.

Evans nodded. "If you wouldn't mind."

The vicar made his way over and used Evans's arm for balance as he stood up on the box and looked over.

"I can't see her face. It's possible she's one of my parishioners but I'll need to see her face before I can be sure." His hands shook as he clasped them together. "What a terrible business."

He looked so distressed, as soon as he stepped down Gabriella walked over and slipped her arm through his.

"Why don't we go make a big pot of tea, Vicar? There'll be a lot of people arriving soon. You can show me where everything is and I'll get on it." She despised the notion that women always hovered in the background, making tea and providing creature comforts while the manly men got on with things, but she didn't think the vicar was going to be able to stay on his feet much longer.

Evans caught her eye and gave her a subtle nod, acknowledging what she was trying to do, and that went a long way.

She gently led the vicar back to the house, but before they got there he pointed to the rear door to the church, and fumbled for and produced a huge set of keys. "The church kitchen," he explained. "It's got a proper urn that we use for church get-togethers. We can let the coppers come in and help themselves as they like."

That sounded very sensible, so she carefully filled the massive stainless steel urn and switched it on, then found the tea bags, sugar and milk under the vicar's direction.

"We just held a fundraiser for the roof last night, so the milk should be perfectly fresh," he told her.

"What happened to the roof?" she asked, stacking cups neatly on the long counter beside the urn.

"Bomb hit it in the war," he said.

Surprised, she looked over at him. He'd taken a seat on a thin, pale yellow formica chair near the door, and he already looked better. "So long ago?"

She wondered how they'd managed until now.

He nodded. "Twenty years, it's been. We had to have a temporary fix done at the time. Some plastic sheeting and some fibercrete over the top, just to tide us over. But we couldn't afford a proper fix for a long time, and months turned to years. The temporary fix finally failed three months ago, and now it simply has to be done."

"You're lucky the whole church didn't collapse," Gabriella said, thinking they'd gotten away lightly if all they got from a bomb was a hole in the roof.

"We were lucky that the bomb never exploded. It fell straight through the roof without detonating, but the tragedy was that sometimes, when the sirens sounded, people would take refuge wherever they were, and that night, a woman must have come into the church for shelter from the bombing raid. The falling debris and slate tiles from the roof landed on top of her and she died."

"That's terrible." Gabriella couldn't imagine the terror of that. "Were you the one who found her?"

The vicar nodded. "First thing the next morning. It took them a while to find out who she was, poor dear. What with the chaos of the war, the police didn't check the missing persons list until a month after her death. Fortunately, she was not yet buried and they were able to identify her by her dental records. Her family came to visit me when they finally worked out what had happened to her." He waved a hand to the door beyond. "They put up a plaque in her memory on the church wall."

As he finished speaking, the urn began to rumble and shake as the water boiled, and Gabriella switched it over to the keep warm setting. "I'll go let the lads know there's tea available, and I'll most likely be off to finish my rounds. Would you like me to walk you home?" she asked.

He shook his head. "I'll stay here. Thank you for your kindness, my dear."

Unsure what to do, but going on instinct, Gabriella walked over and he lifted his hands toward her. She held them in both of hers.

"All the best, Vicar. I hope they find who did this."

She left the door open as she went back to the scene, and caught Evans's eye again.

"Tea?" he asked, hopefully.

"Round the back of the church in the kitchen. I've left the door open, and the vicar is back there, too." She glanced at the tradesman, and then at the hive of activity around the skip. "Is it alright if I go on my way? I haven't finished my rounds."

"Aye." Evans gave a nod. "Just tell me how it was when you got here. Mr. Yates over there says it was as he noticed the body."

She thought it over, gave a nod. "He was chipping bricks off the side of the tower and setting them to one side on the ledge. I could hear the sound of the chisel as I walked down the street and looked up. When there was no room to stack any more bricks, he picked them up and turned, tossed them into the skip below, but as he let go, I think he saw the body. He didn't know that she was dead, and he gave a cry of absolute terror as the bricks dropped down." She'd never forget that sound.

Evans lifted his gaze from his notebook. "That's more or less exactly what he says. He says he saw you on the street and called to you for help."

She nodded. "He did. He climbed down the scaffolding, and pulled the box to the side of the skip and looked in."

"The box wasn't already there?" Evans asked.

She shook her head. "It was set up against the side of the

building. It looked like it was where someone would sit to take a tea break."

Evans scribbled a bit more. "Thanks. You can go. If I need more from you, I know where to find you."

She gave him a grateful smile and left to work her way through the rest of her route. She kept picking at the story of the woman found dead under the roof in the church during the war. At the sheer bad luck of it.

And it stirred something in her memory. Something she'd heard recently, but couldn't quite place.

As she came back down the main road on the final stretch, she caught sight of the Land Rover, parked up on double yellows.

And just like that, she realized she was ready for war.

The Italian temper that lived in her didn't come to the surface often, but today she was Vesuvius.

She circled the vehicle, and when she saw the window was partially down on the passenger side, she smiled. She wrote out the ticket and sealed it in its plastic sleeve, then stepped in as close to the door as she dared, and popped the fine through the window.

It skimmed through the air, fluttering a bit, and then landed on the driver's seat.

She walked the rest of the way back to headquarters feeling a tiny bit better.

She went to find Mr. Greenberg as soon as she got back, and explained about the body.

He carefully put a red pin in his map.

This was the fourth red pin, although only the third in their borough.

The homeless man found dead in Kensington Gardens, and three women.

That seemed like a lot.

chapter
nineteen

JAMES LOOKED at the photograph of Pamela Moresby, and knew they'd found the girl in the ditch. Her family had reported her missing the day her body had been found, and there was no question in his mind this was the same person.

Her mother's hands began to flutter as he stared at the picture, a framed formal portrait taken in a studio. When he raised his eyes, he saw helpless terror on her face.

She said nothing, her lips working as if trying to form words.

"Mrs. Moresby, I would like you or your husband, or both of you, to come down to the pathologist's office, to make an identification, if you could." He spoke gently, and Hartridge sent him a quick, surprised look.

"You . . ." She swallowed. "You have a body . . ." She swallowed again and stopped talking.

"We found someone a few days ago, and their description matches your daughter's. It would be a great help if you could come and see if you think it's her." He looked down at the photograph again. Pamela Moresby looked back at him, eyes serious, face serene.

"My husband's at work. Down the shop." Mrs. Moresby fluttered her hand again.

"Shall we go fetch him, and take him down to the patholo-gist?" James asked.

Mrs. Moresby gave a jerky nod and started to rock, and Hartridge stepped back, out of the room.

James guessed he'd gone to get her older daughter, who had been moving around in the kitchen since they had arrived.

The daughter preceded Hartridge into the room, stopping dead at the sight of her mother, and then folded herself down into a crouch, and grasped her mother's hand.

She tilted her head, staring at James, and he got to his feet.

"We'll be in touch." He couldn't ask this woman another thing. He would see if he could get more out of the husband. He couldn't give his condolences, because they couldn't be sure the body was Pamela Moresby until identification, so he merely gave a formal nod, and left.

Hartridge was waiting for him by the front door of the tiny house squeezed in between two large shops, and when they got outside, he blew out a breath.

"The sister says the victim works in a factory. She's on the late shift some weeks. Comes home around four in the morning." Hartridge followed behind James as he walked to the shop next door.

The green grocer's had baskets of fruit and veg by the front entrance, and green and gold lettering above a door that tinkled as James pushed inside.

A young woman sat at a till near the door, but James spotted an older man stocking shelves who looked up at them as they stepped in.

"Mr. Moresby?" He reached for his warrant card.

From the look on the man's face, he knew exactly why they were here.

"Pam," he said. "My Pam?"

"I'm sorry, Mr. Moresby. Is there somewhere we can speak in private?"

Moresby shook his head. "Here's fine."

James cleared his throat. "We have found a body that matches your daughter's description. It would be a great help if you could come with us to make an identification." He watched Moresby carefully, as the man set down the basket of tins he'd been stacking and stared at the floor.

He drew in a breath. "You've been to see Eunice?"

James nodded. "I've spoken to your wife. She told us where to find you. Can we take you with us now?"

He gave a quick jerk of his head in agreement, and then slowly untied his apron, pulling it over his head and folding it neatly.

The girl at the till had been listening in, and she moved away from her post to take it from him. "I'll sort things here, Mr. Moresby. You don't worry about the shop."

"Close it down, Maureen. Just . . . just close it down." He looked around the shop with blind eyes, and then began to shuffle toward the door.

Hartridge got there before him, held it open, and they accompanied a broken man to the morgue.

"I don't know how she ended up in Fulham." Mr. Moresby sat outside the morgue, his head in his hands, while Hartridge went to get him a cup of tea.

"She wouldn't have gone that way?" James asked.

Moresby shook his head. "The place she worked was ten minutes by bus, straight home. But the buses weren't running like usual that night. That's what we worked out after. When we realized she didn't come home. Because of the fog, you see?"

"So she might have decided to walk?" James asked.

Moresby gave a nod. "Maybe. If there was no bus . . ." His shoulders shook and Hartridge arrived with tea.

James sat with Moresby in silence while he sipped it.

"You think someone offered her a lift?" he asked at last.

"It's possible." James stood. "We'll be in touch, Mr. Moresby. DC Hartridge has arranged for someone to take you home when you're ready."

Moresby nodded, looking down into his mug and hunching his shoulders.

James left, feeling like he was fleeing the scene, even though he still had three other people to interview, two who hadn't been home when they'd called, and one final person they hadn't had a chance to visit yet. He also needed to start looking into Pamela Moresby's last movements.

He and Hartridge were silent as they drove away, until eventually James shook himself out of his funk and looked up the next address on their list.

"I know it's wrong, but I hope this next one isn't a match," Hartridge said as he pulled up outside the row house.

James gave a grunt of agreement. There was no one home, and the curtains were pulled tight.

James tapped Hartridge's shoulder, and pointed to the house on the left. He took the house on the right.

A young woman opened to his knock, a baby held across her body.

"Yes?" she asked on a whisper, lifting a finger to her lips.

"I'm looking for Mr. Clark. Does he still live next door to you?" he whispered back, lifting up his warrant card.

She blinked at the sight of the card, then gave a slow nod. "As far as I know, but he hasn't been around much recently. I heard him last night through the walls, running a bath, but this one keeps me pretty busy, so I can't remember when last I actually laid eyes on him." She gently altered the baby's position. "He in trouble, or something?"

"He filed a missing person's report for a Hatty Clark, and we wanted to follow up with him about it. Do you know Hatty?" James asked.

"Hatty's his wife. But he told me she'd left for the Midlands. To be with her mum. Said his mother-in-law was poorly, and Hatty had gone to look after her. That's why it didn't register so much, you see, not seeing him about. I thought he was eating down the pub most nights, with Hatty not there to make him his dinner."

James looked down at the report and frowned. "All right, I'll have to follow up another time. Unless you know where I might find him? Do you know where he works?"

"He's in sales for soap and shampoo and such. For the big supermarkets. Gives me samples sometimes, which is much appreciated. I'm not sure where his office is, but his local is the King's Arms, down the road. So if you want to catch him later, that's most likely where he'll be." The baby made the cutest sound James had ever heard, stretched and yawned, and then opened impossibly blue eyes.

The woman smiled down at her child, and James felt a lift of the darkness that had clung to him since Pamela Moresby was identified by her father. He hadn't even known how much it weighed on him until now.

"Thank you for your help. It's much appreciated." He left, looking over to where Hartridge was waiting at the car. "Any luck?" he asked as he joined him.

"Clark works in the City," Hartridge said as he got into the driver's side. "He's a salesman. And the wife keeps the house, but the neighbor thought she was just away visiting her mum, not missing."

"I heard the same story," James said. "Also, he's probably eating at the King's Arms every evening, with his wife gone."

"You think he made up the story about her mother because he thought she'd left him?" Hartridge asked.

James thought about it. "Possible. She disappears and he thinks she's had enough, so he makes up a story to explain her absence. Too proud to tell the truth. Only to realize she didn't take anything with her and she's not with her mother or anyone else. So he files a report, but doesn't update the neighbors."

"Or he's done away with her, and this is his way of covering his tracks."

"Or he's done away with her," James agreed. Either way, they needed to speak to Larry Clark.

chapter
twenty

THE PUB WAS NICE.

Gabriella didn't have a wide experience with English pubs, but the King's Arms was clean, had decent seating, and the noise was kept to a low murmur.

James returned to the table with a pint for himself and a shandy for her, and she wondered, as she took a sip, why she didn't just ask for lemonade, because she didn't like the beer half of the shandy. She only ordered it because it was what most women her age drank.

"Is the man you're looking for here?" she asked.

James shook his head. "The publican hasn't seen him tonight. But he says he's usually in at least once a night, so we might as well have dinner here, and see if he arrives."

He settled in opposite her. The booth they'd managed to get was cozy, the wooden back high, which gave the illusion of privacy. She studied his face.

He looked tired. And worried.

She knew he couldn't tell her much about his work, but she wondered what was weighing on his mind so much.

"I'm sorry I can't be off the clock. I really need to speak to this person." James's mouth formed a grim line. "I just missed you, and knew if I didn't ask you to dinner, I wouldn't see you tonight."

"I missed you, too." She hadn't ever missed anyone who wasn't a family member before. It was a strange feeling. "I have a lot to tell you, but let's wait until after you've got your man."

"What news?" He suddenly focused on her, leaning forward, hands reaching to hold her own.

"A lot," she said, curling her fingers around his. Between her father, and Mr. Jaguar, and the dead woman in the skip, a lot had happened since she'd last seen him.

"Tell me." He looked up at the bar and back at her.

She decided to go with the least personal of her news, and most likely the most relevant to his own work. "Did you hear about the woman found dead at that church in Kensington?" she asked. "I was walking past when the construction worker found her."

He went utterly still. "What woman found dead at a church in Kensington?"

She leaned back, but kept her fingers around his own. "She was thrown into a rubbish skip. They're redoing the church roof, and the worker was up a ladder, throwing down bricks, when he saw her."

"And you were there?" James's hold tightened.

She nodded. "The tradesman called me to help him. I called Constable Evans and then waited with the vicar for a while."

"Did you see the body?" James asked. "Could you see how she'd died?"

"It looked like she had a bad head wound, but the worker had thrown bricks down moments before he saw her, so I don't know which injuries were from that, and which ones were from whoever put her in there." Gabriella could see this news was shocking to James. "You didn't know about it?"

He shook his head. "But I've been out all day, interviewing people, or trying to." He leaned back himself. "It's possible the information is on my desk." He released his hold on her hands and rubbed his hair. Since summer had faded the blond strands were a darker gold.

She thought he looked a little rough—stubble obvious on his cheeks and chin, his tie askew and his gray eyes hooded.

He was agitated about the woman found in Kensington. She could see it in the way he gripped his pint. She guessed if he could have, he would have paced up and down and asked her more questions.

The publican set their food down in front of them, steak and chips for James and chicken parmigiana for her. She had been delighted to see it on the menu, thinking it was a solely Australian adaption of the Italian aubergine dish.

As soon as the food arrived, James relaxed a little, and studied her dish with interest.

"Is it what you thought it would be?" he asked.

"So far," she said. "It looks right. I'll let you know if it tastes right."

As she cut into it, the publican came back and leaned closer to James. "Clark just came in. He's at the bar, with the navy jacket."

James gave a nod of thanks. He had made sure he was sitting where he could see the bar, and as the publican moved away, he studied someone behind Gabriella's shoulder. She wanted to turn her head and look, but decided it was probably better she didn't.

"Go, if you need to," she said.

James shook his head, but he was eating faster than he had been. "I'll let him relax a bit, get a pint in him first."

Gabriella held out a fork of chicken parmi and offered it to James. "This is the real deal. I'll bet you they have an Australian back in the kitchen."

James looked at the fork in surprise, as if no one had ever offered him a bite of their dinner before, and then leaned forward to sample it.

"It's good," he admitted, his eyes going from the now-empty fork to her mouth. Then his gaze flicked back to the bar, and his face changed. Became harder.

He slid out of the booth. "He's leaving."

"That was a quick pint," Gabriella said, but James just shook his head and hurried toward the door.

Unable to resist, Gabriella turned to see what was happening, and caught sight of James's tall figure, head and shoulders above most of the other patrons, as he headed out.

He wouldn't want her there for whatever words he was about to have with Mr. Clark, and she had only eaten about a third of her dinner, so she turned back to her food, taking her time, enjoying the soft murmurs of conversation around her and the odd shout of laughter from the bar.

She needed this, she realized. Needed to be around other people, but still able to keep to herself. Just to eat something she didn't have to make or clean up, and forget about the woman in the skip for a bit.

It would be better if James was still sitting opposite her, but he'd be back.

And she would see whether he was going to take another step closer to getting her into bed.

She sincerely hoped so.

James followed Larry Clark out of the pub. He had noticed the moment one of the regulars had leaned in to say something in his ear, and Clark's quick, panicked spin on his chair as he turned to look around.

Someone had told him a copper was in the pub, wanting to talk to him.

It was interesting that his first instinct was to run.

Very interesting.

And annoying, because until that moment, he was having a very good evening with Gabriella.

James stepped out into what was now full blown fog, and heard Clark coughing as he scurried away.

Perhaps he hadn't considered that James had to know where he lived. Either that, or he wasn't thinking at all, just operating on panic and nerves. Because he was headed straight for home.

James followed after him, but he didn't try to hide his footsteps and he moved fast.

Clark didn't seem to understand he was being chased until a few moments before James grabbed the back of his coat. He gave a final, flailing burst of speed when he realized James was breathing down his neck, but it was too late.

"Mr. Clark." James didn't make it a question. "I've been looking for you. Detective Sergeant Archer, of the Met." He pulled Clark back a little, spinning him by the shoulder, and lifted his warrant card. "You in a hurry?"

Clark looked at the card, looked at James, and then swallowed. "No, no. Just didn't want to be caught in the fog. It sets my cough off something awful." He coughed again, but James thought this time it was a little forced.

"Well, we can go back in the pub, if you like?" He didn't want to go back to Clark's house, as it was at least a five minute walk away, but he accepted that if Clark suggested it, he'd have to agree.

"Can't we talk here?" Clark asked.

"Sure," James said, easily. "I'm following up about the report you submitted regarding your wife going missing."

"My wife—" He wasn't putting on the surprise.

James wondered what he had thought this was about.

"Oh. Well, I thought she'd gone to her mother's but then her mother rang up to chat with her, and we realized she was missing." Clark was slowly regaining his composure.

And the mother had threatened that she would report her daughter missing if he didn't, James guessed.

"Any indication that she might have gone somewhere else?" James asked.

Clark shook his head. "After I talked to her mother, I did a more thorough look around, and saw that all her clothes were still in the house, and so was the only suitcase."

This was looking bad, James realized. "Can you think of any reason why your wife might disappear without leaving word of where she was going?" James asked.

"Hatty?" Clark shook his head. "She kept to herself, except for her bridge evenings, where she'd play with a group at the library."

"And when did you see her last?" James asked.

Clark looked down at the ground. "Last time I saw her was the day I left for a short trip three weeks ago."

James's head lifted. "You only filed a police report a week ago."

Clark shuffled his feet. "That's because I thought she was off to her mum's, see?" He glanced up. "I was a day late coming home from a sales trip, and I knew she would be angry about it. I'd forgotten to let her know that I'd decided to stop an extra night on the way back and meet up with a friend."

"Name of the friend?" James asked.

Clark hesitated. "Do you really need to know?"

"Name," James repeated.

Clark sighed. "Just don't tell the missus when she comes back, all right? She'll leave me for real then." He shook his head. "Loretta Smythe." He gave the address, which was just outside London.

"How long were you away?" James asked. "Including the night spent with Ms. Smythe?"

Clark winced at that. "Five days."

"And you never spoke to her on the telephone in that time?" James asked.

"No." Clark pondered. "You're wondering when she might have gone off, are you?"

"I'm trying to ascertain when your wife was last seen. Can you give me the names of her friends?" James saw the reality of the situation was finally dawning on Larry Clark.

He gave a few names, the library where she met her friends for bridge, and her mother's name and number, which he read out from a small address book in his wallet. "She speaks to her mum every week," he said. "So you might have some luck there. Her mother won't tell me anything."

Not surprising, James thought. He was thoroughly unlikeable. "Thank you, Mr. Clark. We'll keep in touch on our progress."

"That's it? That's all you wanted?" Clark still seemed like a man hard-pressed to believe his luck.

"Unless you have something to add?" James asked.

"No. No, no. All good." Clark tipped his hat and hurried away, the fog swallowing him whole.

James wondered what else he was up to, because he was involved in something. As he was in sales, James guessed he might be selling stock under the table or something along those lines. He shrugged, turned back to the pub, and to Gabriella.

chapter
twenty-one

GABRIELLA INVITED James up to her flat.

She didn't want the evening to end, and she wanted to tell him about the news on her father.

James had tried to look for him for her a few months back, as much as it was possible for him to do without abusing his position at the Met, and she wanted to talk to him about the repercussions now that she knew more.

There was silence behind the door of Jerome's flat, but it was Monday, and he might well be tucked up for an early night.

"Coffee?" she asked as she hung her coat on the rack.

"I want to say yes, but I haven't had enough sleep these last few days, and coffee keeps me awake." He hung his own coat up.

"Tea it is." She was slowly developing a taste for it.

"Can you stand to tell me more about the body this morning?" James asked, pulling down two mugs from the cupboard while she put the kettle on.

"The age of the woman, you mean?" Gabriella asked. She thought about it. "I could only see part of her face, but it seemed to me she was around late twenties, early thirties. Wearing a neat tweed skirt and a brown jacket. I didn't see her handbag anywhere."

"And it was in your borough?" he asked.

She nodded. When they each had their tea, she sat down and blew on the surface to cool it. "Constable Evans took my statement, and the statement of the tradie who found her."

He nodded. "I'll go round tomorrow and speak to him." He seemed distracted, moving his cup round and round.

"You think it's the same person who killed the woman at the old bomb site?" she asked.

He raised his head. Gave a brief nod. "And two others."

"The body in the allotment?" she asked, surprised.

"And another one we found just before I went home to Wales." He finally took a sip of tea. "But she'd been dead over a month by the time we found her."

"So four women over two months?" Gabriella set her mug down. "But all left at different places?"

"All hidden, or half-hidden." James lifted a shoulder. "I shouldn't really be telling you about this."

"I won't say anything." Gabriella had a stake in this. Not just because she'd been there for the discovery of two of the bodies, but because it was so clearly dragging James down. "Hidden like the way he left the woman I found on the far side of the debris pile?"

James nodded. "He left the woman we found in the allotment in a ditch, and scooped some sand over her. The first one was thrown into a deep hole at a construction site, and you said today's body was hidden in a skip bin."

Gabriella thought about it. "Not hidden, really. Lying on top. But no one could see her from the ground and he'd put the box he must have used to stand on in order to throw her in back up against the church wall. It was only because the tradie was up the side of the tower, looking down, that he noticed her."

"There seems to be no link between the places, so it could just be convenience, a handy place to put them without drawing immediate attention, but something about it seems more deliberate than that." James rubbed long, broad fingers over his mouth.

"Teddy Roe said he knew the place where I found the woman in the rubble. He helped evacuate that building when it was originally bombed." Gabriella thought back to what he'd said. "He said one of the bodies they recovered was murdered, not killed by the bomb strike."

James straightened. "What?"

She shrugged. "He said the one woman he pulled from the wreckage had been deliberately killed. But no one would believe him, and it was never reported as a murder."

"He's sure?" James asked.

"It's Teddy Roe, so who knows," Gabriella said. "But yes, he seemed pretty sure to me. And sad. I think he knows his erratic behavior meant no one took him seriously." The first World War had done a number on Teddy Roe, and he'd never been the same.

"I'd like to talk to him." James tapped the table, his gaze unfocused, as if he was planning in his head.

Gabriella pushed her mug away. "I only just remembered what Teddy Roe told me because the vicar at the church this morning said they found a woman beneath the rubble when the church was bombed during the war. The bomb never exploded but it crashed through the roof. The next day they found a woman dead inside the church. They said she'd probably taken cover inside when the air sirens sounded, and was very unlucky to have been in there when the bomb hit."

James looked up, eyes suddenly very focused. "They didn't suspect foul play?"

Gabriella shook her head. "Why would they? She was found under the debris from the roof."

"Did they identify her?" James asked.

"Yes. It took a month, but they did eventually, using dental records. The vicar told me there's a commemorative plaque to her inside the church." She tilted her head. "Do you sense a pattern?"

"The allotment." James was back to tapping his fingers. "They told us it used to be a factory that burned down during the Blitz. They found a woman inside it, as well."

"And the first site?" Gabriella asked. She could feel her heart rate increase. The horror of what she was thinking had her in its grip.

"I don't know." James stood. "I'll need to find out."

"And if it is?" Gabriella got to her feet as well. "Are you thinking someone who killed women during the Blitz and hid their bodies in a way that made it look like they died in the bombings is back, and leaving his new victims at the same sites he used before?"

His gaze snapped to her. "That's exactly what I'm thinking." He ran a hand through his hair again. "God, Gabriella. This is huge. If we're right, he's killed at least eight women since the Blitz, maybe more."

"Why now? Why again after all this time?" she wondered.

"I don't know what set him off again, but I think he's using the heavy fog to hunt them down." James stood with fists clenched.

"Or, is the heavy fog what sets him off?" Gabriella wondered. "Like the blackouts during the Blitz, he's got the night to himself."

"Maybe." James looked down at the ground, his whole body held tight and ready.

She moved to him, took his hand with both of hers. "Even if you're right, there is absolutely nothing you can do about it now."

"I know." He blew out a breath. "I'm not sorry for discussing it with you, because you telling me what Teddy Roe and the vicar said has made it fall into place. But it's not fair to put this darkness in your head."

She let go of his hand, slid her arms around his waist. "I've found two of his victims personally," she said. "The darkness was already there."

He bent his head, brushed his lips against her temple. "I want to sleep with you."

He went suddenly still, as if he hadn't meant to say that out loud, and Gabriella leaned back, smiled up at him.

"I know."

He grinned down at her. "Do you, now?"

She lifted up on her toes, kissed his neck, his chin, his cheek—little touches of her lips on his scruff-shadowed skin. "I've known for ages."

"And what are your thoughts on the matter?" He tried to keep his voice lighthearted, but she heard the slight rasp of tension in it.

"I think we need condoms." She held her gaze steady on his. "I'm not getting pregnant, James."

He stared down at her, mouth slightly agape.

She reached up and gently closed his jaw.

"I can get condoms," he told her.

"Good." She leaned in closer, and he closed his arms tighter around her.

"You were going to tell me what has happened in your life these last few days," he said. "Go on. I need the distraction."

She smiled against his chest. "Do you remember the man who I fined in the green Jaguar? The one where you pulled up and got between us?"

"I remember it clearly. I've never seen someone react like that to getting a small fine." He rubbed a hand down her back.

"He's been following me. I think for quite a long time. He even waited outside station headquarters for me. When I tried to approach him, he roared off."

"Gabriella." He pulled back to look at her. "It was definitely the same car?"

"Different license plate—I compared them—but it was the same man. Then, when I got home on Saturday night, he was parked outside, watching the flat." She tightened her hold on him, preventing him from whirling away to pace. "Solomon, George and Jerome noticed him."

James tensed. "Will someone be finding his body somewhere?" His voice was careful.

"No, no. It was all very cordial." She paused. "Well . . . not cordial, but no blood was spilled. On either side. Turns out the car's in his wife's name and she wants to know what he was doing parked in that part of town where I fined him. Apparently she's hired a private detective to ask me which house he came out of."

"He's having an affair?" James guessed.

Gabriella lifted a shoulder. "Probably. Whatever it is, he's dead scared she's going to find out, and he was trying to threaten me into silence."

"I might still have his details." James's eyes were narrowed.

"It doesn't matter. He's been convinced to keep away from me." She sighed, still enjoying the feeling of relief as he drove off. "But that isn't the main news."

"You have more?" He pulled her toward her window seat, the only place other than her bed or the tiny kitchen table where they could sit together, and slid her onto his lap.

She nestled in close. This was nice. "Ruby Everett found my father for me."

His hold tightened. "For sure?"

Her lips twisted. "As sure as possible. My friend Ben works as a junior solicitor at Temple Chambers. He and his senior are going to handle the confirmation for me."

James frowned. "Why so formal? Why not just approach him?"

"Because it turns out he's a viscount. A married viscount." Gabriella watched as the implications hit him.

He blew out a breath. "That's . . . crazy."

"And I'm not exactly going to be popular. With either him or his new family." She thought that was probably an under-statement.

James pulled her back into his arms. "This has to be hard for you."

She sighed. "I think it's going to be harder for him." She listened to his heart beat in his chest for a while, then straightened up. "Now, your news. There's something wrong that you're not telling me." He was too dragged down, too low for it to be simply a hard case.

The look on his face was almost funny. She could see he didn't think he should tell her anything.

"Come on, you know you want to." She held his gaze.

He leaned back against the wall with a sigh. "Whetford set Hartridge up in a compromising situation while I was away. I've always known he was dirty, but Hartridge told me what happened, and it's worse than I thought. He's got another DS working with him, Galbraith, and they seem to be shaking down low level criminals for their own gain."

Of everything she'd expected him to say, this had not been it. It was her turn to gape.

With a small smile, he lifted her lower jaw back up.

She blinked. "What are you going to do?"

"Things have escalated. I think Whetford set Hartridge and me up for an attack yesterday at the CND march."

"What!" Gabriella was outraged. "I've never seen such peaceful protesters as the CND."

James laughed. "Not always, but I agree, they're mostly very law-abiding. I think the people who were going to beat us up were police officers who are in bed with Whetford. And they were going to lay the blame at the CND's door. Don't worry, I managed to put a spoke in Whetford's wheels."

"And now? Do you think he'll give up?" She had met Whetford, and had found him sexist and condescending. She couldn't see him taking being bested very well.

James laughed. "No. I have a plan, but if it goes wrong . . ."

"Tell me," she said. "I'll do anything I can to help."

He shook his head. "If I think of something, I'll tell you. But this is going to be played out inside the walls of New Scotland Yard. And I might be fired at the end of it."

She hadn't realized the stakes, but, of course that could be the outcome. "That doesn't seem fair. Whetford is the one who should be fired. Should be in jail."

"That's unlikely, but if I can get him and his thugs to leave me and Hartridge alone, that will be enough of a win for now." He slid his fingers through her hair, cupping the back of her head. "And I'd prefer to kiss you, and forget about that bastard."

She leaned into him, and lifted her own hands to his shoulders. "Forget about who?"

chapter
twenty-two

JAMES WENT to Dr. Jandicott before he even went in to the Met.

He felt more energized than he had for a week. The time with Gabriella had given him more than just useful information, it had cleared his mind and centered him.

The pathologist was unlocking his office door, briefcase in hand, and raised his brows when he saw James. "Something come up?" he asked.

"There *was* another body," James said. "Yesterday outside St Thomas' Church in Kensington and Chelsea."

"Is that so?" Jandicott pushed his door open and walked behind his desk. "In the church itself?"

"The church is currently carrying out repairs. She was found in a skip bin in the car park. Constable Evans was one of the responding officers." James didn't sit down, he had too much energy.

Jandicott picked up his phone, called someone, and James heard his conversation with half an ear as he worked out a plan of action for the day. He'd already called the barracks and left a message for Hartridge to come straight to Jandicott's office.

"The post mortem is on my schedule for today." Jandicott replaced the receiver. "The body came in yesterday, but I was busy with another post mortem, and had given standing orders not to be interrupted."

"All right, that's good." James relaxed a little. At least the body hadn't ended up with someone like the drunk Doctor Venables.

"Do you want to accompany me, and we can do an initial examination now?" Jandicott asked.

"Yes, please." He got the impression Jandicott was just as alarmed at the number of deaths as he was. The sooner they made progress, the safer the streets would be.

And while he may have worked out the method, perhaps even the circumstances of the murders, he had no idea who was behind it.

"Were you working as a pathologist here during the war?" James asked. Jandicott looked to be in his late 50s, and it was possible.

The doctor shook his head. "I was an army doctor on the Continent during the war." As he walked with James down to the morgue, he shot him a quizzical look. "Why do you ask?"

"There's someone who worked the night crew during the Blitz, and he found a suspicious death in the aftermath of the bombing of the old Billick Building, where the body from the other day was found on the rubble. And the body found yesterday was at a church that was bombed in the Blitz. The vicar found a woman's body after the bombing, even though the bomb didn't explode. Then, the allotment gardens where Pamela Moresby was found used to be a factory during the war, and it caught fire during the Blitz. They found a dead woman in there, too." James couldn't help the sense of excitement that gripped him as he laid it out for Jandicott. This was too much to be coincidence.

"What about the first site?" Jandicott asked. "Was it bombed?"

"Hartridge and I will investigate that. It's possible." He paused. "I need to look into those deaths from the records. See if there was any hint of foul play back then."

"What happened with the body the man on the night crew discovered?" Jandicott asked.

"He was suffering from shell shock from the first World War. He wasn't taken seriously. But he's adamant he was right. I'll have to go have a chat with him, as well."

Jandicott stopped in front of a door, pulled out a bunch of keys, and unlocked it. "Let's see what we have here."

James stood in the doorway, letting the pathologist in first to look the body over. Footsteps sounded in the corridor and he turned his head as Hartridge came toward him.

"What's happening?" Hartridge asked.

"New body. Found yesterday morning." James glanced at him, then focused back on Jandicott.

"Possibly killed at the start of the weekend." Jandicott lowered the sheet that covered her as he turned toward them. "The rate of decomposition would put her time of death around there." He paused. "There's some nasty wounds to her chest and upper arm."

"That might be from the contractor working on the church tower who was throwing old bricks down into the skip before he realized she was in there." James remembered Gabriella telling him how horrified the man had been when he saw her.

Jandicott inclined his head. "That's something, at least. It wasn't a deliberate desecration of the corpse."

"And the cause of death?" James couldn't fight against the hot, burning sensation in the pit of his gut.

"Two hammer blows to the head," Jandicott said.

Their killer had taken four victims in less than two months— that they knew about—and who knew how many during the war.

James stepped back with a sense of purpose. "Let me know if you find anything interesting?" he asked.

The pathologist nodded. "Good hunting."

Gabriella and Liz left headquarters at the start of their shift and parted ways on the Kings Road.

Liz walked away on her rounds like she was dragging a weight behind her, the consequences of partying at Dance-A-Go-Go until late.

Gabriella realized she felt like she was dragging a weight behind her, too, but it was because she was getting closer and closer to the church.

It had taken a long time for her to look inside an illegally parked car without worrying, after she'd found a body inside one in the summer, and she couldn't describe how relieved she was when she'd been taken off her old route, and no longer had to walk past the alleyway where she'd found Patty Little's body.

She didn't like to make waves, but maybe Mr. Greenberg would change her route again, even if it was just to switch this particular street out with someone else.

St. Thomas's came into sight, and she must have been staring at the scaffold-covered spire without a care for her surroundings, because a cyclist almost knocked her down as he came past her on the pavement.

She felt his shoulder brush hers as he sped past, and he looked back at her, as shocked by the contact as she was, his eyes wide, before he turned to face forward and disappeared around the corner.

When she reached the church, though, the skip bin was gone, and the workman was nowhere in sight. The car park was empty. It seemed even worse this way, which made her tell herself there was no pleasing her, but still, she hurried past, not even bothering to check for anyone parked on double yellows. She only felt like she could breathe again when she turned onto the next street.

Up ahead there was a pile of furniture on the pavement, neatly stacked beside a house that looked like it was being renovated, and as she got closer, she saw Teddy Roe and another man standing in front of it.

"Morning, Mr. Roe," she called. "Out looking for something new for your place?"

"Eh?" He turned, recognized her, and touched his cap. "Can you believe this, Gabriella? There's stuff here looks good as new."

It didn't really. Most of it looked worn, but it did look serviceable and clean.

"This is my mate, Jerry." Teddy Roe jerked a thumb at Jerry, who was inching back into a hedge at the sight of her. Teddy Roe realized it and shook his head. "She's not a WPC, mate, she's a traffic warden."

Jerry relaxed a little. Gave her a tiny nod.

Gabriella nodded back. "Do you remember Mr. Archer?" she asked Teddy. "The detective sergeant who rescued me back in the summer?"

"Aye." Teddy Roe gave a nod. "You're stepping out with him, aren't you?"

"Yes." She was surprised at the warm feeling she had at the thought. "I told him what you told me about the body you found in the old Billick Building, and he's very interested in talking to you about it. So don't be surprised if he comes looking for you. It's just about what you can remember from that time, to help him."

She knew Teddy Roe. Knew he would run in a blind panic before he could think things through, if he didn't have advance warning.

"Help him?" Teddy Roe considered it. "I can do that."

"Good." She glanced at the cars parked beside the curb, and just then, a sleek black Mercedes drew up and parked clearly on double yellows. She hitched her bag up on her shoulder. "Have a good day, gentlemen."

She could hear Teddy Roe chuckling behind her, she assumed he was tickled at her calling him a gentleman, and then the two men went back to discussing what was feasible for them to take back to Teddy Roe's little shed, given they were going to have to carry anything between them.

As she got closer to the Mercedes, she began to steel herself for a confrontation. Shiny black cars like the one in front of her were usually owned by rich old men. Sometimes she got lucky, and it was a chauffeur, and they were generally all right, but if it was the car's owner, it often went badly.

She didn't know what enraged them more; that she was giving them a fine, which they didn't like, or that she was a young woman telling them, an older man, that he was in the wrong.

Disrespectful and uppity were two words she heard almost every time.

To keep things short and sweet, she wrote down the license number so she didn't have to ask for it, or waste time looking afterward.

As she reached the driver's door, she'd almost convinced herself it was going to be a chauffeur because the engine kept idling, but the man inside didn't look right. He wasn't in a chauffeur's uniform, but neither was he over fifty and all puffed up.

Instead, he looked a little too sleek, and wore a little too much cologne.

"You're stopped on double yellows," Gabriella said. "You'll need to move along, or I'll have to issue you with a fixed penalty notice."

"That's fine," the man said. "Why don't you get in first for a minute, eh, love? I need a word with you."

Gabriella stared at him. "A word?"

"Just a quick chat about a fine you issued a couple of months back." He smiled and patted the passenger seat.

Gabriella froze. She didn't like that she did, but it was so surprising. So unexpected. "No."

She saw immediately that he didn't like that. She was almost mesmerized by the sudden flash of temper on his face, and then he leaned across, and his hand snaked out and gripped her forearm. "Wrong answer. Tell me about a green Jaguar in Chelsea." The man's eyes were a light blue, and he watched her with cold detachment as she began to twist her arm to get free.

"Are you mad?" She tried to step back, give herself more space to get away, and he ground his fingers into her even harder.

"Just answer the question, girly, and I'll be off." He jerked her forward, closer to him.

"I won't answer anything until you let me go." She stared at where his hand was clamped on her arm, almost unable to believe this was happening.

"Fine." He let go, and the moment she was free she backed away, and then ran around the rear of the car and onto the pavement.

She was cradling her arm close to her chest.

"Now, that wasn't nice. We had a deal." He was out of the car so fast, he was on the pavement before she could even decide which way to run.

She looked up and down the street. The only people to be seen were Teddy Roe and his friend Jerry.

"Teddy Roe," she shouted. "Get help!"

Teddy Roe was already looking her way, and the man from the Mercedes glanced at the two old men and dismissed them.

Gabriella lifted her bag as a barrier between them. "You hurt me," she said.

"I just needed you to concentrate," he said, with a shrug that enraged her even more than the way he'd held her. "The green Jaguar you fined three months ago. Which house did the driver come out of?"

Gabriella laughed in his face. "Do you know how many fines I issue a day? And most of the time, I never see the drivers. The reason they are getting a fine is because they've parked their cars and gone somewhere else without checking the time or whether they're allowed to park where they have."

He hesitated, as if this had not occurred to him. "So you never saw him?"

"I don't even know what you're talking about." She lied without compunction. She was no friend of Mr. Jaguar, but she actually couldn't remember which house he'd come out of, and this man had physically hurt her.

He studied her. "I know it was you who issued the fine. And I was told you did interact with the driver of this particular car. Why are you lying?"

"How on Earth do you know any of that?" she asked. Was there someone at traffic warden headquarters who'd given this man her route?

"I've got my ways." He tapped the side of his nose, which was a gesture she'd have to ask Liz or James about.

"And your ways are what?" she persisted.

"Never mind, just answer the question." He lunged at her, grabbing her upper arms and giving her a shake.

Before she could respond, a chair whacked into his back and he swore, letting her go as he turned to see what was going on.

Teddy Roe was holding a chair from the pile by its back rest, moving the legs back and forward as if he was a lion tamer at a circus.

"What the blazes?" The man tried to grab a leg, but Teddy Roe jerked it away, pulling the man off balance.

There was a sudden sound of metal hitting metal, and with a curse, the man looked toward his car.

Jerry was holding a long poker, slightly rusted at the one end, and once he saw he had everyone's attention, he hit the side of the car with it again.

With an explosive curse, the man ran toward him, but Jerry danced back, over the road to the other side, and waved the poker around from the far pavement. "Bully," he shouted. "Stop hurting that girl."

The man turned back, but Teddy Roe had moved forward, and was thrusting the chair back and forth by the backrest, blocking all access to her.

The noise had drawn attention, and a few people began to come out of their front doors.

With another curse the man got into the car, which was still running, and drove away.

Gabriella realized she was shaking. "Mr. Roe, you've come to the rescue again."

Teddy Roe lowered the chair and turned back to her, a huge grin on his face. "'Twas fun," he said. "Loved it."

Jerry swanned back across the road, waving the poker in some kind of victory dance. "We got him," he said. "Got him good."

"You did. I can't thank you enough." She shivered.

She left them slapping each other on the back, and having what looked like a whale of a time.

She was nervous for the rest of her route, worried that if the man could find her at one point on it, there was nothing stopping him from trying again at another.

But no black Mercedes made an appearance.

As she climbed the stairs to headquarters and stepped inside, she looked toward Mr. Greenberg's office, torn.

Once again, she would be the squeaky wheel, but it was unacceptable for someone to have given out her route. She had a right to feel as safe as it was possible to feel in what was a confrontational job.

She squared her shoulders, and walked toward the boss's office.

The door was open when she got there, and Mr. Greenberg was packing up his things.

"Gabriella." He paused, looking at her with a growing frown.

"Mr. Greenberg." She took a step inside, and realized her fists were clenched.

"Tell me." He sat back down, his things stacked to one side.

She carefully told him, trying to be as objective and unbiased as possible.

When she told him about the Jaguar following her, and waiting outside the building for her, then outside her flat, he leaned forward in his chair.

He knew Teddy Roe, and when she moved on to the events of the day, he smiled a little at her description of how he'd come to her rescue and eventually pushed his chair back and stood. "I'm changing your route, and it will be between you, me, and the person I switch you with, until I get to the bottom of this. Is that acceptable to you?"

She gave a nod. "I'm sorry, sir. I seem to always be getting into some kind of bother."

"No." He rose. "You were doing your job. And someone here made that job much more difficult." He looked at her and she realized she was cradling her arm again. "Let me see."

She reluctantly pulled her sleeve up, and looked down at the dark purple bruises. They were worse than she'd thought.

Mr. Greenberg was quiet, and then he bent down and pulled a camera out of a drawer. "Hold still, please."

She waited while he took a few shots.

"You and I will go and lay a formal complaint tomorrow, but I'll make some calls first tonight. No one hurts my people without consequences, Miss Farnsworth."

She looked at his face and then began to back out. "Thank you, sir."

"Wait." Mr. Greenberg set the camera down and lifted a pen. "Did you get the license plate of the car?"

She leaned against the doorjamb. "As it happens, I did."

chapter
twenty-three

JAMES STARED at the plaque in the church to commemorate the life of Valerie Jones, and then stepped back.

"I'm still in touch with the family, if you need an address," the vicar said.

"That would be very helpful," James said. "Do they live locally?"

"One borough away. They attend their usual church most of the time, but on Valerie's birthday and at Christmas, they take part in the service here, in memory."

"Can you recall who came to help when you found the body? Which nick they came from and so on?" James asked.

The vicar frowned. "I wouldn't know exactly which nick. It was during the war, so it was mainly the day and night crews, clearing up. All the bobbies I knew were off fighting, and I didn't know the ambulance crew. It was a chaotic time."

"Even an exact date would be helpful," Hartridge said.

"That I can give you." The vicar moved through to the tiny office at the back, and pulled out a book. He flipped through it. "There you go." He pointed a gnarled finger at an entry, and Hartridge bent over the tome and copied the information.

As they left, James felt the vicar's eyes on them, and he turned and gave a final wave farewell.

"He wonders why we're asking for this information," Hartridge said. "He's putting it together."

"As long as he doesn't tell anyone else, there's not much I can do about that." James agreed, though. The vicar came across as mild and welcoming, but he was nobody's fool.

"What now?" Hartridge asked.

"We need to go back to headquarters and start looking through records, phoning people up, and generally looking back twenty years for like crimes." James knew it wasn't going to be easy. The war had strained resources, and he didn't know how well the records had been maintained. "But first, we look for Mr. Teddy Roe."

James hadn't been round to Ruby Everett's house for a while. He knew Gabriella visited her often, and that the widow had given Teddy Roe a place to stay at the back of her garden.

He knocked on the front door, but there was no response, so he gestured for Hartridge to follow him around the side.

Teddy Roe and another man were at the back shed, trying to maneuver a large armchair through the door. Ruby Everett was watching their efforts, her expression bemused, offering advice as they moved this way and that.

"Can we give you a hand there, lads?" Hartridge asked as they walked toward the trio.

The man helping Teddy Roe dropped his side of the chair and looked around wildly, as if for an exit.

"Ow! Jerry, you idiot. That landed on my foot." Teddy Roe's face was red with anger.

"It's all right, we're just here to ask for Mr. Roe's help about something he saw during the war." James could see Jerry was still in panic mode.

"He thinks you're here to collar him for hitting that bloke's black Mercedes with a poker," Teddy Roe said. "But he doesn't know you're sweet on Miss Farnsworth, and you'd be fine with us doing a little damage to the paintwork to get him away from her. He was hurting her, he was."

James blinked. This had taken the strangest turn. "Sorry, someone attacked Miss Farnsworth today, and you got him away from her by . . .?"

"There was a pile of stuff being tossed. Like this lovely armchair." Teddy Roe patted the mustard velvet with affection. "Miss Farnsworth was coming by, doing her job. She said hello to us, went on her way, and this bloke grabs her. He hurt her arm. So Jerry grabbed a poker from the pile and I got a wooden dining chair. I went for him, Jerry started hitting the nice shiny paint on his fancy car." Teddy Roe grinned, showing a few missing teeth. "Stopped him right quick."

Jerry looked like he was about to faint at the confession Teddy Roe had just given.

"Thank you, gentlemen. I appreciate your helping Miss Farnsworth. Did you get a good look at the man in question?" James eyed Ruby Everett's house, and wondered if she'd mind him using her phone. He needed to call the Traffic Warden HQ.

"Sure, and his car, too. We chased him off." Teddy Roe patted the armchair again. "Miss Farnsworth was all right, though, not to worry."

"You never told me this, Teddy." Ruby Everett had been observing from the sidelines, but now she stepped forward. "Do you know why he attacked her?"

"She was giving him a fine." Teddy Roe shrugged.

It could be as simple as that, or it could be to do with the story she'd told him the night before. About the green Jaguar.

"Well, thanks again. Actually, I'm here to ask you to remember the details of an incident you told Miss Farnsworth about. The bombing of the Billick Building during the war." James saw Jerry shuffle back and slowly begin breathing again. He looked like he couldn't believe his luck.

"That woman I found." Teddy Roe nodded slowly. "Something very wrong there. She was under some ceiling panels, but there were no injuries on her anywhere except her head, and only on the back. It looked to me like someone had picked some ceiling board up and set it on top of her, not that the ceiling board had landed on her, if you know what I mean?"

"Do you know if there was an autopsy?" James asked.

Teddy Roe shook his head. "I was night crew. I didn't have anything to do with the bodies after the ambulance took them away. I did tell the coppers about it, but no one took me seriously." He shrugged. "I thought I found another woman in similar circumstances a few weeks later, and that put the nail in my coffin. They were sure after that that I was making it up."

"What other woman?" James asked, keeping his voice steady.

"Down near Holland Park," Teddy Roe said, and gave a street name. "Can't remember the exact number, but there was a big mansion of a house third down from the corner that had its back garden bombed, and I found a woman under the shed. Piss poor job of hiding her, like whoever left her there didn't have the time he needed."

"Did you see her injuries?" James asked.

Teddy Roe nodded. "Head wound, back of the skull, like the other one."

There was silence in the garden for a moment.

"Well, thank you, Mr. Roe. Why don't DC Hartridge and myself move this in for you, and then, Mrs. Everett, if you don't mind my using your phone?"

They lifted the chair easily and got it in, much to Teddy Roe's delight, then left him putting the kettle on for him and Jerry.

"You'll phone to see if Gabriella is all right?" Ruby asked as she led them inside.

The house was warm after the cool of outside, and James slipped off his coat as he walked to the telephone. Ruby took it from him and hung it on the coat rack, and did the same for Hartridge.

He heard her murmur something about tea as he dialed the

Traffic Warden Center. He was put through to Mr. Greenberg immediately.

"Gabriella's arm is badly bruised where the brute grabbed her, but she seems to be more angry than shaken," Mr. Greenberg said. "I've photographed her injuries and we'll go in tomorrow to formally report it, but I've already called a few people about it."

"And what was it about?" James asked. He was gripping the receiver so hard he heard it squeak, and forced himself to relax his hold.

"It seems to be related to a fine she issued back in the summer. The man who accosted her today works for the wife of the driver." Mr. Greenberg paused. "He intimated that someone in this office had given out her details, as well as her route. Her signature is on the fine, so if this man is a private detective, which she thinks is possible, then he may have been able to get some information about her from her name, but I don't know how he could know her route without someone in this office telling him."

"Could he have followed her?" James asked, then realized he couldn't possibly have known who to follow unless he had been given the information by someone. "Sorry, that still means he knew who to follow."

"Precisely."

"Unless the man she fined told the wife's private detective," James said. He didn't want someone in her office to have put her in danger.

There was a short pause. "I hadn't thought of that possibility. It's a comforting one," Mr. Greenberg said. "But why would he?"

"This man is obviously not shy to physically intimidate someone," James said. "He could have done the same to the husband. I was there when Miss Farnsworth fined the husband, and he seemed like a typical bully to me. All bluster when he was trying to intimidate her, but when I arrived, he couldn't run away fast enough."

"I hope you're right," Mr. Greenberg said. "It would ease my mind to know no one here did something like share personal and route details to someone who did one of my wardens harm."

"If you need any assistance in your search for answers, just let me know," James said.

There was another pause. "That probably won't be strictly within the rules, DS Archer, but if I think of anything, I'll let you know. Miss Farnsworth has gone home, if you want to go round and see she is well for yourself."

James replaced the receiver and followed the sound of conversation to the kitchen. Hartridge was sitting at the table, a cup of tea and a piece of cake in front of him.

"Any word?" Ruby asked.

He nodded. "She's gone home. Mr. Greenberg says her arm is bruised but she's otherwise fine."

"Why was she attacked?" Hartridge twisted in his chair to look up at him.

"It's a long story." He shook his head as Ruby lifted the teapot to him in the offer of a cuppa. "I'm going to go see if she's all right, and then I'll meet you back at New Scotland Yard," he said to Hartridge. "You all right to get yourself back to the office?"

Hartridge gave a nod, and Ruby let him out the front door.

As he drove toward Notting Hill, he tried to remember where he would have put the information about Mr. Jaguar, given he hadn't pursued charges, and what he would do with it if he could lay his hands on it.

Nothing Mr. Jaguar would like, that was for sure.

chapter
twenty-four

GABRIELLA HEADED to Ruby Everett's house from the bus stop, and as she turned into Ruby's street, she thought she caught sight of the back of James's Wolseley driving away.

She wondered if she'd just missed him.

As she got to the front door, it swung open, and she stepped back in surprise at seeing DC Hartridge.

"Gabriella." Ruby leaned around the detective constable. "DS Archer just left to visit you, and check that you're all right."

"I thought I saw his car driving away." She cast a curious glance at DC Hartridge, wondering why he wasn't with his boss.

Hartridge cleared his throat. "I'm off, back to the Met. Thank you for the tea and cake, Mrs. Everett." He grinned at Gabriella and then walked down the path, whistling.

Ruby caught sight of the basket hooked over Gabriella's arm, and ushered her in. "Whatever's in there smells amazing."

"I baked Teddy Roe some bread as a thank you for helping me this morning. He—"

"He told us." Ruby drew her through the house to the kitchen. "It sounded as if he thoroughly enjoyed it."

"So did Jerry," Gabriella said. "I'll come back inside to have a chat, if you have time?"

"I definitely have time, but just hang on a sec." Ruby went

into her pantry and came out with a jam jar. "For them to have with their bread. I know Teddy Roe has butter already."

The jam was so dark, Gabriella couldn't begin to guess what type it was, but it looked homemade, so it was probably from the strawberries Ruby grew in her garden.

Gabriella took the wrapped loaf out of its basket and crossed the garden to the shed.

She could hear Teddy Roe and Jerry chatting away through the partially open door, and called out a greeting.

"Gabriella?" Teddy Roe poked his head out.

"I baked you some bread to say thank you, Mr. Roe. For you and Jerry." She held it out to him and he took it, lifting it to his nose to give a deep sniff.

"Freshly baked?"

"Just came out the oven an hour ago," she confirmed. "And Mrs. Everett has thrown in some homemade jam."

"Lovely! We can have bread, butter and jam for our tea." He nudged the door open and put the bread on the table. "What do you say, Jerry?"

"I say you're a useful person to know, Miss Farnsworth. That copper was right pleased with us helping you this morning. Always good to have a marker to call in with a copper." He smiled a gap-toothed smile.

Not really knowing what to say to that, she simply nodded. "Hope you enjoy it, and thank you again."

"You find out who he is?" Teddy Roe asked her as she backed out.

She shook her head.

"Don't you worry. He'll be found out. That copper will make sure of it." Teddy Roe gave a sage incline of his head, and then lifted up a bread knife and waved it. "Thank you again."

She left them to their feast, and she could hear their crows of delight all the way to the back door.

When she sat down with Ruby, it was to espresso from a stove top pot.

"You know the way to a girl's heart," she said, and took a happy sip.

Ruby raised her cup and clicked it against Gabriella's. "Will you show me where you were hurt?"

For the second time that day, Gabriella rolled up her sleeve. The bruises were darker now, a purple blue that looked ugly against her skin.

"I have frozen peas." Ruby got up and fetched a bag, and draped it over Gabriella's forearm. "Bastard." She was glaring at the marks.

"He wanted information out of me, and he didn't like me refusing to give it to him." Gabriella gave a one-shouldered shrug so as not to dislodge the peas. "I think he's working for the wife of someone I fined a while back. Trying to find out which house he was in when I fined him."

Ruby's face was a picture of astonishment. "Really?"

"Yes. It sounds ridiculous, doesn't it? I think the wife wants to track down his mistress." She couldn't think what else it could be. "And I actually can't help her, because I can't remember which house he did come out of."

"But you could narrow it down to a section of the street?" Ruby asked.

"Yes." She gave a slow nod. "That's probably all she'd need." She finished her espresso. "Not that I'd help her now. Not after this." She looked down at her arm.

"No. Your detective sergeant was very keen to check up on you." Ruby leaned back in her chair. "He'll be disappointed to miss you. I'll wager he'll be around tonight."

She hoped so, but she knew he was neck-deep in his case and there was also the trouble with Whetford. "Maybe."

Ruby tapped the table with impatient fingers. "I've been dying for you to come round and tell me what's happening with your father."

She had meant to come sooner. She knew Ruby would be curious. "Sorry, since we spoke I've been able to get my friend Ben to take the case. His senior has offered to take it pro bono, and they're going to send a letter to my father this week."

Ruby made a face. "That's going to stir up a hornet's nest. But I'm glad you're using lawyers. They should shield you from the worst of his reaction."

She shrugged. "I'm expecting it to be bad. He thinks he's gotten away with hiding his marriage to my mother, and now his reputation will be destroyed, along with the life of the woman who thinks she is his wife, and his children."

"All of them might blame you," Ruby warned. "People aren't always logical or fair in these circumstances."

"I can't help that." Gabriella shook her head. "My mother has been living in limbo for years. She can't get on with her life. My father needs to divorce her, so she can marry Gino."

"I agree." Ruby looked grave. "I'm just saying, watch your back."

The police files between 1939 and 1955 were being stored in the basement of a government building now used by the Home Office.

James looked up at the high atrium and listened to the echo of the receptionist's high heels on the parquet flooring as she led them to the back of the building and then down some stairs.

When he'd returned to the Met from his failed mission to see Gabriella, he'd made enquiries to find out where the old case files could be found. He'd discovered they were stored in government buildings all over London, but the most recent files down here were over a decade old, so James supposed it wasn't surprising the receptionist had handed over the key in surprise. There probably wasn't much traffic to this basement.

He unlocked the heavy wooden door and once he and Hartridge were through, he locked it behind them again as

Hartridge flicked the light switch and a sickly, yellow glow blossomed and then flickered a few times before holding steady.

"Gloomy," Hartridge opined.

It was.

There were rows and rows of shelves, which looked like they could be accessed from both sides, holding large evidence boxes. Along the wall, though, were filing cabinets, and James turned there first. Hopefully, this was the catalogue for where to find what lay amongst the stacks.

"The blackout laws lasted almost the whole length of the war, and we know he used the blackouts to hunt." James ran a hand along each cabinet as he read the dates listed on the drawers. "But he also used the Blitz as a way to hide what he'd done to his victims, so let's focus on that time period first." He came to a stop at September 1940 and pulled out a drawer.

Hartridge took the next cabinet over, which started at December 1940, and they worked in silence for the next hour.

"I've got something." Hartridge held out an open file to him. "A woman was attacked at night during the Blitz by a man in uniform. Says he came up alongside her and asked her directions to the local pub. When she turned away slightly to point in the right direction, he swung something at her head. She never saw what it was, but she caught the movement out of the corner of her eye and jerked away. He shoved her, and she screamed as she fell down. A bystander coming out of an alleyway ran to her aid, and the attacker took off."

"That sounds exactly what we're looking for." James took the file, scanning through the details. "We need to speak to this woman. And the bystander, if we can."

He saw the attending officers had found a few items near where the attack had taken place.

"Stack 7, box 45," James said, checking the inventory list. He found the right stack and had to reach to the top shelf for box 45. He brought it back to the scarred wooden table that was set between the cabinets and the shelving units, and opened the box.

"Anything useful?" Hartridge asked.

He carefully tipped the items out. "A used ticket for the cinema. An empty book of matches from a pub. A glove. And a half-empty pack of cigarettes." He studied the cigarettes. "During the war, I have a feeling these were expensive and I don't think someone would have just thrown a packet away with so many left inside."

"You think it was the killer's?" Hartridge asked.

"Most likely, but I don't know how they could have traced them back to an individual person." James wondered if there were any fingerprints that could be lifted off the box, though. He used a pen to shift it to the side.

"What about the glove?" Hartridge asked.

"Same, I'd imagine." He slid the pen into the glove and lifted it closer to the terrible light.

"No. That glove looks like the one my Dad had as part of his Air Force uniform. I played dress up it in often enough when I was younger, and that one looks just like his." Hartridge tilted his head. "There's a number inside, I think. Tells you who it was issued to. They're leather, and not cheap, and if you lost yours, you had to report it and pay for a replacement. My Dad was proud to have never lost a single piece of uniform, which is how I know."

James stared at him. "Are you being serious?"

Hartridge nodded. "Absolutely."

"The victim said he was in uniform. It was dark, obviously, with no ambient light, so she couldn't tell which service he represented. But this could be his." James set the glove down. "Where's the serial number?"

Hartridge took the pen from him, and pointed to the top of the glove opening, just inside. "Should be there."

James held out the box and Hartridge dropped the glove back inside. Then James carefully slid everything else on the table into the box as well. "Take this to the forensic laboratory, get them to dust for prints on everything in here, and get that serial number."

Hartridge took the box, the excitement clear on his face. "You're going to keep looking for more cases?"

"This case was from March 1941, and the Blitz only went on for two months after that, so just to be thorough, I'll go through the rest." James wanted to tick all the boxes now they were on the scent.

He let Hartridge out, then locked the door again. But he didn't go back to the cabinets just yet. He walked back to stack 7 and lifted box 91 from where it sat, on the shelf below box 45.

It was in the wrong place, which had caught his attention, and then, as he'd reached up for box 45, he'd noticed the name of the officer-in-charge on the side. Whetford.

He pulled it down, took it back to the table, and then went to the cabinet to find the matching file. Surprise, surprise, the box had been placed in the wrong stack completely. It should have been in stack 17, not stack 7, he saw, and gave a cynical smile.

If it was someone else, he'd chalk it up to just a filing error. Just a simple administrative mistake. But it wasn't someone else.

The case was from 1955, the second year Whetford had been on the force.

He flipped open the file, then decided to take a look at the evidence box first. The contents gave him pause, and he pulled his gloves from his pocket and put them on before lifting out the evidence, piece by piece.

Bloody clothes. A bloody knife. And a five pound note with smudges of blood on it.

He stared at them for a bit, and then put them back, setting the box down at his feet before he began to page through the file.

Whetford had caught the case because his boss had been off sick. It looked like a gangland killing, one thug murdered by another. Or that was the conclusion Whetford had come to, reading from his notes.

And because it was Whetford, James suspected it was all bollocks. Except, this was very early in Whetford's career. Maybe he had been straight back then.

Maybe he was seeing corruption and spin where there was none.

According to the file, no one had ever been arrested for the crime. So why had Whetford hidden the evidence in the wrong stack?

Could this just be exactly what it looked like? A misfiled box?

He lifted the box back onto the table and studied its contents again. He held up the five pound note and saw there weren't just smudges of blood on it. There were two clear prints.

He went back to the file.

The five pound note was in the evidence list. No mention of the fingerprints.

It was impossible that they could have been missed.

So. This whole setup was insurance.

Whetford had stashed the box here in the archives, where no crook had access, and hidden it away in the stacks to keep it safe.

It was unlikely to be discovered where it was and keeping it here was certainly safer than keeping it at the office or his home.

James thought of the letter in his inner jacket pocket that he had planned to send to the Police Commissioner, as well as the Police Board, about Whetford and his schemes, and wondered if there was a better way to deal with the situation than literally sticking his neck out and jeopardizing his career.

He mulled it over as he set the Whetford case aside and went through the last of the files from 1941 that seemed relevant.

There was no mention of either of Teddy Roe's cases, nothing at all about his concerns that he had reported any suspicious deaths, but James wasn't that surprised.

The search was still worth his time, because he found another report about an attack on a woman outside a pub. The man had come 'out of nowhere' the woman said, and just a moment after he'd attacked her, the air raid sirens had sounded.

As people poured out of the pub, he'd run away, pursued by a couple of the pub-goers, but he disappeared and they had to get to cover.

The woman was only slightly injured, her arm badly bruised as she lifted it to defend herself against a blow.

This man had come at her from the front, so in that respect, it didn't fit with the other crimes, but he might have been acting on impulse, James thought. He had seen his prey and couldn't resist, so he didn't take the time to get behind her.

Maybe this mistake had reinforced to him to always take his victims completely unaware.

He noted down her name and address, although chances were she had moved on since then. It was still worth checking out.

Then he picked up the Whetford evidence box, placed the file on top, and let himself out of the basement.

If he did what he was thinking of doing, he would be exposing Whetford. Possibly to deadly retaliation.

There was no other reason to bury the case, ensure it went cold, other than he'd taken a bribe, or gotten some favor from the killer. If the case was dug back up, like James was considering doing now, whatever deal Whetford had made was done. Finished.

He turned over the implications. If Whetford had used this murder to put a gangland killer in his debt, if he'd let them get away with the death of a rival in order to profit from it, then did James really care what the fall-out was?

As he climbed the stairs, he decided the answer to that question was no.

chapter
twenty-five

GABRIELLA STOPPED at the grocer's on her way home, buying ingredients for a nice dinner. She didn't want to call James at the Yard, she didn't feel comfortable doing that, so she made a meal for two, knowing he might not come by.

If he didn't, she wouldn't have to cook tomorrow night, which was fine, too.

But when at six there was a knock at her door, she smiled as she walked over and opened it.

"Hello, again." The man from earlier, the one driving the black Mercedes, shoved her inside, locking the door behind him and putting the key in his pocket.

Gabriella backed away, adrenalin prickling under her skin at going from happy anticipation to cold fear. She edged around the table she had set for two, and saw the man's glance land on the place settings.

"You're expecting someone." He looked over at the tiny kitchen, and gave a sniff. "Smells good."

"They're due at six," she said, her voice wobbling a little. "That's why I opened the door so quickly."

He looked down at his watch. Grunted. "Then we'll make this quick. I don't like being messed around, so trust me when I say I have no patience for any more of your nonsense."

"*My* nonsense?" The fear gave way to outrage for a moment.

He stared at her. "You're mouthy. I'm sure you've been told that before. Let's just get through this, shall we?" He walked closer and placed his hands on the table, leaned over it. "Just tell me what house he came out of. That's all. No mess, no fuss."

"Why do you think you're entitled to shove your way into my home and question me like this?" Gabriella was breathing fast, her chest tight, but she wanted to make sense of it.

"My business is looking up right now, love. The client that wants this information is my ticket to bigger things." Mr. Mercedes clicked his tongue impatiently. "Now, which house?"

"You know the road I fined him on," she said. "It would have been on the ticket."

"Sorry, that won't do. It's a long street. Too many houses and flats to investigate them all." He narrowed his eyes, like she was testing him.

She felt her fear spike, her chest tighten. Because she couldn't remember. She really couldn't.

"I had my back turned to him. It was near the end of the road, just a few hundred yards from where it ends in a t-junction. He shouted at me from behind, and I turned, but I honestly don't know which house he came out of." She lifted both hands. She saw they were both shaking.

He hesitated. She knew the story sounded reasonable. It was almost the truth. She actually had noticed him coming down the path of a white Georgian townhouse, although she had no idea of the number, or could even point to the exact one, as there had been several in a row. She wasn't about to send this thug to the wrong person's door, that's for sure.

"How far was he from you when you noticed him?" he asked.

"He was close enough that I heard him shouting, far enough that I couldn't make out what he was saying," she said.

He pulled out a London A-Z from his coat pocket, and she could see there was a bookmark sticking out of it. He flipped to the page, and turned the book to face her, setting it down on the table and jabbing a finger at the spot. "Give me the general area."

She didn't want to get closer, because he would be able to grab her, but she leaned forward a little. Hesitated.

"Show me, or I will become very unpleasant," the man said. He glanced at his watch, and Gabriella flicked her own gaze to the old wall clock hanging in the kitchen.

Amazingly, only five minutes had passed.

A knock sounded at the door, light and friendly.

They both froze. Her eyes snapped to his face, but he was staring at the door. The knock came again, at the same time that she moved, edging around the table, and he panicked.

He lifted his arm and there was suddenly a gun at the end of it.

Gabriella had never had a gun pointed at her. Had she ever even seen a gun in real life, she wondered?

The thought seemed to come from some far away place.

She moved her gaze from the barrel to the man's face. His lips had almost disappeared into his mouth, and his eyes couldn't seem to stay still.

Up until now, he could have claimed she'd let him in to her flat, and they were just talking, but now, he had crossed a very big line.

"Gabby, you home?" It sounded like Jerome, although he never called her Gabby, only Gabriella. She had thought it was James.

The man held a finger to his lips. It shook a little. "Who?" he whispered.

"My neighbor," she whispered back, terrified he was going to pull the trigger by mistake, out of nerves. "He'll have seen my light is on."

"Gabby?" Jerome knocked on the door again.

The man shook his head and made a zipping motion across his lips.

"Gabby, Mr. Rodney said you were hurt today. Are you all right? I'm worried." Jerome knocked harder.

"Hurt?" the man frowned, voice very soft.

She held out her arm and lifted her sleeve, saw him dismiss the bruises with a shake of disbelief.

"Gabby, I'm worried you're lying hurt. I'm going downstairs to Mr. Rodney to get his key to your place, I'll be back." Jerome shouted the words through the door, and then there was the sound of feet pounding down the stairs.

"Quick, show me the section of road, and I'll be off." He lifted the book and held it out to her.

She took it and tried not to look at the door, at the handle slowly turning. She got a little distance from him, moving toward the small kitchen cupboard. "Can I get a pencil to draw it in?" she asked softly.

"Quickly, and don't make me take this up a notch," he said, and the gun wobbled a little.

She made it to the drawer and pulled it open on a loud squeak, and at the same moment, the door swung open.

"Police." James threw the door wide, and she saw his eyes widen in shock at the sight of the gun.

The man spun, but he didn't forget where she was, either. He moved a few steps deeper into the room, where he could move the gun easily from her to James.

"Now how did she get the police here?" he asked.

"Miss Farnsworth's boss put in a complaint about you with the Met this afternoon. I'm here to interview her. Part of the file contained your car's registration number, and I saw your car parked outside. You were visible through her window from the street, and her neighbor gave me the spare key he keeps for her to let me in." James spoke in an even, reasonable tone, but she saw when he stopped talking that his jaw was clenched tight.

"Bad luck." The man shook his head, and she thought he muttered a few choice swearwords under his breath. "I don't want this going any further. Get the neighbor in here, too."

James turned. "Jerome, he's got a gun. Please come in."

Jerome peered in, saw the gun and swore. Stepped in with both hands held up in front of him.

"Go stand in the kitchen," the man motioned with the gun, and Jerome came to stand beside her.

James began to move as well.

"Uh, uh." The man shook his head. "You go stand right up against the wall over there." He pointed with the gun. "I'm going to walk out of the flat, and you are not going to move, or someone might get badly hurt."

James nodded, lifting his hands like Jerome, and did as he asked.

The man edged to the door, keeping them all in sight the whole way. He pulled out the key he'd pocketed when he'd locked himself inside with her, and with the gun still trained on them, slid it in to the outside lock.

Then he stepped out, slammed the door, and she heard the key turn.

"Damn," she said, as James ran to the door and tried to put in the spare key. "That won't work. Someone will have to pull the key out before we can unlock it from this side."

James ran back to the sash window, and shoved the lower half up and leaned out. She and Jerome joined him, and saw the man run to his Mercedes and drive off.

"We thought we were so clever," Jerome said, and he sounded disgusted.

"You were, though," she said. If he hadn't had a gun, it would have been masterful.

The ruse had worked beautifully. They had given the man the impression he had enough time to get his answer and leave before Jerome returned, and then they had quietly opened the door.

"I never thought for a moment he'd have a gun." James turned to her, and she blinked at the harsh line of his mouth.

"How could you?" she asked. "He never even showed it to me

until you two knocked on the door. I don't think he wanted to use it."

"Where did he even get it?" Jerome wondered.

"My guess is during the war. He's old enough to have served." James gave a sharp shake of his head. "He was the man from earlier today?"

"Yes." She turned away from the view of the street and sat down on the deep window seat.

"When I saw the black Mercedes with some paint damage in the street, I guessed it was him." James leaned against the window, hand in a tight fist.

"You were cooking dinner?" Jerome said, suddenly noticing the table.

"Yes." She got to her feet.

"Who were you expecting?" James asked, also studying the table.

"You." She shot him a look. "I thought it was you at the door, when he knocked."

She went to the kitchen, got out another plate and cutlery, and set it on the table, ignoring the fact that her hands were shaking. "Help me move this to the window seat so we can all sit down. Unless you've eaten, Jerome?"

"No." He looked bemused. "We're having dinner?"

"Well, we're stuck in here," she said. "And dinner is ready."

The two men exchanged a look and then lifted the table between them and set it down close enough for someone to use the window seat as a third chair.

"Sit," she told them both. She dished pasta at the tiny kitchen counter and ladled sauce over it, sprinkled basil on top, and then carried it over. "Will you grate the parmesan?" she asked James, turning to fetch the grater and cheese.

He closed his hand gently around her forearm to stop her. "You all right?"

She lifted the back of her other hand to her cheek, and realized it was wet. "I'm all right." She gave a slightly gurgling laugh. "Really. I'm fine."

He let go of her, and she came back with her own bowl and the cheese. Took a seat.

"This looks good," Jerome said. His words broke the tension and she flashed him a quick smile.

They started to eat, and she felt herself relax as a comfortable silence descended.

They had just finished when James turned at the sound of voices below.

"Solomon," he called down from the open window.

"Hey, Mr. Detective." Solomon stood below, looking up.

"We're locked in Gabriella's flat. Do you mind coming up and letting us out?" he asked.

"Now that's a new one." Solomon gave a chuckle as he headed inside, and Gabriella caught a murmur from someone who sounded like George.

The key turned in the lock moments later, and both men stepped inside, George looking around with interest. She realized it was his first time in her flat.

"Jerome?" Solomon must have expected it to be just the two of them. "What's up, man?"

"Man with a gun locked us in, is what's up." Jerome said, head tilted.

There was silence, and Gabriella thought a lot was being exchanged between the two with not a word spoken.

"Not the green Jaguar man?" George asked.

Gabriella shook her head. "Connected, though. I think it was the private investigator he didn't want me talking to. The one he said his wife hired."

"And he came here, with a gun, to make you talk?" Solomon made a face and turned to James. "What are you going to do about it?"

"Now that I can leave the room without damaging Gabriella's door, I'm off to find out his name and address off his car registration, and I'm going around to arrest him." James shook his shoulders, as if loosening up before a fight.

"Need some help with that, man?" George asked, politely.

James hesitated, as if he was considering it. "Better not."

"Pity." George inclined his head.

James turned to her, and she thought he was uncomfortable with the audience they had. "Thank you for dinner." He leaned in and kissed her cheek. "I'll be round tomorrow evening. I don't think I'll be able to come back at a decent enough time tonight."

She gave a nod, and watched him grab his coat and disappear down the stairs.

"What car does this gun-toting man drive?" Solomon asked.

"A black Mercedes. It's got a scratch on the side." Gabriella couldn't believe that that had happened just this morning.

"Number plate?" George asked.

She looked it up in her notes and told them.

"He comes here again, we'll be ready," Solomon said.

There was definitely some comfort to be taken in that.

chapter
twenty-six

"HE'S NOT HERE." Hartridge rounded the side of Ronny Tanner's house, shaking his head. "No lights, car's not in the garage. I think he's done a runner."

James forced himself to admit that that was the only play Tanner had left, after drawing a firearm on a police officer. "I want a warrant to search his house," he said, although he didn't know if he had enough cause for one. "But we will definitely alert the port authority, in case he decides to leave the country."

He probably wouldn't, though. He'd find somewhere to hunker down and wait them out.

"His office is about ten minutes from here. Let's go there next." He yawned on the last word. It was already one in the morning, but he didn't want to leave it until tomorrow.

Hartridge didn't complain, and they were soon parked in front of a row of houses converted into businesses in a quiet street.

"Nice," Hartridge commented. "He wasn't scraping the bottom of the barrel, was he?"

"No." James had had the impression the client who'd hired him had money, especially if she owned the green Jaguar, and she would have chosen a reputable investigator, probably through a recommendation.

They looked around, but the firm was locked up and there were no lights on here, either.

"It'll be easier to get a warrant for the business than the house, so let's get on that first thing tomorrow." James turned back to the Wolseley just as he heard a car come up the street.

The headlights illuminated him and Hartridge, and there was a sudden squealing of tires as a black Mercedes sped away.

Tanner.

"He was coming back for something," Hartridge said. "And we got here first."

"Yes." James felt a sudden lift in his spirits. "Let's get a few uniforms to stand front and back here until the warrant's issued. I don't want him getting in for whatever it was he came for."

It meant there was something here he wanted. And now he couldn't get it.

The energy of that fueled him enough to get home before he crashed into bed. As he lay, looking at the ceiling, he remembered the silent tears dripping down Gabriella's cheeks as they'd eaten dinner, and admitted he might have to take a step back when they took Tanner in. Because he wanted to hurt him.

Very, very badly.

"Where the hell were you, yesterday?" Detective Inspector Whetford loomed in James's office, blocking the way out.

James slung his coat over his arm, the warrant he'd been waiting for finally in his hand, and considered his boss.

"Sir?" he asked.

"I came past at least three times, and you were never once in your office." Whetford waved a hand in the direction of Hartridge's cubby hole. "Neither was your bagman."

He was shaking a little, and James could see he was working himself into a rage.

It could be manufactured, a way to build up a head of steam

in order to punish James for his failure to fall in line on the weekend, but James thought the shakes were genuine.

"As I mentioned in the report I put on your desk last night," James said, sure—beyond sure—that Whetford had not checked a single file on his desk for weeks, "we've managed to link the four murders over the last two months to murders that happened during the Blitz. Given that every day this bastard goes undetected, more women are at risk, I've literally worked between sixteen and eighteen hours a day since I caught the first case."

"What?" Whetford took a step back as if James had struck him. "What case?"

"The one I've been involved in since before I went on leave, sir." James had gone around Whetford to get the case, but he'd covered himself later by giving the details to the pool secretary who worked for four DIs, Whetford included.

She would have entered it into the system and Whetford would have assumed it had been a random assignment. If he'd even looked.

"You went on leave during this?" Whetford grabbed onto the one thing that was a bad look.

"Dr. Jandicott couldn't say how that first victim died, sir, who she was, or even how long she'd been dead before she was found. It was only after I returned and the second body turned up that we established the link." James studied Whetford, and thought his hands might be shaking a little.

"Jandicott?" The pathologist's name seemed to take the wind out of Whetfor's sails. "And he thinks the same person is responsible for four deaths in the last two months?"

"We both do, sir. Our reasoning is in my report." He had used the pretext of dropping the hastily drawn-up report to Whetford's office last night as a way to get in and set up his plan to discredit his boss, before he'd headed over to Gabriella's. He'd slid the report under a few other files, so it looked as if he'd dropped it off earlier than he had. He'd known Whetford wouldn't be at work. He preferred to do his business in a noisy pub, where no one could see who he talked to and hear what was said. "Have you had time to read the report yet, sir?" James asked. "If we're right, he's responsible for a lot more than just four deaths."

"My God, man." Whetford stared at him in horror. A multiple murderer was so rare as to be major news in the Met. "Why haven't you briefed me before now?" Whetford's neck was red.

"Sir, I went to your office a number of times, and eventually left the report when I couldn't speak to you personally." James rubbed a hand on his brow. "I've been burning the candle at both ends to catch this monster, sir. Along with Dr. Jandicott and DS Hartridge."

Again, Jandicott's name gave Whetford pause. He might have power over James, but Jandicott was the head pathologist and had access to far more ears than Whetford did. "Give me the short version, right now, so I can brief the Commissioner." Whetford pulled his collar away from his neck, and James felt a quiet satisfaction at the display of nerves. Because no DI should be this out of the loop with his subordinates' cases—and Whetford knew it.

James spelled it out in simple terms, wondering if Whetford would realize that he would fall short of even the most basic questioning by the Commissioner, but Whetford was too focused on getting the broad strokes committed to memory.

Whetford fiddled with his collar again, and the flush moved up from his neck to his cheeks. He took out a handkerchief and wiped the sweat off his brow.

"You coming down with something, sir?" James asked.

"Maybe." Whetford coughed into the handkerchief. "Maybe I am." He stepped back into the passageway and then finally focused on James's coat. "You're off again?"

"I'm afraid so, sir." James decided not to tell him he was busy on a different case this morning. The smog had come in heavily in the early morning hours, and he felt a rising sense of pressure, that lives hung in the balance.

But after they went to look through Tanner's office, they had three visits connected to the current case lined up. First, a meet-up at a library with the ladies who were friends with Hatty Clark, the missing wife of Larry Clark, which Hartridge had set up through the librarian, and then they had the names and addresses of the two victims during the Blitz who might be survivors of their killer's first attempts at attacking women. James hoped they still lived at the addresses they'd given during the war.

And they had also put in a request to the Air Force to get back to them about the origin of the glove that had been recovered from one of the scenes, and were waiting to find out if any finger-prints on the evidence the police had gathered back then were a match to a current, known offender.

"As long as you keep me informed, Archer. A briefing once a day, no exceptions." Whetford's gaze flicked away from him.

He would know how difficult that would be for James, given the negligible time he spent in the office.

"Certainly, sir." James stepped out into the corridor with him, and closed his door. Hartridge was lurking just inside his own office, unwilling to make himself known. James couldn't blame him.

He pretended Hartridge wasn't there. "Are you off to speak to the Commissioner now?"

"Yes. And I mean it, Archer. Daily updates." Whetford walked to the staircase and disappeared.

James looked after him, and wondered if it was stress, or whether his boss was hitting the bottle. Whatever it was, it didn't look good on him.

"We off to Tanner's office?" Hartridge asked, finally stepping out into the corridor.

"Yes. Let's see if we can find whatever it was he was after last night."

chapter
twenty-seven

GABRIELLA STARTED HER ROUTE LATE.

Mr. Greenberg had insisted they go and lay a formal complaint at the closest police station to where she was attacked, although she had told him about the incident the night before, and that James was following up.

"I am adding my weight to it, then," he said. "These are separate incidences and they warrant separate charges."

She'd meekly agreed and gone along. Now that she was on her new route, she realized how much she appreciated Mr. Greenberg making sure she was in a completely different section of Kensington. Mr. Mercedes may still be on the loose, but he had no way of tracking her down.

She walked along a tree-lined street of mansions that butted up against Holland Park, and then slowed in surprise when she turned left to go up the side of the park and saw the cyclist who had nearly run her down yesterday half-in and half-out of a telephone box. He was holding onto his bike with one hand, awkwardly keeping the door open so he could hold the phone with the other.

He turned his head slightly, saw her through the dusty window pane of the door, and quickly looked away.

She frowned as she got closer.

Maybe he thought she was going to confront him?

She walked past him, and he had his back firmly turned, murmuring into the receiver too softly for her to hear the conversation, despite the open door.

For some reason, she didn't like the idea of him being behind her, so she crossed the road, saw a car parked in a way that partially blocked a driveway, and stopped to write out an FPN.

As she affixed the fine to the windscreen, she saw the cyclist riding away, toward a footpath set between two houses that led into the park, and felt a quick sense of relief.

Ten minutes later, she was halfway down the long, eastern side of the park, when she caught sight of the black Mercedes.

It was coming towards her.

The man from the night before was behind the wheel, and his eyes narrowed the moment he saw her.

He pulled the Mercedes to a halt, double parking on the other side of the street to where she stood.

There was nowhere to run. To her back was the tall, black metal railings of the park fence. To her right and left, the long street that ran down the east side of the park.

At least going right would head her back down to Kensington High Street, and from there, to her headquarters. To safety.

If she was going to run, it would have to be now, she decided, as the Mercedes engine shut off.

She turned right and ran down the street. She heard the man swear, and then the car door slammed shut.

He was getting back in the car, and before he could start up the engine, she darted across the road into a narrow lane, a street with high hedges and fences on both sides. Her bag slammed against her side as she sprinted, and she glanced back. Saw the car turn in after her.

She needed to turn right the first chance she got, knowing it would take her to the high street. He would be mad to try to attack her there.

She heard the engine growl behind her and she put on a little more speed, but the car easily drew level with her.

Mr. Mercedes leaned out of the window.

"I'm not going to hurt you," he shouted. "I just want you to call the coppers off. I can't even get back into my office."

She chanced a quick look at him, then ran even harder. There was a screech of brakes and she couldn't resist looking back.

He had mounted the pavement to avoid hitting a badly parked Mini Cooper.

A car door slammed, and then she heard the heavy tread of running feet.

Damn, he was chasing her on foot now.

She could see a road to the right up ahead. She just had to make it there.

She put on extra speed, but he was gaining. She took the turn, and then saw the dusty blue Land Rover.

She almost stumbled to a stop in surprise.

It was parked illegally in front of a fire hydrant, and as she jogged closer she listened for and just caught the faint hum of electricity.

She looked back and saw Mr. Mercedes had slowed himself. He was walking toward her as if she were a wild animal he wanted to grab.

"Listen, last night didn't go the way I wanted it to. And it was bad luck that copper arrived when he did." He moved closer, and Gabriella stepped right next to the Land Rover. "There weren't any bullets in that gun. It's just for show. For protection, see? You were never in any danger."

"Please leave me alone." She didn't like how breathless she sounded. She got angry, just hearing herself. Hearing how much he had frightened her.

He took another few steps. "Come now. You don't look hurt. You're fine, love. Maybe a bit shaken up, but you'll live. I want you to drop the charges. If you refuse to cooperate with the Met, they'll be more inclined to drop things."

She stared at him in total disbelief.

"There's bobbies guarding the doors to my office. I can't run a business that way." He lifted his hands, as if making a reasonable request. "I need you to call them off."

She looked down, judging the height of the Land Rover's wheel base to the road. She'd have to move quickly.

"Do you understand what I'm saying?" Mr. Mercedes spoke to her as if she were a child, and took a step forward.

Gabriella slid her bag off her shoulder and let it fall to the pavement. She didn't need to get caught in the straps. Then she dropped to the ground and rolled.

The road was dirty, and she felt the grit under her palms. She lifted her head slightly once she was fully under the car and on her back, and looked for the switch she guessed powered the electrification.

She saw it was on the street side, under the rear wheel.

"Are you mad—?" Mr. Mercedes crouched down beside the Land Rover, and for a moment she thought he wasn't going to touch it.

But then he leaned his head down to look under the car, and put his hand against the side door for balance.

She heard the crack, saw him fall back. She rolled out the other side, got on her haunches and reached under the back wheel and flipped the switch.

Then she ran back around the front to pick up her bag.

Mr. Mercedes was lying on the ground, and he groaned and turned, pushing up onto his hands and knees.

The sound of bicycle brakes screeching made her look up, and she saw the cyclist from earlier.

A lightbulb went off.

Gabriella ran, heading for the high street up ahead, and as she turned left onto it, she looked back, and saw the cyclist helping Mr. Mercedes to his feet.

There was no one giving out her route. She'd been followed

yesterday and today by the man on the bike, and he'd called Mr. Mercedes to let him know where to find her.

She disappeared into the crowd of pedestrians, heading toward headquarters. It was close by, and she walked at a fast clip, weaving between groups until she turned into the cul-de-sac.

She could see the double doors of headquarters up ahead, but she was the only person on the street.

When she glanced back, the cyclist was turning in behind her.

She slid her bag off her shoulder, holding it by the strap, and faced him.

If she swung it hard enough, she could probably dislodge him from the bike.

The cyclist came to a stop, brakes screeching again.

"He wants to talk to you," he said, gripping the handlebars. He was wearing trousers with bicycle clips to keep his hems from catching in the chain, and a light jacket. He looked around her age.

"He had a chance to talk to me twice yesterday, when he grabbed me on the street, and later, when he forced his way into my flat and then held a gun on me. I'm not giving him another." She got a better grip on her strap.

"I don't know anything about that." He blinked a little. "I'm just paid to let him know where you are. He wants you to call off the cops."

"I got that," Gabriella said. "I don't have any say in what the coppers do."

"But if you withdraw the complaint, they'll back off. He didn't mean to frighten you and he can't run a business if the cops are going to come down on him."

"He didn't just frighten me, he hurt me. And if he wanted to keep the cops off his back then he shouldn't have waved a gun at one, should he?" She shrugged, and began to walk backward, toward the steps.

"Did he really wave a gun at a copper?" the cyclist asked, voice rising a little in disbelief.

She nodded, and the cyclist swore softly under his breath.

She reached the bottom step, turned, and ran up and through the doors.

Then she looked out the window set in the wall beside the doors, and saw him cycling away, shaking his head.

Mr. Mercedes would be lurking nearby, she guessed, waiting to hear what he had to say.

The question was, would he realize he'd failed and leave her alone, or would he try to approach her again?

twenty-eight

"SO, Tanner's client is the Honorable Mrs. Fitzgerald." James looked up from the folder in his hands and frowned.

He was inside Tanner's office, which was messy, but the furniture and fittings looked expensive. From a few of the bank statements he'd found, the man liked the finer things, but didn't quite yet have the income to pay for them.

"A lady?" Hartridge shook his head. "That'll go down well."

It would be more difficult to hold her to account, but James was aware she herself hadn't done anything wrong so far. It had been her husband and her private detective who'd stepped over the line.

James jotted down her phone number and address from the file, and then gave a quick read of the contents. "Tanner's job was to find out which house her husband had been visiting when he'd gotten the parking fine. Doesn't say he's to threaten anyone, or anything else. So there's nothing to charge her with." Even her husband, who James could see from the file was Mr. Reginald Fitzgerald, hadn't done enough to warrant a charge. He'd followed Gabriella around, but he hadn't touched her.

That had been Tanner.

And Tanner had waved a gun at a police officer. There was no getting around that.

"I think this is probably what he was after." James slid the file into an envelope to take into evidence. "Let's put a note on the door informing him there's a warrant out for his arrest, and telling him where to hand himself in."

He checked the time.

They hadn't spent as long as he thought they would searching Tanner's office, so he got Hartridge to drive to one of the Blitz witnesses before they were due at the library to meet Hatty Clark's bridge friends.

Her house was on the way—or at least, the house she'd lived in at the time of the attack in April 1941. Her case was the one James had found after Hartridge had left with the evidence from the March attack, and he steeled himself for disappointment when he knocked on the door.

"Lucille Bourne?" he asked, when a woman opened it. Her hair was pulled neatly back in a bun, her dress covered by a flowered apron.

She nodded cautiously. "I was. I'm Lucille Hammond, now."

In that case, they were lucky to find her at the same address, James thought. He held up his warrant card. "I'm sorry to bother you, but I'm here to ask you about an attack you experienced during the war. Outside a pub in Earl's Court?"

The shock was obvious on her face, and she stepped back to let them in, offering them tea as she did.

They ended up in a sunny kitchen, watching her put on the kettle.

"You know, I haven't thought about the attack in years," she said as she put tea bags into a teapot. "What brings you to my door now?"

"We can't go into the details, but we've come across new information that might lead to his arrest." James didn't want news of a deranged killer getting out. "Can you remember anything from that night?"

"How he looked, you mean?" she asked, then turned as the kettle whistled. She seemed to be thinking it over.

"He was taller than me, but normal height for a man, not heavy set but not particularly slender, either." She poured out the tea, and handed them their teacups—delicate fine bone china with roses around the rim, on saucers with the same pattern.

"He approached you from the front?" Hartridge asked.

Lucille Hammond glanced at him, gave a nod. "I think he came out of a side street, but I was jumpy, it was dark and I was afraid, so the moment I heard footsteps, I turned to see who was there. I was facing him, with my torch switched on, and he seemed to reel back in surprise."

"This was near a pub?" James asked.

Lucille Hammond nodded. "I was meeting some friends there after work. I was only nineteen when I was attacked." She shook her head. "So young. When I saw the man, he looked like he was in uniform—a serviceman, I thought—and I immediately relaxed."

"What did he do?" James asked.

"He swung something at me." She shook her head, as if still baffled by that. "I didn't see what. It looked short, not a stick, or anything like that, more a cosh, maybe?" She shrugged. "I leaped back, so whatever it was only caught me a glancing blow on my arm. I screamed." She finally sat down at the table with them, took a sip of her tea. "I had a piercing scream. Honestly, they called me the banshee at school." She gave a low chuckle. "Scared the life out of my attacker."

James tilted his head. "What did he do?"

"He swore, I can't remember exactly what he said, but almost like my scream brought it on, the sirens started blaring, and he was sort of frozen in place." Lucille Hammond set her cup away from her. "And people just poured out of the pub, and I pointed at him and screamed again." She lifted her hands. "I don't even think I spoke an intelligible word, but somehow a few of the men understood he needed catching."

"They didn't catch him, though?" James asked.

She shook her head. "He turned and ran, and the sirens were

still blaring, so the men had to get to shelter." She leaned back in her chair. "My friends came out the pub, and they took me with them into the underground. When we were safe in the tunnels, I found a copper and told him what happened."

"Did you notice hair color, eye color, anything like that?" James asked, aware this was twenty years later.

"Dark hair, maybe, but he was wearing a hat or a cap. No idea of his eye color. In the dark, it was impossible to see." She sighed. "I honestly don't know what he wanted."

They thanked her for her time and got into the Wolseley before they spoke again.

"She doesn't understand that he wanted to kill her," Hartridge said.

"And I'm glad she doesn't." James was happy she'd managed to survive the encounter so unscathed.

He hoped Hatty Clark had managed to survive unscathed, too. Or wasn't missing at all. As Hartridge drew up outside the library, he had to believe these ladies would know if she had simply left her husband, or had disappeared in suspicious circumstances.

The bridge club was set up in the reading room, a small chamber off the main library, with hard wooden chairs set around the edges of the room, and a low coffee table in the middle.

They were chatting amiably to each other when the librarian showed him and Hartridge in, which made the sudden silence at the sight of them all the more pronounced.

"I appreciate you coming to speak with us," James said, sitting down close to the door. "My colleague and I are worried about Mrs. Hatty Clark, and wonder if you have anything you can tell us about her whereabouts."

There was a moment of shifting bodies, hands gripping handbags, feet shuffling.

"Did her husband ask you to ask us?" One of the women leaned forward. She had a tight perm of mouse brown hair and bright red lipstick, and James thought he wouldn't like to meet her down a dark alley. She had the eyes of a cut throat.

"He did make a missing persons report, but it seems it was under duress from Mrs. Clark's mother." James gave her an easy smile. "We want to find out if she's come to harm, either by a stranger's hand, or by someone she knows."

"Someone like Mr. Clark, you mean?" A small, bird-like woman who had a lap full of knitting shifted in her chair.

"Perhaps," James conceded.

One of the other women sighed. "We can't keep this up, Mavis. They're the police."

The little one glanced over, made a moue with her mouth, and then turned back to him. "She's staying with me."

James breathed out a sigh of relief. "You won't believe how happy I am to hear that. Please ask her to get in touch with me when she has a chance, so I can strike her off the missing persons list." James took out a card and handed it to the woman.

"Easy as that?" the woman asked.

He nodded. "She can do what she likes, but if she isn't missing, no one needs to spend time looking for her, do they?"

"Sure, and I will do that," the woman said, taking his card with a cheeky grin.

"Good." James walked out, feeling a lightness he didn't anticipate.

"That's happy news, at least." Hartridge slid into the car.

"Yes. Clark was so shifty, I was worried the outcome would be worse." James thought about it. "I'll pass on the tip to Vice or Fraud. There's something wrong about that man."

Hartridge gave a snort, to which James guessed he didn't believe either department would do anything about his tip, but he would pass it on, anyway.

They headed for their final interview of the day.

Shepherd's Bush had suffered a lot of damage during the war, but Mrs. Gallagher's house was one of the ones that had made it through unscathed. She was down a smaller street behind the new shopping center, and they couldn't find parking.

Hartridge let James out and went to find a spot as close by as possible.

He walked up the little path to the door, and had his hand up to knock when a voice came from the side.

"Can I help you?"

He tried not to jump, and turned to find a woman crouched down in a garden bed, a little trowel in one gloved hand, with a basket full of weeds beside her.

"Sorry, I didn't see you there." He showed her his warrant card. "DS Archer. Are you Mrs. Gallagher?"

She rose to her feet, dusting her skirt, and then stripped off her gloves. "I am." She suddenly took a step back and her hands clasped together. "My Johnny?"

"Oh, no, Mrs. Gallagher. This is about an attack you experienced during the war. I wondered if you would mind me asking you a few questions about it?"

"Well." She picked up the basket and walked toward where he was standing on the steps. "I wasn't expecting that."

He stepped aside, and she pushed the door open and invited him in.

"Do you remember the incident well?" James asked her.

"Someone tried to kill me, that's not something that goes away, DS Archer." Mrs. Gallagher waved him into her front room. "I've thought about it often these last twenty years."

"It was March 1941, is that right?" James asked her.

She nodded. "I was working for the Ministry of Agriculture during the war, and I was on my way home. We'd had some crisis and I was late getting on my way, so it was already dark." She clasped her hands together loosely, and James saw she was wearing a massive diamond ring.

"My husband was away, fighting in the war, and so when what looked like an officer came up to me, I honestly didn't feel even a twinge of nerves." Her lips quirked to one side. "He asked me for directions to the pub, and I turned to point the way." She shrugged. "That's when he swung at me."

She stood suddenly, as if she couldn't remain still, and James thought her agitation was telling. Even after all this time, the memory affected her.

"With his fist?" James asked.

She shook her head. "Something else. I felt the air pass by my cheek as I jerked back, and something, maybe the way he held it, or his angle, told me it was a hammer or something like a hammer." She leaned against the wall and looked out the front window, then turned to him. "If he had managed to land that blow, I have no doubt I wouldn't be here, talking to you now."

James thought she was probably right. "What happened next."

"He shoved me to the ground, and it was like my throat was paralyzed, my voice was gone." She grimaced. "And then, when I hit the ground, I suddenly drew in a huge breath and screamed."

James saw her hands were fisted by her side. On the mantelpiece, near where she stood, was a series of photographs of her, with what looked like her husband and children.

"Someone came to the rescue?" he asked.

She smiled for the first time since they had begun speaking. "Someone came to the rescue. A woman coming home, like me, cutting through an alleyway to the main road."

"A woman?" James thought the bystander had been a man, but he realized now that the report hadn't specified.

"Jessica Tate. Still my friend, to this very day." Mrs. Gallagher smiled again. "She was like a dervish, swinging her handbag like it was a mace from the Medieval period."

"And he ran off?" James asked.

"He ran, but when he realized Jessica was a woman, and a small one at that, he paused." Mrs. Gallagher caught his eye, gave a nod when she saw he understood what she was saying.

"You think he was going to come back?" he asked.

"Until Jessica's screaming roused a couple more people," Mrs. Gallagher said with a nod, "definitely."

"To finish the job?" James asked.

Mrs. Gallagher shook her head. "To pick up his glove, which he'd dropped."

"It was definitely his?" he asked. Excitement prickled down his arms.

She nodded. "Definitely. He wanted it so badly, but when Jessica's antics brought more people, he gave up and ran."

"That is very helpful. Thank you very much." James stood. "Did you notice anything about him regarding the way he looked?"

"Dark hair, brown eyes, medium build," she said, without a moment's hesitation. "He stood over me with murder in his eyes, DS Archer. His face is burned into my memory."

He gave a nod, and she took him out to the hall and opened the front door.

James saw Hartridge doing a slow drive past, and gave him a wave.

"Why have you come to ask me about this now?" Mrs. Gallagher asked.

"We have some new information," James said. "And the case was never closed."

"That's good," she said. "I'm pleased to hear it. And I hope you get the bastard."

chapter
twenty-nine

IT WAS long past the end of her shift, but Gabriella had been persuaded to wait in Mr. Greenberg's office, and so she was standing in front of his map when James knocked on her boss's door.

Mr. Greenberg rose from behind his desk and came round to shake James's hand. "Terrible business, what happened to Gabriella," Mr. Greenberg said. "But the one thing that has put my mind at ease is that she was able to discover no one in this office shared her route. She was being followed by a cyclist employed by Mr. Tanner."

"That's his name?" Gabriella asked, surprised.

"Yes, sorry, I forgot to tell you DS Archer found out his name during the course of his investigation." Mr. Greenberg gave James a satisfied smile. "I am going to let the Commissioner know how pleased I am with the quality of the investigation into this," he said. "It's very heartening to know the Met takes threats to the Traffic Warden division seriously."

Gabriella caught her lower lip with her teeth. Would they have, though, if she and James weren't stepping out, as Liz called it?

"Of course," James told him. "I've had bobbies keeping an eye out for him in this area since you called me about Tanner's interaction with Miss Farnsworth earlier, but there's been no sightings. I think he's gone, but I'm going to get Miss Farnsworth's statement at the Met, and then make sure she's escorted home."

"Good man." Mr. Greenberg beamed.

James indicated the map on the wall. "I have to say how impressed I am by this, sir." He stepped closer. "It really gives a great perspective on things."

"Thank you." Mr. Greenberg rocked back on his heels. "Helps me to see if there are problem areas."

"The red are deaths?" James asked. "And the yellow?"

"The yellow are attacks on my wardens." Mr. Greenberg tapped the pin on the street near Holland Park where Gabriella's final confrontation with Tanner had occurred.

"Very helpful. Can I ask where you got the map? I would like to set something like this up for myself." James pulled out his notepad, and Mr. Greenberg gave him the details.

When they walked out to the Wolseley, Gabriella thought James had made a friend for life with her boss.

When they were both inside the car, James turned to her. "Tell me."

She knew Mr. Greenberg had not given him a lot of detail, but had assured James she was fine. She supposed if the tables were turned, she'd have been worried, too.

"You remember the electrified Land Rover?" she asked.

He gave a slow nod.

"While I was running from Tanner, I saw it. I rolled underneath it, and he got down on his haunches to grab me and pull me out, and put his hand on the door."

James blinked. "Pow?" he asked.

"Pow." She knew her smile was slightly evil. "Gave me time to roll back out, and leg it."

"But the cyclist still came after you?" James must have heard that from Mr. Greenberg as well.

"Tanner was obviously not up to running after me, so he sent his lackey, but the bloke didn't really seem to know about Tanner waving guns around or anything like that." She recalled the surprise on the cyclist's face. "He pled Tanner's case again—for me to drop the charges against him—and when I told him it wasn't up to me, that he'd threatened a police officer with a gun, he left, looking pretty confused."

"Well, Tanner can't stay in the wind forever. We've sealed his office with a notice telling him to turn himself in, and I think he'll probably do that soon." James wove carefully through the late afternoon traffic, and when he turned through the imposing gates of New Scotland Yard, she felt like she was entering a castle.

He parked, and when she reached for her door handle, he put a hand on her arm. "I want to hold you," he said. His gaze lifted and focused beyond her shoulder, and he sighed. "But that will have to wait."

He released her, and when she turned to look out of her window, she saw two men approaching.

"Wait for me to open your door," James said, and there was something tight in his voice that held her in place.

It wasn't a gentleman thing, she realized. He wanted to intercept the men coming toward the car. He got out the car and intercepted the men, blocking their view of her, in a studied, casual way that made Gabriella worried.

These men were dangerous. And he didn't want them to see her.

She slid a little way down in the car seat, keeping her gaze on what was happening.

James was bigger than both of the men. He was bigger than almost every one she knew except for maybe George and Melvin, and even then, he and George were probably close to the same size.

Melvin was in a class of his own.

Whatever the conversation was, it wasn't friendly. One of the men's hands fisted by his sides, and he threw down his cigarette and crushed it beneath his shoe as if he'd like to be doing the same thing to James's face.

James, on the other hand, moved as if he was simply passing the time of day. Then he looked at his watch, and whatever he said next had both men turning and stalking off.

James went back to the car and opened the boot, and Gabriella turned in her seat. He looked at her through the window on the rear door, and mouthed "Stay" before he pulled out a box, and did a complicated juggle to close the boot with one hand and keep hold of the box with the other.

Finally, he came round to her door and gave a nod, and she opened it and stepped out.

"What was that?" she asked.

He shook his head. "I didn't want them seeing you. They are not nice men, and if things happen the way I'm planning for them to happen, I don't want them looking your way, for any reason whatsoever."

She wanted to ask more, but she guessed this was to do with Whetford, and James's plan to extricate Hartridge and himself from his clutches. The courtyard of New Scotland Yard probably wasn't the place to ask about it.

"What are their names, in case I bump into them?" She'd rather know, and both had been wearing hats and coats, so she might not recognize them immediately.

"DS Galbraith and his partner, DC Bartholomew." James led her across the courtyard to a door set in the back. "Never speak to them, and get away from them as fast as you can."

She was curious as to why there was so much animus between James and the two men, but a few other officers passed them, coming the other way, and she swallowed her questions.

When they got to James's office, DC Hartridge stepped out of a small room to the left of it, excitement on his face, which morphed into surprise at the sight of her.

"Miss Farnsworth." He glanced over at James, and she saw he was holding a file in his hands.

"Tanner had another go at her," James said, and Hartridge's attention swung back to her.

"You all right?"

Before she could answer, the door at the far end of the corridor opened, and DI Whetford stepped through.

"Why don't you take Miss Farnsworth's statement about the incident," James said to Hartridge. "I need to talk to the boss."

Hartridge looked so relieved, Gabriella wondered again what on earth was going on here.

Hartridge stepped back into the small room he'd come out of, and inclined his head.

She glanced quickly at James, but his face was stony as he stepped out into the passageway to meet Whetford head on.

She followed Hartridge into the tiny office, and he shut the door behind her.

"What's going on?" she asked, keeping her voice soft, but Hartridge just shook his head.

She played along, giving him all the details of the incident with Tanner, and even managed to smile with him when she described how she'd gotten him to shock himself.

All the while, she strained to hear what was being said outside, but the drone of voices never got loud enough to make anything out.

Whatever it was, she remembered James saying his job could be on the line, and she felt sick to her stomach that Whetford could win this unspoken battle between them. He had the power to push James out.

She wondered if Ben's senior, the silk who'd taken on her case, would be interested in representing a DS from the Met. Maybe it wouldn't come to that, but there was no harm in asking.

chapter
thirty

JAMES SETTLED in behind his desk. "I was planning on coming to you a little later, sir," he said as he set the file Hartridge had given him down in front of him.

"I asked you to give me a daily briefing." Whetford was spoiling for a fight. James had seen it on his face the moment he'd stepped into the corridor.

"Yes, but I've literally just come in from the field. I'd planned to write out the main points before I briefed you, so you had the facts in writing as well, sir." He pulled a notepad closer and picked up a pen.

Whetford hadn't taken the seat that was offered to him, and he was prowling the office, looking at the board James had up to one side. Right now, it was clean of any notes. James didn't want Galbraith or anyone else coming in to read his case notes, and possibly interfere.

"You aren't very organized, are you?" Whetford said, waving at the board.

"To be honest, sir, I've done most of my analysis with Dr. Jandicott, given so much of this case rests on the forensics." He lifted his hands. "It's been more useful to carry my notes with me, and Dr. Jandicott and I have then had all the information at our fingertips."

Whetford stopped, and James could see he'd forgotten that Dr. Jandicott was fully involved in this case. It would be difficult for him to throw James under the bus if Jandicott spoke up for him, and he knew it.

"Right, well, that's not SOP." He frowned down at James. "Needs to be justified."

"I'm sure Dr. Jandicott will back me on our methods. This is a complex case and we've needed to be flexible." He leaned back in his chair.

"Has Galbraith spoken to you?" Whetford ignored what James had just said, and turned to look at him, hands on the back of the chair he refused to sit in.

"I met DS Galbraith and his bagman a few minutes ago in the courtyard when I came in," James said. "They seemed upset."

That was an understatement. Galbraith looked frightened, and he'd been looking for someone to lash out at. James had let him know that he was not a good candidate for that.

Whetford went still, looking down at his hands, and when he lifted his gaze, his eyes were hot. "What did he say?"

"Galbraith said someone had made trouble for you, sir. I'm not sure I understood him. Something about an old case? That you've handed an investigation over to them to look into?"

Whetford narrowed his eyes. "Someone submitted evidence from an old case of mine to the lab, and they managed to get some new leads. Galbraith is taking over the reopened case."

"And that's made trouble for you?" James asked, hoping he looked confused.

Whetford was silent, and James wondered whether he'd over-played his hand.

His plan had counted on Whetford never reading what was put in front of him by his secretary—something he suspected but couldn't be a hundred percent sure of.

He'd slipped a request for service to the lab for signature into the pile of letters and forms in Whetford's To Sign pile the night he'd gone in to drop off his report on the murder case.

It had been the only weak link in his plan, but as he'd already dropped the evidence off at the lab, leaving it with a number of other boxes from other detectives to be processed, the signature was merely a nice-to-have, rather than a deal breaker.

It looked as if he had got his nice-to-have.

He had put the Commissioner's name down as the person to receive the results, as well as Whetford, on the lab form, and now that he had confirmation the lab had found something, he'd find a way to let someone in the press know, as well.

Whetford wouldn't be shelving this quietly away. James wanted whoever he was covering for to hear about it.

"Was it you, damn it?" Whetford's voice was suddenly low and mean.

"Did I find old evidence in a past case of yours and submit it to the lab?" James asked, as if trying to clarify. "I'm not sure I understand."

Whetford's face twisted. "Don't play coy. I'm sure it was you."

"What exactly am I supposed to have done wrong, even if I did do this?" James asked. "Which I didn't."

Whetford opened his mouth and then closed it. "Never mind." He turned on his heel and walked to the door, throwing it open.

"Don't you want my verbal report?" James called after him.

"Send me your notes within the hour." Whetford stalked away.

James leaned back in his chair. Whetford was rattled, and Galbraith had been almost as jumpy. Not because he was on the line if whoever Whetford had protected from a murder charge decided to take action, but because if Whetford was gone, so was Galbraith's money train.

James had known Whetford would suspect him, but he'd been very careful to keep his name off any documentation. Whetford could suspect all he liked, but he had no proof.

He wondered what the retaliation for this might be, and

hoped Whetford was too busy covering his arse to be bothered with it.

He looked down at the file Hartridge had given him before Whetford had stormed his office, and flipped it open. Inside was a message from the Air Force, giving the name of the pilot who'd been issued the glove found on the scene of Mrs. Gallagher's attack. And on the next page was the confirmation of fingerprint evidence matching a man with the same first name, but a different surname. He was on file for attacking a man in a pub, and had been given a two month sentence for assault.

"So, are Harold Blythe and Harold Linaker one and the same?" he asked, tapping the page. "My guess is yes." He looked for an address, and saw that Linaker had given an address in Kent after he was released from prison. That had been ten years ago.

Maybe he was traveling in to the city to commit his murders and then going back to Kent, or maybe he had moved. Either way, they'd have to go out to Kent and see who was at the address now, and what they had to say about Linaker's current whereabouts.

There was a soft knock at his door, and he looked up to see Hartridge and Gabriella.

He caught Gabriella's gaze. "Ready to go home?" he asked.

She nodded. "My statement is done."

He gathered up the file and put it in the slim case he had begun taking around with him.

"You read the file?" Hartridge asked, watching him.

"Yes. Good work, Ian. This means we're off to Kent tomorrow."

Hartridge nodded, but James could see he was dying to ask what Whetford had said, but didn't want to discuss it in front of Gabriella.

Well, they'd have the car journey out to Kent tomorrow to talk all they liked.

"I'm going to take Miss Farnsworth home. I'll fetch you tomorrow morning from the barracks." He got his coat, and he could see Hartridge wanted to argue, to suggest they get someone else to take Gabriella home, but when he met James's gaze, he closed his mouth and gave a nod.

Gabriella walked back down the stairs with him in silence, although he noticed her casting quick glances his way. He put a finger to his lips, and she nodded, giving him a smile before her expression smoothed to neutral as someone came up the stairs toward them.

When they stepped out, he saw the fog had come in.

He could see the Wolseley, but only just. Even though it was late afternoon, the fog made it dark enough to seem like dusk.

Their killer might be hunting tonight.

The thought sat like a rancid stew in his stomach.

He'd already seated Gabriella in the Wolseley and was getting in the driver side when Hartridge came running toward them, exploding through the swirling white waving his arms.

"What is it?" He knew from Hartridge's face it wasn't good.

"Thames Division just called. They've found a woman's body in the river." Hartridge was out of breath.

James thought immediately of Tamara Davies. He noticed Hartridge had a file in his hand.

"That the Davies file?" he asked.

"Yes."

"Get in." He wasn't letting Gabriella go home on her own, but he needed to find out if this could be Tamara Davies. As Hartridge got into the back of the car, he slid into the driver's seat. "I have to go to a scene, but I don't want you going home on your own. Do you mind waiting in the car while we check something out down by the river?"

"I can take the bus," she said. "Go stay with my friend Dominique until you're done."

He liked the idea of her not having to wait for him in the car, but . . . "I know this sounds unreasonable, but you'll have to walk to the bus stop, and once you get off, walk from the bus stop in Earl's Court to Dominique's flat—and you'll have to do it in this fog."

She studied him. "The killer uses the fog. You think he'll be out tonight." She spoke thoughtfully. Exchanged a look with him. "All right."

"Thank you." He started the car, and when he glanced in the rear view mirror, he could see Hartridge studying him with interest.

Whatever his bagman thought, he didn't care. He would not be able to concentrate on anything tonight if Gabriella walked off alone into the fog.

thirty-one

THE FOG WAS THICKER on the banks of the Thames.

Gabriella knew it was to do with being in a valley, and the cold coming off the water mixing with warmer air, but that's as far as her knowledge went.

Whatever the reason, she could not see James, or anyone else for that matter.

When they'd arrived, they'd been greeted by someone with a torch, and so she'd caught a glimpse of a wall, stairs leading downward, and a man in uniform, but that was all.

She felt as if she were in a cloud-like cocoon, where no sound or light could penetrate.

According to the clock on the dashboard, forty minutes later four figures emerged beside the car, and she straightened in her seat, unaware until now that she had slumped right down.

"It's definitely her," James was saying. "We have a case file. I've brought it with me, if you need any of the details right now."

"You have a suspect, don't you?" one of the men asked, and she realized his bulk was due to the life jacket he was wearing.

"I think it was the father. I don't know if it was premeditated, but my information is that he liked to hit his wife and daughter around, and the daughter had had enough and was saving up to move out." James lifted his shoulders. "I think they might have both been drinking, and he hit her harder than he meant to. Or maybe he did mean to kill her. That can be up to the pathologist to decide. And you. But you'll have trouble because he's a big man at the docks."

The other man swore. "That's great."

James shrugged again. "We conducted interviews with the family, and with the victim's friend, and we'll give copies of those to you."

"Appreciate it, mate." Both men turned and were gobbled up by the white fog.

James and Hartridge got into the car, bringing with them the smell of river water and, faintly, of decomposition.

"What's your preference, Ian?" James turned around in his seat. "Do you need to get back to the office or can I drop you at the barracks?"

"The barracks," Hartridge said, and then leaned back and closed his eyes.

Gabriella said nothing, having a feeling both men were decompressing after seeing something terrible, and Hartridge slid out of the car when they reached the barracks where he lived with barely a murmured goodbye.

"Thank you for being so patient." James glanced at her as he pulled away. "I know it was asking a lot."

"I know why you asked." Gabriella left it at that. There could surely be nothing constructive to say about whatever James had had to deal with at the river, so she asked the question both she and Hartridge had been desperate to know the answer to. "What did your boss want? Are you all right?"

James was silent for a moment. "I did something . . . unusual."

She waited for him to elaborate.

He sighed. "While I was looking into some old cases, I stumbled across information that pointed to Whetford covering up a murder case he'd been in charge of years ago."

"Covering up?" She frowned. "So the murderer would go free?"

"That's what it looked like. And given his *modus operandi*, I guessed he had gotten a kickback for doing it." James swore as a car suddenly appeared in front of them, brake lights glowing red. He stopped, waiting for a bit, but the car didn't move and he swore again and got out.

When he came back, he was shaking his head. "The high street is backed up to Holland Rd, it looks like."

There was no one behind them, yet, and they had just passed a side street, so James reversed and turned the car up it. She couldn't see the street name, but this was her new patch, and she knew it was only a street or two over from Holland Park, but on the other side of the park to where she'd had the run-in with Tanner this morning.

What little of the houses she could see were large, with deep front gardens, just like the ones she'd run past to get away from Tanner.

To shift her thoughts, she went back to James's problem. "If Whetford was covering for a murder, he's playing a dangerous game, surely?" She wondered why Whetford would trust a murderer not to tie him off as a loose end.

"He gave himself some insurance. He hid the evidence on police property in a place where he thought only he could find it again," James said.

"But you found it?" Gabriella turned to him, but he kept his gaze firmly on the thick white fog in front of them.

"I found it," he agreed. "And I submitted the hidden evidence to the lab."

She gasped out loud. "You took his insurance away."

His lips quirked up for a quick smile. Then he shook his head. "And there will be repercussions."

"So does he know it was you? Was that why he came to see you?" She thought there would have been more shouting if that was the case.

"He suspects, but he isn't sure. And because he isn't sure, he's dancing around the actual accusations he wants to make, because they're confessions of sorts." James sighed. "He's still capable of doing damage to both me and Hartridge. But hopefully I've given him something else to concentrate on." He suddenly slammed on the brakes, but they were going so slowly, they stopped almost immediately.

The headlights illuminated a man, waving both his arms.

James pulled over to the side of the road and got out, and Gabriella did the same.

"I hit a van head on," the man said. "I'm afraid the road is blocked."

The smell of burned rubber and petrol hung in the air, and that, along with the smog, make Gabriella cough.

James had taken his torch out of the car, and played it across a large sedan, crumpled into the front of a grocer's truck.

There was no one else around.

"Where's the truck driver?" James asked.

"Gone to find a telephone," the man said. "I'm here to stop anyone driving into us."

James sighed and turned to her, speaking low. "This is going to come under the local nick's remit, but we're not getting any further tonight in the car. Are you up for a walk?"

Getting home would probably take an hour on foot, Gabriella guessed, but even that might be safer and quicker than taking the car. "That's fine."

They returned to the Wolseley to fetch their things, and by then two coppers had arrived. James spoke to them quietly to one side, and the man who'd hit the truck sidled up beside Gabriella.

"What's he saying, do you think?" he asked.

"He's with the Met. Probably professional courtesy," she said.

"Gotcha." The man seemed relieved. "Rum conditions, eh? Wish I hadn't decided to drive."

Before Gabriella had to find a response to that, James appeared beside her. "Ready?"

She nodded, walking with him into the swirling mist as the conversation behind them faded.

It was eery. Gabriella felt as if she were in some kind of inbetween world. The glow of house lights to her left allowed glimpses of a gate post or a low hedge, and occasionally glinted off the window of a car parked on the street to her right.

James was closed in, saying nothing, and what little she could see of his profile seemed tight and clenched.

"You think tonight's the night, don't you?" she asked, and was surprised at how soft her voice sounded. "You think he's going to hunt another victim."

He turned to look at her, his expression grim. "Yes."

To know someone was going to be hurt, but not who or where, was torturous.

"And he's kept to Kensington and Chelsea, and Hammersmith and Fulham?" That would narrow the where.

James gave a jerky shrug. "That we know of. Teddy Roe told me there was another body he found that looked like a murder, under the rubble in a house near here." He pulled a notebook out his pocket and shone his torch down on it. Gave a nod. "If tonight is the when, then Harborne Close might be the where."

"Would it be worth having a look?" she asked.

"More than worth it." He played his torch light to the right, as if hunting for a street name in that direction. "The address Teddy Roe gave me is the most likely lead I've got right now."

She was about to ask him if he wanted to go straight there when suddenly there was a shriek of brakes and then a scream from up ahead, and they both broke into a run, the light from James's torch bouncing up and down.

They reached the scene of the accident in less than a minute, and while Gabriella had seen a few pedestrians being hit by a car during the course of her work, there was something about the light from the headlamps spilling over a crumpled body, surrounded by swirling white, that shocked her.

"Teddy Roe?" She realized she knew who the body was, the shock deepening, and she crouched beside him and took his hand.

It trembled in her own, and she felt a wave of relief that he was still alive.

James crouched on Teddy Roe's other side, moving his jacket off his chest to check for injuries, and feeling his pulse.

Then he looked up at the car, and the headlamps illuminated his face. It glittered in the light as the tiny droplets of mist that clung to his stubble reflected the glow.

He looked like a Viking, about to go to war, or the archer he was named after, standing, bow drawn, on the battlefield.

Whatever had been keeping the person in the car, they suddenly scrambled out.

"I didn't see him," the man blurted.

That was probably true. It was very difficult to see, but Gabriella was inclined to dislike him because he'd hit Teddy Roe and then stayed in the car.

If they hadn't been here, would he have driven around the body and left?

It was difficult to make out the driver in the fog and darkness, and James rose to his feet, hand going into the inner pocket of his coat to produce his warrant card.

"DS Archer," he said. "And you are?"

Teddy Roe groaned, and Gabriella brushed his hair off his face in a soothing motion.

"Can you tell me where it hurts?" she asked him.

"Gabriella?" He half-opened his eyes, and she realized, now she was so close to him, they were almost arctic blue. "Legs," he said, then closed his eyes again and went limp.

James and the driver had gone quiet and turned to listen to her and Teddy Roe's exchange, but as soon as Teddy Roe seemed to lose consciousness again, James turned back sharply.

"Name?"

"Colonel Johnson." The driver snapped it out, irritated.

"Do you live nearby?" James asked.

"No. I was visiting a friend, and was on my way home," Johnson said, almost affronted. "Why?"

"So my friend can get help by calling the ambulance," James said. "That would be easier if you lived nearby."

"Oh." Johnson sounded chastened. "No, unfortunately not. And my friend doesn't have a telephone."

It could be true, but Gabriella was more inclined to believe he was lying because he didn't want them going to his friend's house —either out of embarrassment, or because he was uncomfortable with his friend's name going into any official report.

"I'll go to this one here," she said, pointing to a house right opposite them. "The lights are on, so someone's home."

James nodded, and she gently untangled her fingers from Teddy Roe's and ran.

chapter
thirty-two

GABRIELLA DISAPPEARED INTO THE FOG, but James could hear her running up the path and knocking on the door.

"What's a Met detective doing walking around on a night like this?" Johnson asked, in a jocular way that made James think he was trying to get chummy.

"I was taking my girl home when the road was blocked by an accident further down the road," James said. "It was either walk or wait for the road to be cleared."

"Right." Johnson rocked back on his heels. "Down toward the high street?" he asked.

"Yes. And the high street's blocked, too. Either an accident or just very slow traffic."

"God, what a mess." Johnson glanced at where Gabriella had disappeared then studied Teddy Roe, prone at his feet. "She knows this tramp, does she? Your girl?"

"She does." James wasn't going to elaborate. "He's a friend of hers."

"Looks like a rough sleeper."

Teddy Roe used to be a rough sleeper, but James studied him carefully now. His clothes were a little worn, for sure, but he was clean, and he looked like he got enough to eat. Since he'd moved into Ruby Everett's shed, his life had taken a massive turn for the better.

Still, to a person like Johnson, he probably looked destitute.

"He fought in the first War," James said. "And he was night crew in the second."

"Ah." Johnson's voice changed, and he cleared his throat. "Known a few like him. Hard to get some of the bad times out of your head."

Teddy Roe groaned and tried to turn on his side, then screamed in agony as whatever was broken made itself known again.

"Shh, shh, Teddy. Help's coming." James grabbed his hand like Gabriella had, and Teddy Roe's eyes flickered open again.

"I was following," he whispered.

"Following?" James wondered if he'd gone into a fever state.

"Holland Park," Teddy Roe's voice cracked. "Remember? I told you about Holland Park."

James went still, alarm bells ringing in his head. "The body," he said. "The body in a bombed out garden near Holland Park." Just what he'd been thinking about before they heard Teddy Roe scream.

"Yes." Teddy Roe reached up with his free hand and gripped James's shoulder. "The body in the shed. Thought I'd have a look when the fog came in, thought I'd have a wander over and check it out, and there he was . . . acting all nervous and shifty."

"Who, Teddy? Who was doing that?" James asked.

"Dunno." Teddy Roe's hands went slack, and he dropped back to the road. "Maybe not him, but maybe it was."

James looked up. Johnson was staring at them both, his face a picture of confusion.

"Is Harborne Close near here?" he asked Johnson.

Johnson pointed to the right. "There," he said, and James lifted his torch, and sure enough, there was the street sign for Harborne Close.

"Where did the man go, Teddy?" James crouched back down beside him.

But Teddy was out again, moaning softly.

"Stay with him," James said to Johnson, rising to his feet. "I just need to check something."

He didn't give Johnson a chance to reply, he jogged across the road, and then slowed, keeping his footsteps as quiet as he could as he followed the street sign.

Harborne Close was quiet, and there weren't very many lights on here.

James counted the houses, came to a stop at an old stone mansion. It had been missed by the bomb, Teddy had said. Only the back garden had been hit.

It stood utterly dark, and from what he could make out of the front garden from the street lights, it was neglected and overgrown.

Teddy Roe hadn't said where the man he'd been following had gone, and to be fair, he may have followed a completely innocent stranger who was just trying to get home, and who had not liked Teddy Roe trailing after him.

James checked his watch with his torch. It was only eight thirty. Even in the current smog conditions, surely the killer would wait until the early hours of the morning to move a body?

But if, as he suspected, their killer was going to strike again, this would not be the worst place to wait and try to catch him.

The only problem with that was his victim would most likely already be dead, and James wanted to catch him before he killed again.

Still, given he had no idea where the man was and where he would strike, at least narrowing down where he might leave the body was far better than nothing.

He would take Gabriella home, and then he would come back here and wait.

It eased the sick feeling he'd had in his stomach since he'd walked outside of New Scotland Yard and seen how thick the fog was.

The sense of impending doom wasn't gone, but even if the worst happened, and a woman was killed tonight, James was glad there was a chance he could make sure she would be the last.

chapter
thirty-three

GABRIELLA STOOD UNCOMFORTABLY in the hall.

It smelled of vinegar and lemon, and she could see her face in the polished end post of the massive staircase on her left that swept up and curved to the right overhead.

The door to the house had been opened after a long delay by a young woman a few years younger than herself, dressed in a bright orange ensemble Gabriella guessed would be called loungewear.

It was made from stretchy fabric, and if she were a betting woman, she'd say it was designed by Mary Quant. It was, no doubt, unspeakably expensive.

The woman had stepped out onto the porch when Gabriella had explained the situation, trying to see the accident for herself, and then, faced with the impenetrable fog, invited Gabriella in on a wave of Faberge Tigress perfume.

"The telephone is in my father's study. I'll have to go and ask him if you can use it." She strolled away, unhurried, and Gabriella had to clamp down on her urge to tell her again that it was an emergency. That someone was injured.

The room the woman had come out of was to the right of the front door, and she'd left the door slightly ajar.

Gabriella caught a glimpse of a man lounging back on a pale gold sofa within. He shot her a grin, and got lazily to his feet.

Something about him screamed smug self-satisfaction, as if he'd never met a consequence he wasn't able to dodge, and she stepped past the room, heading further down the hall in the direction the woman had taken.

"Who're you?"

The voice came from above, and Gabriella looked up. A young girl was peering at her through the balusters, about halfway up the stairs.

"Gabriella Farnsworth," she said. "There's been an accident on the road in the fog, and I need to call an ambulance."

"Did Victoria let you in?" the girl asked, rising to her feet and running lightly down the stairs.

"I'm not sure who let me in. She was wearing an orange jumpsuit."

The girl reached the bottom and laughed out loud at that. "I'll get Daddy. He's a doctor, and the telephone's in his office." She ran past Gabriella, and a moment later she heard two feminine voices arguing up ahead, then someone hammering on a door.

"Daddy, there's an accident on the road. They need to call an ambulance!" The girl's voice was urgent.

"Why didn't you tell me that's what you wanted, Victoria?" The shock and exasperation in the man's voice was clear. "Where's the woman who came in."

"She's waiting in the front hall," the girl said. "Where Victoria left her."

Gabriella heard the door to the parlor creak open behind her, and she glanced around in time to see the man sneaking out.

She turned fully in his direction.

He paused at the front door, lifting a finger to his lips as if they were in on a prank or joke, silently asking her to keep quiet.

She gave in to the temptation to put him on the spot.

"It's nice of you to go out and see if you can help," she called, just as all three members of the household appeared.

Gabriella turned back to look at them.

"What's Robbie still doing here?" The man with the two girls sounded shocked. He was large and bluff, wearing shirtsleeves and tweed pants. The young girl was holding his hand. Victoria hung back a little, fiddling with the collar of her jumpsuit.

"Victoria's been canoodling with him in the front parlor for *hours*," the girl said.

At that, Robbie mumbled something and slipped out the front door.

"I really need to phone for an ambulance," Gabriella said into the sudden silence his exit created. "There's a man severely injured on the road, broken legs are a definite, and I'm not sure what internal injuries he's sustained."

Her words snapped the man out of his bemusement. "Right, Poppy will show you to my office so you can call 999. I'm a doctor. I'll go out and see how I can help. Victoria, you'll come with me so that you can run in to fetch whatever I may need."

Victoria looked a little sick, and Gabriella wondered if she'd been deliberately slow-walking her trip to her father's office to give Robbie a chance to disappear.

She followed after Poppy, who ran back down the passageway and into a dark, heavily-furnished space with a massive desk. She pointed to a telephone, and Gabriella asked for the address as she dialed 999.

When that was done, she left Poppy in the study and went back through the house to the front door. She had to step to the side as Victoria came in from outside, face pinched.

They shared a glance, and Gabriella could see dislike in the young woman's eyes.

They said nothing as they passed each other.

Gabriella navigated the path carefully and followed the voices to a little group of two: the driver, Johnson, and the doctor.

"Where's James?" she asked, and as soon as she said it, he appeared out of the swirling fog.

"Just checking something," he said. He looked over at the doctor, crouched beside Teddy Roe.

"This is the man who lives in the house I went to. He's a doctor," Gabriella told him.

"Dr. Jenkins." The man looked up. "Did you see what happened?"

"No. We came across him after Colonel Johnson had already hit him," James said. "I'm DS Archer." He took out his warrant card, and Gabriella saw Dr. Jenkins' demeanor change. He had been suspicious of James, assuming he was at fault, but now he turned to look up at Johnson.

"How fast were you going when you hit him?" he asked.

"I was hardly going any speed at all. Do you see this fog?" Johnson sounded indignant. "He just jumped in front of the car, I tell you."

Gabriella listened to the back and forth and guessed that Teddy Roe probably had run out in front of Johnson, but the colonel had definitely been contemplating leaving the scene, and she didn't like him on those grounds alone.

"How long will the ambulance take?" Poppy's clear, high voice cut across Johnson's excuses, and everyone turned to her, surprised to find her watching them all.

"Poppy. In the house now. Your mother will have something to say about you being out at a scene of an accident in the dark like this." Dr. Jenkins pointed toward the house. "Go."

With a put-upon sigh, Poppy flounced away, and then Victoria appeared, carrying a blanket.

Jenkins took it from her, and from his demeanor, Gabriella guessed he was angry and disappointed in her. As soon as she handed it over, Victoria spun on her heel and disappeared back into the house.

"I'd give him something for the pain, but the ambulance crew won't thank me for that. They like to assess their patients for themselves. I'm just going to make him a little more comfortable." As Jenkins spoke, the sound of a siren came from the Holland Park Avenue end of the street, and as it got closer, the red lights on the ambulance roof danced strangely in the fog.

James strode out, waving his torch to slow them down when they got near, and Teddy Roe was soon strapped up and on his way to hospital.

"I've got your details," James said to Johnson as the ambulance left, sirens wailing. "You can go home now."

Johnson muttered something under his breath and disappeared into the fog, and she, James and Dr. Jenkins stepped onto the pavement to allow him to drive slowly past them, in the wake of the ambulance.

"Bad business," Dr. Jenkins said.

"Thanks for your help." James held out a hand to shake, and then they watched Jenkins go back toward his house. He disappeared in the fog before she even heard his garden gate squeak open and then closed.

Gabriella slipped her arm through James's and they carried on walking.

"Where did you go?" Gabriella asked, when they were far enough away from the Jenkins' house to be sure no one could hear them.

"Teddy Roe had the same idea as me. He was hanging around Harborne Close and claims he saw someone acting 'suspicious' and followed him. Whether it was the actual killer or not, we'll never know. I quickly nipped down the street to check things out." James tugged on her arm, and they started walking again.

"And everything looked fine?" she asked.

"Yes. But it's only nine now. Too early for our man to be dumping bodies. I'll walk you home and then I'll go back and keep watch."

She was silent for a good minute, thinking of reasons why he should take her with him, when someone coughed up ahead.

Her grip on James tightened, and she tried to see through the smog.

A figure coalesced from the mist, and she stopped in surprise, loosening her grip as James moved to stand in front of her.

"Robbie?" she asked, peering around James. "That's your name, isn't it?"

Robbie cleared his throat, his gaze darting from her to James.

"Thought you were on your own," he said, then tilted his head to James. "Where'd you come from?"

He wouldn't have seen James when he'd left the house, Gabriella realized, because James had been checking out Harborne Close.

"This is Victoria Jenkins' boyfriend," Gabriella explained to James.

"How did he get ahead of us?" James wondered.

"He ran off as soon as he heard Dr. Jenkins coming out of his study," Gabriella said.

"Hey, hey, thanks for that, by the way, making sure the old killjoy saw me," Robbie said. He tried to make his voice jocular, but he failed.

Gabriella felt a frisson of fear. He'd been waiting for her, thinking she was on her own. What had he been planning to do?

"Full name?" James asked suddenly, pulling his warrant card out of his inner jacket.

"What?" Robbie stumbled back a step. "You're a copper? Look, I was just going to tell her it wasn't very nice to out me like that, and . . ." He trailed off.

"And?" James asked, voice sharp.

"Never mind." Robbie turned and disappeared, and they both heard his footsteps fade as he ran away.

Gabriella stayed standing for a moment. "If you weren't here . . ."

He had looked at her in a way that made her skin crawl when she'd gotten a glimpse of him in the parlor, and that was before she'd said a word to him. She wondered if she hadn't called to him as he'd tried to sneak out—outing him, as he put it—whether he would have waited for her like he had.

Her guess was there was a strong chance he would have done

it anyway, and come up with another excuse why he should waylay her.

James took her hand, and they started walking again.

"I'm going to call Dr. Jenkins and ask for Robbie's full name," James said. "And let him know about this incident."

That would certainly make Robbie's life a little harder. Gabriella approved.

"I don't want you waiting for the killer on your own," she said as they reached Holland Park Avenue and turned left toward Notting Hill.

"I'll call Hartridge to meet me, don't worry. I'll need him if the killer does turn up." She could hear the suppressed excitement in his voice. Like he was looking forward to it.

"If he comes tonight, it means he's killed someone," she said.

"I know." His voice dropped an octave. "But I can't guess where he might attack. The best I can do is use Teddy Roe's information to watch where he might go afterward. Even though stopping him from hurting someone would be the main prize."

She got it. James had to work with what he had, with what he could feasibly do. She just wished she could shout to everyone who was out and about on this filthy night to stay in, wherever they were.

Because a killer was on the hunt.

chapter
thirty-four

JAMES KEPT an eye out for Robbie as they turned off Holland Park Avenue into Ladbroke Grove.

The surprise on his face when he'd realized Gabriella wasn't alone had chilled James. Robbie had planned to do something to Gabriella, and James had a sick feeling he had lain in wait for unsuspecting women before.

It seemed Robbie had kept going, though, because he wasn't following them that James could see.

He walked Gabriella all the way up the stairs to her flat, and stepped inside with her when she unlocked her door.

"Can I make you a coffee to take with you?" she asked. "I think I have some paper cups."

He had planned to go right away, because the temptation to stay was already tugging at him, but hot coffee on a night like tonight would be a life saver. "Thank you."

She got started, and to keep his distance he walked to the window and looked out, watching what little of the street he could see.

Even if Robbie had wanted to follow them, he'd have had a difficult job of it, James realized. The fog tonight was a true pea souper, and suddenly, he was itching to get going. Because the killer was out there, James was sure of it.

Tonight's conditions were perfect for him.

When Gabriella turned away from the stove, James left the window and walked back to her, waited while she opened a cupboard and took out some paper cups.

When she straightened, he took them from her, set them down, and drew her close.

She slid her arms around his waist with a sigh and rested her head against his coat, which he hadn't even taken off.

"Please be careful tonight."

"I will." He ran a hand down her back, smoothing her long, dark hair. He forced himself to stop when he got to her waist.

Since they'd spoken of sleeping together, he had not been able to get it out of his mind, and the box of condoms he'd found the time to go and buy had been in his coat pocket ever since.

The coffee pot rattled on the stove as it began to boil, and Gabriella turned away and set about making him strong, Italian coffee in a paper cup. She put it inside another cup so it wouldn't burn his fingers, and he took it gratefully.

"Don't open the door to anyone. Tanner's still out there." He spoke from the top of the stairs, waiting for her to close and lock her door.

"He won't be back, surely?" she asked, pausing with the door half closed.

He shook his head. "It would be crazy for him to do it, but I never discount crazy behavior."

She shot him a grin, then closed up and locked, and he walked out, careful not to spill his drink on the stairs.

As soon as he was outside, he headed for the telephone booth on the corner and phoned the barracks, sending the officer on duty to rouse Hartridge. While he waited, he sipped his coffee and looked out into the fog.

A man walked past, hat low, collar up against the weather, and something about him made James straighten and take notice.

"Hello? Sir?" Hartridge's voice drew his attention, and when he glanced back, the man was gone.

"Sorry. Someone just walked past who reminded me of Tanner." James hadn't seriously considered the private detective would come back. He'd told Gabriella he never discounted crazy, but in this case, there really was no reason for Tanner to return.

And it may well not have been him.

"What would he gain?" Hartridge asked.

"Agreed." But still, he didn't like it. He explained his plan to watch the Holland Park house, and heard the eagerness in the detective constable's voice at the thought of action.

"I'm just going to walk past Gabriella's, make sure that wasn't Tanner and he isn't hanging around, and then I'll walk back to Harborne Close. It will take you some time to get from the barracks to Holland Park, especially with the chaos the smog is causing on the roads, but try to hurry and I'll meet you there." James hung up and stepped out of the booth. He stood quietly, surrounded by dense white, listening for any suspicious sounds, and then headed back to Gabriella's.

When he got close, he slowed, walking as silently as possible.

He could just make out the old Victorian that Gabriella lived in through the fog.

Mr. Rodney's ground floor flat was in darkness, but Gabriella's flat, two floors up in the eaves, was still lit with a warm glow.

He leaned against the fence, looking up at it, until the sound of footsteps drew his attention. He heard the faint click of dog's nails, and an elderly man walking a Jack Russell appeared like an apparition. The man drew back sharply in surprise at the sight of him standing still on the pavement, then gave an embarrassed nod as he continued on, shooting James a few suspicious side glances.

The light in Gabriella's flat went out suddenly, and James was left standing in darkness.

Tanner was nowhere in sight, and he'd caught a few glimpses of Gabriella moving around before the lights went out, and she was alone.

He waited another minute, listening, sipping the last of his coffee, but eventually he turned and headed back to the main road.

To wait for a killer instead.

———

Gabriella rose up out of the hot bath, flushed and with wrinkled fingers. She seldom spent long in the tub, but tonight she had looked forward to a good soak.

The fog had chilled her to the bone, and the water made her feel warm again.

She pulled on her pajamas—red and white striped flannel pants and a red button up top that had stripes on the cuffs—a present from Dominique for her birthday in June. Dominique had been open about buying them in the end of spring sales, and this was the first time the weather had been cool enough for Gabriella to wear them.

They were almost too warm after the heat of her bath, so she didn't put her dressing gown on over the top as she cleaned the bath. She shared the bathroom with Jerome, but she'd checked that he wasn't home before she took her time.

She had thought tonight would end differently.

Before the fog had stopped the traffic and forced them out on foot, she had been half nervous, half excited to see whether James would stay over.

She wanted him to, but years of conditioning by her conservative family made it a bigger step for her than it seemed to be for others.

Liz, for example, had no qualms.

She was glad to be away from Melbourne, away from the stifling, watchful eye of aunts, uncles and family friends that never seemed to give her a moment of privacy.

She had privacy here, and she reveled in it.

When this killer was caught, she would invite James over, and make it clear what she meant by that.

She didn't know now if the flush on her cheeks was from the bath or her thoughts as she gave the tub a final rinse and gathered up her toiletries.

She stepped out into the narrow hall that separated her flat from Jerome's, reached back into the bathroom to switch off the light, and then paused, frowning, when she was enveloped in darkness. The light that illuminated the hallway had blown.

She shrugged and reached back into the bathroom again to switch the light back on, running her fingers over the wall to find it in the darkness.

Suddenly she was pressed against the doorjamb, the corner of the wooden frame digging into her collarbone.

"Be very quiet."

Tanner. She could smell his strong cologne.

She had been so careful, switching off the light in her flat before she'd gone to take her bath, making sure to lock her flat door behind her.

And he'd been waiting outside the bathroom all this time.

The agony of the sharp edge pressing into her chest warred with her fear.

"How on earth do you think this will help you?" she asked on a wheeze as at last he pulled her back against his chest.

The relief from the pain made her lightheaded.

"You will drop the charges, or I'll keep coming back. And I also need to know what you've told the coppers. Everything you've said to them, so I can prepare a defense. Do that, and I'll walk away, no harm, no foul." Tanner shoved her down the short passageway to her door in the dark. "Where's the key?"

Gabriella looked back toward the bathroom, at where she'd dropped her robe and her toiletries. "In the pocket of my bathrobe."

He swore in her ear, spun her back to the bathroom, and shoved her in front of him until they reached the fallen items.

"Get it," he told her.

She tried to bend to pick it up, but his grip tightened.

"No funny business."

She waited, and after a beat he loosened his grip, allowing her to reach down for it. As she dug in the pocket of her robe, she held onto his forearm for balance, and then crouched suddenly, spinning with her elbow out and slamming it into his crotch.

He gave a keening grunt, bending at the waist, and she shoved him to the side.

He fell through the open bathroom door, and Gabriella ran, taking the stairs two at a time. Long familiarity made her footing sure, even in the pitch dark.

As she flew down, she considered her options.

Mr. Rodney was most likely asleep, and it would take too long to rouse him for help, so she headed straight out of the front door.

The fog was still thick, and she had a good chance of losing Tanner in its white embrace.

She raced toward Holland Park Avenue, glad she'd put her slippers on before she'd left the bathroom. They were pretty sturdy and matched her pajamas, a gift from Ben and Trevor she knew full well Dominique had organized.

She and James had passed a few people on their walk back to her flat, but now, more than an hour later, the streets seemed empty. She reached the main road and listened for cars, but she could hear someone running behind her, and she chanced it and darted across to the other side.

A big lorry suddenly lumbered by, and using the noise from its passing she ran down the first street to the left she could find.

She knew the street name where James was waiting—but she didn't know exactly where it was, especially in the fog.

She would have to head in the general direction of Holland Park and figure it out.

When she reached an intersection, she went right, but before she continued on, she stood in the lee of a large oak tree on the corner and listened for Tanner.

There were no footsteps behind her any longer, and she

leaned against the tree in relief, closing her eyes and catching her breath. Her heart had been pounding, trying to fight its way out of her chest, but it slowed at last and she was able to take her first real breath since Tanner had grabbed her outside the bathroom.

Slowly she realized she was cold, and moisture was seeping into her flannel top from the tree bark, so she pushed away and carried on down the street, looking for a road sign so she could work out where she was.

When she got to the next intersection, she found a pole with a sign on it, and had to go right up to it to make out what it said, but the street name meant nothing to her. It wasn't Harborne Close, and she didn't know the area well enough to find it from here.

Still, she had to be near the park, and as soon as she reached it, she would hopefully be able to orientate herself. She walked down the road, glad to have a destination in mind.

Most of the houses along this street were in darkness, and she didn't want to knock on a stranger's door. She slowed when she heard a sound up ahead, and stopped, head tilted, trying to work out what it was.

The squeak, squeak, squeak was rhythmic, and for a moment she wondered if it was a gate, swinging back and forth.

Then, just for a second, the fog thinned, and she saw a man up ahead, pushing a wheelbarrow. An arm hung, limp, over the side of it.

She stayed frozen in place as the fog swirled back to cover him. She thought something was lodged in her throat, and her hands crept up to rest, all twined together, between her breasts.

A man had used a wheelbarrow to transport the victim she'd found at the Billick Building.

And James was waiting for a killer tonight.

She had been so pleased to be headed toward him, so happy to get away from Tanner, that she had forgotten why James was out here in the first place.

The killer was in front of her, but she knew for sure they were not in Harborne Close, where James was waiting.

Perhaps the killer would be turning down into that street soon. Either that, or Teddy Roe had given James the wrong address.

She could not let the wheelbarrow get too far ahead, but she wanted a safe distance, as well.

She looked down at her slippers and took them off, and immediately felt safer now that she could walk silently on bare feet.

Up ahead the wheelbarrow continued its squeak, squeak, and Gabriella hurried after it.

THE WHEELBARROW WHEEL FELL SILENT, and Gabriella stopped dead.

Either the killer was taking a rest, or he'd reached his destination.

She waited, unsure how far behind him she was. Her feet were icy, and she wished she could put her slippers back on. She lifted a foot, pressed it against her flannel pants, and then did the same with the other while she considered her options.

The rattle of a lock made her flinch, and then she heard the high screech of rusted hinges.

There was a sudden silence, and she imagined the killer was wincing, listening for any reaction to the noise. After a minute, the screech came again and then the squeak squeak of the wheel-barrow told her he was back on the move.

Gabriella tiptoed forward and almost walked face first into an old wooden door set in a high stone wall. It stood open—the killer had not risked closing it after the high-pitched screech it had made before—and she moved around it and looked into an over-grown garden.

She hesitated, torn.

She still didn't know where Harborne Close was. It had to be near, but the fog had her turned around, and James could be anywhere.

Should she wander around and look for him, or follow after the killer and at least see what he was up to, first?

The wheelbarrow had gone silent again, and in the sudden quiet, Gabriella heard a low moan.

Her heart felt like it was about to leap out of her chest.

Was the victim still alive?

Unable to do anything else, she stepped through the gate.

The grass was long, and what little of the paved pathway she could make out in the fog had weeds growing through the cracks. She could see where the wheelbarrow wheel had crushed them.

Her feet were almost numb with cold, now, and she took a moment to put her slippers back on.

A light shone from the house, from a ground floor room, and as the fog swirled away, she caught a glimpse of a decrepit mansion. She also saw the killer, just for a moment, his back turned to her, as he moved toward what looked like a tarp-covered frame.

The wheelbarrow stopped again, and then she heard another moan.

A man's voice swore softly, and adrenalin tingled in her arms.

The victim was definitely alive.

She began to edge to the right, away from the killer, because in the brief glimpse she'd gotten, she realized they'd entered the property through the rear garden.

If James had the correct house, he could be waiting, on watch, in the front. Just yards away.

She needed to get around the side of the house, go through the front garden, and find him.

Right now.

The killer coughed, and as she moved away, she kept looking in his direction. He had left the wheelbarrow and was moving to the tarp-covered shed.

As she reached the corner of the house, she caught a glimpse of him coming back, carrying a shovel.

She couldn't stand the thought of running for James while he either buried his victim alive or hit her with the shovel to make sure she was dead.

She couldn't do it.

"Stop!" She shouted it as loudly as she could. "Put down the shovel."

The killer's head came up. She could barely make out his face but he was wearing what looked like a tweed coat under an open trench coat.

What did she do now? She hovered at the corner of the house, then turned her head toward the front. "James," she called out. "Come right now."

When she turned back, the killer had taken a step toward her.

That was good, she assured herself. She was distracting him from his plans. She took a step back herself, then glanced down the side of the house again, hoping James was coming.

Hoping that he'd heard her.

The back door of the mansion suddenly opened, and a man stood in the doorway, shining a torch out into the garden.

He was in a red brocade dressing gown, a shock of white hair standing up around his head. "What's going on?" His voice was annoyed and a little creaky with age. "Who're you?" The light from his torch landed on the killer, and for a moment, before the fog shifted and hid him, she saw the killer's face clearly for the first time.

She didn't know him.

He was thin almost to the point of being gaunt, his nose a sharp blade in his unremarkable face. He turned toward the old man, shovel shifting in his hands in a way that spoke of violence.

"Get back in the house," Gabriella shouted to the old man. "Phone the police."

She spun and ran through weeds and long grass growing down the side of the house, into the front garden. "James!"

She heard the sound of running behind her, and glanced back. It was a mistake.

She tripped over something and cried out as pain shot up her leg. She went down, banging her knee as she did on whatever it was she'd run into.

She sprawled face down, and then rolled over onto her back, feeling lightheaded with the white hot agony in her shin and foot.

The killer slowed, swinging the shovel up onto his shoulder as he stalked forward.

"What have we here?" His voice was what she thought of as BBC lite. Someone trying hard to sound like they grew up on an estate with a butler, and just not quite meeting the mark.

"That's what I want to know."

Gabriella twisted around as James stepped out of the fog.

She took the opportunity, while the killer was distracted, to push herself up, get her feet under her, and stand.

As she straightened, the front door opened, and the same old man in the dressing gown stepped out, this time with an ancient shotgun in his hands. In fact, it looked more like a blunderbuss.

"Now see here, I've called the police, and I want you off my property."

"That's very good, sir," James called back. "Did they say how quickly they can be here?"

The old man seemed to blink in surprise. "Why? Do you need to know how quickly you need to get out of here?"

"No, sir. I'm Detective Sergeant Archer with the Metropolitan Police, and I would be grateful for some assistance from fellow officers."

"Oh." The old man disappeared inside, and with a sinking heart, Gabriella guessed he hadn't actually called the police.

At least it seemed he was going to do so now.

She wondered where Hartridge was. It was possible he was still on his way, given the mayhem the fog was causing to traffic.

The killer turned to look at the still-open door thoughtfully, and began to back away.

"Harold Blythe, I presume?" James asked. "Or do you go by Linaker now?"

The shock on the killer's face as he stumbled to a stop told Gabriella James had struck a direct hit.

"Why are you here, Gabriella?" James didn't look at her, his focus was on Blythe, but she could hear the frustration in his voice.

"Tanner attacked me when I came out of the bathroom," she said. "I thought I'd run to you, but then on the way, I heard the wheelbarrow, and followed him into the back garden." She pointed down the side of the house. "The woman is still alive. I heard her groaning."

Blythe took another few steps backward, spun, and ran toward the house. When he reached the door, he slammed it shut behind him.

James ran after him, fetching up against the door and yanking the handle. "Locked. The old man must have left the key in the door." He banged his fist against it.

"Let's go around the back." Gabriella took a step and then stopped, taking in a deep breath to manage the pain.

"What is it?" James ran over and reached out to steady her.

"Banged my leg," she said, and forced herself to start limping forward. She noticed a fallen garden statue on the ground, and realized she'd been tripped up by some sculptor's rendition of either Eros or Cupid, complete with bow and arrow. She resisted the strong urge to kick it as she passed. "We need to hurry."

"When I heard you shouting for me . . ." James shook his head as he helped her move a little faster.

"Sorry, but when I heard the wheelbarrow, I thought I had to follow it to find out where he was going, and when I heard the woman moan, I had to call out to you to distract Blythe, because he was coming toward her with a shovel."

"He's got a hammer somewhere on him, too," James said, voice grim as they rounded the corner. "And now he's in the house with the old man."

The fog seemed to be thicker in the back, and there were no useful streetlights to diffuse the darkness. The downstairs light was still on, though, and that helped a little.

"The backdoor might be open," Gabriella said quietly. "That's where the old man first came out."

James left her and ran toward it. As he put his hand on the handle it swung open, and Blythe exploded out, shovel half raised.

James jerked back, and Blythe misjudged his swing, missing James and staggering forward.

He didn't see the two short steps down into the garden, and he tripped. As he fell, the shovel flew from his hand, and he rolled twice before he got up on his hands and knees.

James ran to stand over him, leaning down to grab one of his wrists, handcuffs in one hand. Blythe threw himself backward, trying to hit James in the face with the back of his head, and suddenly the two men were rolling around, grappling with each other.

Gabriella grabbed up the shovel, watching carefully for any sign of the hammer James had spoken about, but if he had it on him, Blythe was too busy wrestling with James to get it out.

She held the shovel handle two handed, looking for a chance to hit Blythe with it.

Blythe was shorter than James, but he was clearly strong, and fighting for his life.

From behind her, she heard the woman moaning again. She needed help as quickly as possible, and so did the old man, because Blythe had most likely attacked him, too.

She turned the shovel around, and brought the end of the handle down hard on Blythe's leg, scared the shovel head might hurt James by mistake. She began to circle the two men, jabbing Blythe whenever she could.

James finally got him face down, one wrist in his hand, but Blythe twisted up, elbow slamming into James's stomach.

James briefly lost his hold, rearing up and away, and Gabriella spun the shovel the other way round and brought the blade down hard on Blythe's head.

He fell forward, and James grabbed his wrist again, snapped on the handcuffs, and wrenched his other arm back.

When he was finally secured, James leaned back on his heels, breathing hard.

"Thanks," he managed.

Gabriella dropped the shovel and ran toward the wheelbarrow, and as she reached it, she heard the first wail of sirens in the background.

chapter
thirty-six

JAMES WATCHED Blythe being loaded into a police car.

The lights of the ambulance treating the woman in the wheelbarrow were muted by the fog, and he realized this was his second ambulance of the evening.

He hoped Teddy Roe was all right. The old man deserved some kind of commendation for his help.

"Do they think she's going to survive?" Hartridge appeared beside him as the ambulance doors closed. The sirens started up as they sped away.

"Touch and go," James said. That she was alive at all was amazing.

"And Mr Somerville?" Hartridge glanced back at the mansion.

"He wouldn't go in an ambulance. One of the uniforms called his local GP to come round to see to him, and—" He stopped as a man in a coat and hat, carrying a doctor's black leather bag, came down the street. "Dr. Jenkins." He gave the doctor a wave.

"Archer, is it?" Jenkins came to a brief stop, glancing at the chaos around him, and then continued forward.

"Yes, I was just telling my constable that Mr Somerville's GP had been called, and then saw you coming down the street. We offered him an ambulance, but he absolutely refused to go to the hospital."

"Damn fool." Jenkins glanced at the door and shook his head. "He was attacked, the policeman on the phone said."

"There was an assault on him in his home, yes." James began walking toward the door, and Jenkins and Hartridge fell into step with him. "He was shoved over, fell and hit his head."

James didn't say it, but Somerville was lucky Blythe had been in a hurry and hadn't had the time to use the shovel he'd been carrying, or the hammer they'd found in his large trench coat pocket.

They entered the house, and James nodded in approval at the PC holding a warm, damp towel to Somerville's head.

"Evening, Ned, I see you've got a spot of trouble." Dr. Jenkins moved toward Somerville with confidence, and the PC stepped back. James tilted his head toward the door, giving him permission to escape.

"Now that your doctor is here, I need to go interview my suspect," James said. "Detective Constable Hartridge will be round tomorrow for a statement, if that's possible?" James looked at Jenkins, rather than Somerville.

"We'll see. If you could call me first, Detective Constable?" Jenkins fished a card out of his pocket and handed it over to Hartridge. "I'll let you know."

Hartridge took the card with a nod.

"Where's that girl?" Somerville suddenly asked. "The one who told me to run inside and call the police?"

"Gabriella?" Jenkins asked, his head coming up in surprise. "She was caught up in this, too?"

"Yes." James left it at that. "She went in the ambulance with the victim."

"What victim?" Jenkins sat back, frowning.

"The chap that came in and had a go at me, he had bludgeoned some poor woman half to death. Was planning on burying her in my old shed." Somerville huffed out a breath. "Bloody nerve."

Hartridge cleared his throat suspiciously.

"Well, sounds like there was a lot going on here tonight." Jenkins wisely didn't ask any more questions, and James and Hartridge left him to his patient.

"How did the doc know Gabriella?" Hartridge asked as they walked out.

"She knocked on his door by chance, asking for help when Teddy Roe was hit by a car. He lives around the corner." James ran a hand through his hair. He made a mental note to call the doctor tomorrow and warn him about Robbie, but now was not the time.

It had been a very long night, but he couldn't be happier with the outcome.

He clapped Hartridge on the shoulder. "You stay here with forensics. I'll get a lift back to the Yard and make sure Blythe is tucked up in a cell for the rest of the night." James wanted to make sure all the formalities were observed. "Then tomorrow, I want you to take someone with you and head out to the address we have for Blythe in Kent. He's going by Linaker there, so find out as much as you can, and call me with any updates that might be useful before I question him."

Hartridge nodded, looking pleased about running down a lead on his own.

As James flagged down an officer and organized a lift, he felt a grim sense of anticipation for the interrogation tomorrow.

Whatever they could prove or disprove about Blythe's past killings, they had him bang to rights over this attempt at murder. No matter what, he wasn't going to be walking free any time soon.

"There's a rip in your pants."

Gabriella lifted her head with a start and blinked bleary eyes at the matron in front of her.

She looked down, studied the rip, and then lifted the hem of her right pant leg up. Her shin was covered in blood, long since dried.

"Ran into a statue," she said.

"Come on, then. Let's fix you up." The matron began walking away, and Gabriella rose stiffly to her feet from the uncomfortable chair in the corridor and hobbled after her.

"You're waiting for word on the woman who was attacked?" the matron asked as she showed her into an examination room.

"Yes. I was running away from her attacker when I tripped over the statue." Gabriella sank down with relief into another chair, and the matron got busy cleaning the wound.

Gabriella winced.

"I'd also like to hear how another friend is doing," she said, when the job was done and she had a neat bandage around the scrape. It wasn't deep, but there was a massive bruise. "I'm not sure if he was admitted to this hospital, but it's likely."

"What happened to him?" Matron asked.

"He was hit by a car crossing the road in the fog," Gabriella said. "I think his legs were broken. His name is Mr. Theodore Roe."

"Ah." Matron gave a nod as she went to wash her hands. "Yes, he's here. Sleeping now, I expect. Got plaster on both legs and he'll be in a wheelchair for a good month, but he'll live."

"Thank you." She would call Ruby Everett in the morning and let her know what had happened to her tenant.

"Do you have a name for the woman who was attacked?" Gabriella asked.

James had been excited to see her handbag was with her, under her in the wheelbarrow, and she remembered there had been no bag near either of the two victims she had seen.

He must take them after he had hidden their bodies, she thought. But he hadn't been able to, this time.

"Her name's Katie Brompton." Matron wiped her hands on the towel at the sink, and then turned back to Gabriella. "The police will need to find her next of kin."

Gabriella nodded. "Can I visit her when her surgery is over?"

"Of course, love." Matron escorted her out. "But now I have to insist that you get home to bed. You're already dressed for it, after all."

Gabriella had totally forgotten until that moment that she was wearing her pajamas. She looked down at the dirt-smeared red and white stripes, then looked back up at the twinkling eyes of the senior nurse.

She trudged out of the main hospital entrance, into the night. The fog had lifted a little, but it didn't matter. She didn't have a way to get home.

She had not thought about that at all.

"Gabriella?" The voice behind her was astonished.

She turned, and saw Ruby Everett.

"The hospital called you?" she asked, although, they must have. There was no other explanation.

"Yes. How did you know about it?" Ruby stopped beside her, and then seemed to realize she was wearing pajamas. Her eyebrows went up.

"James and I were walking home when we found Teddy Roe on the road. I called an ambulance, but they wouldn't let me go with him."

"So how come you're here?" Ruby asked. "Are you injured?" Her gaze was on the rips in Gabriella's pants.

"It's a long story." She almost didn't have the energy to explain it all, but she managed to outline the main points.

"So this Tanner could still be waiting for you?" Ruby asked.

Gabriella stared at her. That had not even crossed her mind.

"Come." Ruby waved a hand, and a taxi pulled up beside

them. "I'm going inside with you to check he isn't still there," she said.

She peppered Gabriella with questions on the short journey home, and when they pulled up, the taxi driver, who'd introduced himself as Jimmy, and who'd been listening to their conversation with avid attention, switched off the engine. "I'm coming along, ladies. Can't have too much muscle."

They got out, and Gabriella stopped. Pointed.

"That's Tanner's car."

The black Mercedes was parked a little way down the road.

"All right. Time to get serious." Jimmy leaned back into his cab and pulled out a tire iron. "Always have one handy. Just in case." He sent Ruby a wink, and she smiled back.

"I like a man who comes prepared," she told him.

They climbed the stairs quietly, Gabriella in the middle, with Jimmy in front and Ruby bringing up the rear.

When they reached the landing, she saw her dressing gown was hanging from her door knob, and her toiletries had been put back in their bag and were on the ground in front of her door.

She put her hand in the dressing gown pocket, and found her key. Then she glanced at Jimmy, waited for a nod, and then tried the door.

It was locked.

She sagged with relief. "He can't be in there. It can't be locked from the inside without a key."

She opened it up and pushed the door open, but the interior of her flat was exactly as she'd left it. "He must have not come back after he lost me in the fog," she said, feeling a little light-headed with relief. "Jerome must have put my things by my door."

"And he didn't come back for his car, either?" Ruby wondered.

"Maybe he was afraid to. He would assume I'd run straight to the police." Gabriella leaned back against the wall.

"Well, you look dead on your feet, so I'll get Jimmy to drive me home. Come for dinner tomorrow night, and catch me up on everything." Ruby handed her her toiletries, and then she and Jimmy withdrew.

Gabriella closed the door, locked it, and walked to her bed.

She'd never felt so happy to be home in her life.

chapter
thirty-seven

JAMES COULD HEAR the phone in Hartridge's office ringing.

He hurried out of his office, hoping it was Hartridge calling with information from Kent, and lifted the receiver. "Hello?"

"DC Hartridge?"

"No, he's not in. This is DS Archer." James recognized the voice as the sergeant from downstairs.

"Right. DS Archer, there's a man tied up and gagged in a car in Notting Hill, found by a bobby this morning on his rounds. The car registration has a flag on it, attached to a case you're involved in."

"What type of car?" James suddenly realized he'd forgotten all about Tanner. "Where in Notting Hill?"

He could hear the sergeant turning pages. "Black Mercedes." He gave the registration number and the street it was found in.

Gabriella's street.

"Have they released the man who was tied up?" James asked. "He might be the person of interest we've been looking for for the last few days."

"No, the bobby didn't know what to do, so he called it in." The sergeant flipped a few more pages. "Do you want to go fetch him?"

James looked at his watch. The lawyer Harold Blythe had insisted on could only make it in this afternoon.

He had time.

"I'll come. Tell them to wait for me." He went back to his office to fetch his coat, and found Whetford hovering just inside his door.

"Sir." He reached for his coat, and began shrugging into it. "If you need to discuss something with me, do you mind if we walk and talk? I have to pick up a suspect, but I also need to go over information before I question Harold Blythe this afternoon, so I'm unfortunately pressed for time."

"Certainly." Whetford didn't sound happy about it, but he stepped out of James's office. "Well done on the arrest last night. Will it hold water?"

"For the abduction and assault on Katie Brompton, it definitely will. The same goes for the assault on Mr. Somerville and on me." James shrugged. "The rest is something we'll have to work on. DC Hartridge is in Kent this morning, looking over Blythe's house. Maybe we'll find something there that links Blythe to the murders we believe he committed." He kept quiet about the glove that linked Blythe to the attack on Mrs. Gallagher. No point letting Whetford know that he'd been down in the archives, looking through old evidence boxes.

James wondered briefly how the reopened murder case was going for Whetford. Whether he was in any danger.

He gave Whetford a more thorough look, and under his scrutiny, Whetford shifted a little, as if nervous.

"Very well. That's good work." They had reached the stairwell, and Whetford started up the stairs to his office. "Keep me informed."

"Yes, sir." James ran quickly down the stairs and thought maybe Whetford did look a little gray. He found he had no twinge of conscience about it at all.

When he reached Notting Hill, he felt something go cold inside him at how close Tanner's car was to Gabriella's house.

There was a small crowd gathered on the pavement, trying to get a look at what was happening. The bobby had been joined by a colleague, and they were starting to look a bit desperate.

When the Wolseley pulled up, James could see them breathe a sigh of relief.

"DS Archer? PC Naigle." Naigle gave him a nod. "This the man you're looking for?" He stepped back, allowing James a look inside the car, and there was Tanner, furious eyes snapping above a black fabric gag which was tied around his mouth and nose.

"That's him." As he took out his handcuffs, he glanced at the crowd.

Jerome was among the group, and when he caught James looking at him, he gave a sly wink and then backed away.

Mystery solved.

James fought a quiet battle not to smile as he helped the PCs untie the rope around Tanner's wrists and ankles, and cut off the gag.

"Let me at least stretch out before you put those on me," Tanner said, giving the handcuffs a dark look as he shook out his limbs. "I was the victim of an assault."

"Do you know the identity of your attacker?" James asked, ignoring him and getting on the handcuffs.

"Attackers. Plural. And no, they wore masks. But they were Jamaicans or something. Black fellows." Tanner's gaze scanned the crowd, which was a representative mix of the British Empire.

James looked up at Gabriella's flat, but her curtains were closed and he wondered if she even knew what was going on down here.

He wanted to run up and knock on her door so badly, but the clock was ticking and he hoped Hartridge had some news for him. He didn't want to be away from the phone too long.

"Let's go." He put Tanner in the back of the Wolseley, and headed back to Scotland Yard, grateful that the fog had blown away with the wind this morning.

"So you went back to Miss Farnsworth's house in your car

after you chased her in the fog?" he asked. He would have seen the Mercedes if it had been there last night, he was sure of it, and if the man he'd seen last night really had been Tanner, he'd been on foot.

"You know about that?" Tanner asked, surprised. "About running after her in the fog?"

"I spoke to her about it shortly after she managed to evade you." James still recalled the shot of fear that had crackled through him when he'd first heard Gabriella call his name. He never wanted to feel that way again, and Tanner was responsible for it.

He lifted his gaze to the rear view mirror and sent Tanner a quick look.

"See, I just wanted her to drop the charges. She wasn't harmed, right? I also wanted to know what she'd told you. That's all. I wasn't planning on doing anything to her." Tanner moved his shoulders, as if he couldn't get comfortable.

"Tanner, are you sane?" James couldn't believe a man in his position was seriously arguing that holding a person against their will and forcing them to talk was a harmless endeavor.

Tanner blinked. Shuffled around on his seat. "I went too far, all right. I saw my whole career in shreds, and when I realized she was in the bathroom, I thought it would be an easy matter to get her to talk. After the adrenalin wore off, I went back to apologize for scaring her. When she wasn't there, I guessed she'd have gone to you again. I lost my grip there for a bit, I don't mind admitting it." He heaved a sigh. "And then when I was walking back to my car, these blokes jumped me and left me tied up. I'm not sure why."

"Your client must be paying you big money to have you trashing your reputation like this," James said. "Mrs. Fitzgerald, is that right?"

Tanner's gaze lifted. "You got a warrant to search my office?"

"We did." James sent him a cold smile. "And we will be talking with Mrs. Fitzgerald, you can be sure of it."

"She's paid me a lot, but not enough to lose my license." Tanner shook his head. "She insinuated that she'd recommend me to her posh friends, and I thought this could really be an in for me with the moneyed set, you see?"

"But why the aggressive hounding of Miss Farnsworth?" James had never understood that.

"Mrs. Fitzgerald is desperate to know who her husband was visiting that day. A desperate client who looked like she would be very grateful if I found out what she wanted to know." Tanner shrugged. "I need the money, and I don't mind admitting I could see a nice rosy future if I got it right."

"And you thought Miss Farnsworth was the answer." James tightened his grip on the steering wheel.

"When Mrs. Fitzgerald saw the fine, and that her husband tried to hide it from her numerous times, she became convinced he was having an affair with her cousin, who lives on that street." Tanner grimaced. "He, of course, refuses to admit it. He insists he wasn't in any house at all, that he'd parked there to go shopping because he couldn't find a place to park on the high street."

"And do you think he's having an affair with Mrs. Fitzgerald's cousin?" James asked.

"Given the fear I've seen in his eyes at the thought of being found out, yes." Tanner shifted on his seat again. "And I should probably clarify that Mrs. Fitzgerald's cousin in this instance is a man."

"Ah." That did make things clearer. Both the fear on Fitzgerald's part, and the relentless chasing after the issue by his wife.

"You have to see that I didn't set out to hurt or frighten Miss Farnsworth." Tanner leaned forward as James drove through the massive steel gates of New Scotland Yard. "I've learned my lesson."

James parked in front of a side door, and an officer emerged.

He opened the passenger door, and watched Tanner struggle out.

"Holding?" the officer asked.

"Yes, please take him to holding." James stepped back. "Am I going to have other people coming forward after what's happened in this case hits the news, Tanner? Others who you've held against their will, grabbed, or chased through the streets of London to get them to withdraw charges or give you information?"

Tanner's look, startled and fearful, told James there probably would be, and he was silent as he was led into the building.

James parked the Wolseley and then went in by the front entrance. "Any messages?" he asked at the desk.

He was handed a note phoned in by Hartridge, asking him to call a Kent number, and he ran up to his office to make the call.

Hartridge answered on the second ring. "This is definitely Blythe's residence," he told James. "We found four handbags in a cupboard, all in a neat row, and behind them, we found another five."

James sat down slowly. "So Katie Brompton was his fifth. Was he matching his old body count, murder for murder, I wonder?"

"We couldn't find records of anyone killed during the Blitz at the place where the first body was found over a month ago," Hartridge said. "But now we have the handbags, we should be able to work out who he might have murdered and left there."

"Good work, Ian. I want all evidence collected by the book, everything labeled and put in separate bags. And keep looking for anything else that would tie him to the crimes."

"We've got him either way, don't we?" Hartridge asked.

"We've got him," James agreed. He leaned back and looked up at the ceiling, then closed his eyes.

This was why he was a copper, despite the poison that Whetford brought to the Met. He and Hartridge had made a difference, and Whetford could try to push them out or corrupt them, but he would not succeed.

thirty-eight

"JAMES, Jerome has a message for you from me."

James stared at the neatly-written note stuck to Gabriella's door, and turned to knock on the door opposite. There was no sound from within, and so he walked down the stairs and out into the chill autumn evening, wondering what his next step should be.

He heard talking coming from the small private garden to the right, and felt a surge of relief as he followed the sound and stepped into the well-kept space.

"James!" Jerome leaned back in the cast iron garden chair and gave him a wave.

"Good evening, Jerome. Mr. Rodney." James always had the sense he was addressing Gabriella's grandfather when he interacted with Mr. Rodney.

"Mr. Archer." Mr. Rodney scraped back his chair and stood. "Would you like some tea?"

"No, thank you. I'm looking for Gabriella. Apparently Jerome has a message for me from her?"

Jerome nodded. "She waited for you for a bit, but she was invited over to Mrs. Everett's house for dinner and says if you are able to, you're welcome to join them."

"Thank you." He hesitated, wanting to ask Jerome about

Tanner, but as if he had read his mind, Jerome shot a quick glance at Mr. Rodney and gave a minute shake of his head.

"Well, I'll be off to Mrs. Everett's. Thanks for the message." He'd have a chat with Jerome later and get the full story. He was looking forward to it.

He drove the five minutes to Ruby's house, and as he parked beside the front gate, he saw the house was lit up, but the curtains were drawn.

As he reached the front door, he could hear Teddy Roe's gravelly voice from within.

He rang the bell, and Ruby came to answer it, wiping her hands on an apron.

"James." She gave him a warm smile. "We hoped you'd get away in time to join us. Come in."

He stepped inside, suddenly aware that he had never been invited to dinner at anyone's house in London until he'd met Gabriella. Nor had he been invited to tea, as he had just been at Mr. Rodney's.

"I should have stopped to buy something," he said, belatedly realizing he was empty-handed. "Can I go out and get you anything?"

"No." Ruby led him into the kitchen, and turned to look at him over her shoulder. "I know you've come straight from New Scotland Yard, and that you didn't know about this dinner until you got to Gabriella's. Your company is enough."

"Thank you." James decided next time, he would be sure to buy flowers and whatever drink Ruby favored.

He stepped into the kitchen after her, and there was Gabriella, crouched beside Teddy Roe in a wheelchair, drawing on his plaster cast.

"It's your copper," Teddy Roe said, elbowing Gabriella gently, and she rose to her feet with a smile.

"I'm glad you got off in time," she told him. She took a step in his direction and then paused awkwardly.

He moved to her, leaned down and kissed her forehead. "Me, too. It was a busy day."

"But you got him?" Gabriella asked.

"I got him, and I got Tanner." Ruby handed him a drink, and he took a sip, froze, and darted her a look.

"Gin and tonic," she said.

He had never had one. He took another sip and realized he liked it.

"Well, dinner's ready, so let's sit down and you can tell us everything you're allowed to tell us." Ruby pulled a pie dish from the oven with big oven mitts, and set it on the kitchen table.

Once they were all dished up, Ruby leaned forward. "How did you get Tanner, what with everything going on? That's what I'm dying to know."

"His car was found parked near Gabriella's house this morning, with him tied up and gagged inside." James savored the tenderness of the meat from the beef and mushroom pie.

"No?" Teddy Roe crowed. "Someone trussed him up and left him for you to find?"

"They did." James tried to keep a straight face. "A bobby found him this morning on his rounds."

"Really?" Gabriella frowned. "Who would . . .?"

He saw the moment she figured it out.

She threw back her head and laughed. Then sobered up. "He didn't see who it was, did he?"

"No." James had also been a bit worried about that. "They wore masks."

"Well." Ruby looked from one to the other. "You know who, by the looks of things?"

"Maybe." Gabriella smiled. "I'll thank them later."

"He wasn't there when you got home from the hospital?" James had only thought about the fact that Tanner could have been waiting for her when she got home from the hospital after he had the call about Tanner being found tied up.

"His car was parked near the house, but we didn't think he

was in it. Ruby was at the hospital to sort out Teddy Roe's paperwork, so we took a taxi back to my flat together, and even the taxi driver helped check to make sure he wasn't lurking inside the house," Gabriella said.

He should have considered the possibility, but he didn't say anything. His apology needed to be a private one.

"What about Blythe? Can you tell us anything there?" Gabriella asked.

"He went to the garden shed, Gabriella tells me," Teddy Roe said. "I was right, weren't I?"

"I'm recommending you for a commendation, Mr. Roe." James had submitted the paperwork that afternoon. "Without your information, another woman would be dead, and the killer would not have been caught."

"Well." For once, Teddy Roe was speechless.

"I think that's a wonderful thing to do." Ruby was a little teary-eyed.

Gabriella glanced at him, and he saw a sheen in her eyes, too.

"It's very justified, Mr. Roe." Gabriella reached out and patted the old man's hand. "Your information was a life-saver."

"Makes up for what happened in the war, a bit." Teddy Roe brushed his cheek, and James realized that Teddy was crying, too. "They didn't listen to me, and I was too messed up in the head to be believed. But you believed me, all of you. But especially you." He looked over at James. "You're the law, and you took me serious, you did."

Ruby cleared her throat, and they all started eating again.

"We found evidence at Blythe's house that links him to the Blitz murders, and to the more recent deaths." James worded his comment carefully. "I can't say more than that, and I'll ask you to keep what I've said confidential, but we have a strong case for prosecution."

"What did he have to say for himself?" Gabriella asked.

James shook his head. "Not much. His lawyer tried to keep

him quiet, but he said a few things under caution that show a . . . disturbed mind, and a hatred for women."

"He didn't tell you why he did it?" Ruby asked.

"He said the darkness gave him permission. There were no eyes on him, and he could be himself." James wasn't sure whether to believe that, but he was afraid that might be the clearest reason they would get.

James couldn't see the man he'd spoken to for hours that afternoon ever explaining the dark fantasies that drove him. He was too much of a coward.

"What about Katie Brompton, his victim?" Ruby asked. "We tried to find out how she's doing but they wouldn't tell us."

"She came through surgery in a stable condition, but she's still in a coma. They need to wait for the swelling to go down before they can see whether she still has brain function." And James thought it would be a miracle if she did. Her skull had been indented by Blythe's hammer strike.

"What news do you have about your father?" Ruby turned to Gabriella, skillfully changing the topic.

"Ben's boss has sent him a letter. He reckons my father will pass it on to *his* lawyer, and we might hear from them as early as next week." Gabriella twined her fingers together, and he could see the thought of a response made her very nervous.

They finished dinner, ate a light and airy mousse for dessert, and then James offered Gabriella a lift home.

As they waved goodbye and drove away, James realized he wanted this to be a permanent thing.

Him and Gabriella. On their way home. Together.

thirty-nine

GABRIELLA FELT James hands on her shoulders as they walked into her flat, and then glanced back at him as he helped her out of her coat and hung it on the rack.

"You're quiet."

He'd said hardly anything on the short drive from Ruby's, and she was pleased that he took off his own coat and hung it beside hers.

He was at least planning to stay for a bit.

"I'm sorry I forgot about Tanner after everything that happened at Somerville's mansion. I should have realized he might be waiting for you to come home." His hands flexed.

"You can't remember everything. Be responsible for everything," she said. "It was up to me to think of it, and it didn't cross my mind until it was time to leave the hospital."

He glanced down at her leg, but she was wearing trousers and the bandage was hidden. "I noticed you limping."

"I have a new dislike of Cupid," she said. "But my shin is only bruised, and I'll be fine soon enough."

"And what about Tanner? He frightened you." James's mouth was a hard line.

"Yes." When he'd pressed her up against the doorjamb, she had never been more frightened, except when Blythe had started running after her. "Then Blythe showed up to snatch the prize in that contest, so I don't feel so upset about Tanner anymore. Not that he doesn't deserve the full charges."

James studied her. "You're making light of it."

"It's the only way to get through it." She shrugged. "I'm safe, and they're both facing charges. Will I be nervous coming out of my bathroom again? Yes. Will I flinch when I see a black Mercedes or a green Jaguar? Yes, again. And I don't think I'll ever walk on my own in a thick fog, let alone look at a wheelbarrow the same way."

"I don't like that any of this happened to you." He didn't get any closer to her, as if his presence alone was the cause of her troubles.

"I don't, either. But that's not on you. Tanner and both the Fitzgeralds would have come after me, whether I knew you or not, and having you in my life helped me significantly where that was concerned. How quickly would the Met have been on the case if I'd gone to them as a private citizen, and you hadn't been involved? If you hadn't been on the receiving end of his nonsense? My guess is they wouldn't have done anything about it. That's why he's so surprised to be suffering consequences now. Because he's surely done this before and gotten away with it. The way he spoke to me, the logic he used, tells me he's used to operating this way. His victims have no doubt complained and my guess is the Met just looked the other way." She was breathing hard by the end of her little speech. She hadn't realized until now how angry that made her. Tanner had been allowed to behave like he had for long enough he thought he was untouchable. James had put an end to that.

"You look angry," James said with interest.

"Yes." She almost said *sì*. Like her grandmother would.

"Very Italian." He gave a slow smile.

She took a step forward and grabbed hold of his shirt. "And here you are, all English stiff upper lip. I thought you were a Welshman?"

He tucked her hair behind her ears, eyes laughing. "You want me to sing?"

"Oh, yes," she whispered, and went up on tiptoe, lips hovering just short of his own. "I want you to sing."

———

The sky was clear but it was almost winter-cold at the building site.

The press shivered in a huddle, looking like they wished they were anywhere else.

Dr. Jandicott came out of the tent they'd set up to shield the body from view, and gave James and Detective Superintendent Halberd a nod, carrying the last of Iris Johnson's bones, all wrapped up, to the big black car he'd arrived in.

His appearance had energized the journalists, and they all moved a little closer.

"It seems as if the final remains of Iris Johnson have been recovered." Detective Superintendent Halberd addressed them, his voice cutting across the whistle of the wind. "Thanks to the fine work of DS Archer and his team, we can now assign these terrible deeds to London's history. Harold Blythe is under lock and key, and he will hang for his crimes if he's found guilty."

Halberd's tone made it clear there was no doubt about that.

The press exploded into a rowdy crow-fight, shouting questions over each other.

Neither James nor Halberd responded, and eventually they settled down and took turns.

When they left, some running for their cars to beat their competitors to the front page scoop, Halberd rocked back on his heels.

"This is what I like, Archer," he said. "You kept this low key enough those hyenas never had so much as a sniff of the story while you were investigating, and then we could come out with a fully solved case when the villain was already behind bars.

Very good look for the Met." He clapped a hand on James's shoulder.

Hartridge stood a little way away with Iris Johnson's family, and as soon as the press left, he walked them over to the place where the builders had uncovered her remains, just the day before.

"You happy with your bagman?" Halberd asked, eyeing Hartridge and the weeping mother, sister and her husband who were all that was left of Iris's family.

"Very, sir." James glanced at him, sure he was hearing an offer for someone else in that tone. He shut it down immediately. "DC Hartridge's help on this case was absolutely invaluable. As it was for that affair in the summer."

"Good, good." Halberd settled back down. "And Whetford?"

James froze. "DI Whetford, sir?" What was he being asked here?

"He seem alright to you?" Halberd didn't look at him, his gaze settled into the middle distance.

"He seems a little animated by some old case of his that was reopened," James said carefully. "Otherwise, he lets me get on with my job, which I like."

"Yes, that's a good strategy with a go-getter like you, Archer." Halberd nodded sagely. "I heard about the Pollock case. Bad business that, and it's good to hear there's some movement."

"The lab is definitely more advanced now than it was then," James said, knowing full well the new evidence was nothing to do with scientific progress.

"Very true." Halberd sounded thoughtful. "That's a good line to feed the press, actually. I got a couple of press requests just this morning, although I'm not sure how the vultures heard about it. The Met leaks like a sieve."

"I think the case being reopened is quite widely known," James agreed.

"Can't be helped." Halberd clapped him on the shoulder again. "Job well done, Archer. Keep it up." He walked away, and his driver got out of his car and went to open the rear door for him.

James stood quietly for a moment.

It sounded like Whetford was not in a good place. Not if Halberd was asking questions about him.

Hopefully that meant the games he and Galbraith were trying to play with Hartridge and himself would stop.

Hartridge was shepherding the Johnson family back to the car the Met had arranged for them, and he could see they were thanking him for his and the Met's kindness.

Iris Johnson's body had lain beneath the rubble and then the ground for nearly twenty years, and it was fitting that her body was found by the building site crew now, with the belongings Blythe had taken from her so recently in their custody.

They could lay her to rest.

Even though the last few days had been a blur of activity, he walked with a loose-limbed stride over to Hartridge, who was standing next to the Wolseley, watching the Johnsons drive away.

He only needed to think of Gabriella, warm beneath him, skin so smooth he couldn't get enough of touching her, and his mood improved.

"Halberd seemed like he had a lot to say," Hartridge said as James came to stand beside him.

"He made a few comments about Whetford," James said.

Hartridge looked over at him sharply. "About?"

"Nothing specific. Like he was testing the waters. Like Whetford is on the out." James wondered how much Halberd was compromised. He didn't doubt that he was.

"And?" Hartridge asked.

"And he's got reporters asking him about the reopened case. He sounded unhappy."

"How did the press find out about it?" Hartridge wondered.

James was silent.

Hartridge turned. Stared. "You?"

James shot him a grin. "It's a triumph for the Met. Reopening an unsolved case and finding good evidence to convict."

Hartridge frowned. "It sounded like Whetford was unhappy about it, though. Galbraith certainly looked unhappy."

"Maybe it wasn't solved because someone didn't want it solved," James said. "Maybe Whetford made some promises about keeping that case cold, and now, whoopsie, it's heating up."

"In the archives," Hartridge breathed. "You . . ." He trailed off, speechless. "That's why you haven't sent the letter to the Commissioner about what he's up to. You decided to do this instead?"

"I think Whetford might be too busy covering his arse, or watching his back, to worry about either you or me for a while." James shoved his hands into his coat pockets. "Come on, let's get back to the office. It's freezing out here."

"I thought you seemed happier," Hartridge said. "Now I understand why."

James laughed as he slid into the car. "Sure," he said. "That's probably the reason."

author's note

The incidents in this book with the electrified Land Rover are based on a true story in London in the early 60s of a farmer who hated the new traffic warden system and the fines that came with it.

Though it may sound incomprehensible to us, laws against reckless endangerment only came into effect in England and Wales in 1971, and there were no legal consequences for him electrocuting the numerous police officers and traffic wardens who tried to give him parking fines.

The smog mentioned in this book is based on the 1962 London Smog incident. Smog enveloped the city for four days, and resulted in the deaths of 700 people. In the 1950s, deadly pea souper fogs had plagued London and led to the deaths of an estimated 12,000, resulting in the 1956 Clean Air Act. People were given time to switch over to the cleaner forms of energy and heating set out in the Act, and so the problem continued, to a lesser extent, into the 1960s.

I got a lot of inspiration for the police corruption in the 1960s that is a main thread in this story from the three part documentary series (available on YouTube) entitled Bent Coppers: Crossing the Line of Duty.

As for the blackout killer plot, there were several "blackout killers" that operated in World War II. One in London, Gordon Cummins; one in Berlin, (also known as the S-Bahn Murderer) Paul Ogorzow; and one in Melbourne, Australia, (known as the Brownout Strangler) Edward Leonski. There are numerous documentaries available on all these serial killers, many available on YouTube.

also by michelle diener

Historical Fiction Novels

Traffic Warden Mysteries:

Ticket Out

Susanna Horenbout series:

In a Treacherous Court

Dangerous Sanctuary (A short story - available for free, exclusively to readers who sign up to Michelle Diener's New Release Notification List)

Keeper of the King's Secrets

In Defense of the Queen

Regency London series:

The Emperor's Conspiracy

Banquet of Lies

A Dangerous Madness

Other historical novels:

Daughter of the Sky

Fantasy Novels by Michelle Diener

The Rising Wave series:

The Rising Wave (Prequel novella to THE TURNCOAT KING and now included as bonus material in The Turncoat King)

The Turncoat King

The Threadbare Queen

Fate's Arrow

Truth's Blade

Truth's Blade Bonus Short Story (Available free to newsletter subscribers)

Other fantasy novels:

Mistress of the Wind

The Dark Forest series:

The Golden Apple

The Silver Pear

Science Fiction Novels

Verdant String series:

Interference & Insurgency Box Set

Breakaway

Breakeven

Trailblazer

High Flyer

Wave Rider

Peace Maker

Enthraller

Sky Raiders series:

Intended (Short Story Prequel Available Free to Newsletter Subscribers)

Sky Raiders

Calling the Change

Shadow Warrior

Class 5 series:

Dark Horse

Dark Deeds

Dark Minds

Dark Matters

Dark Ambitions: A Class 5 Novella

Dark Class

Dark Class Epilogue: Free on newsletter signup

Collision Course

Short Paranormal Fiction

Breaking Out: Part I (Short story)

Breaking Out: Part II (Novella)

To receive notification when a new book is released, and to receive exclusive copies of numerous novellas and a free audio book, sign up at michellediener.com.

about the author

Michelle Diener is an award winning author of historical fiction, science fiction and fantasy romance. She has released 32 books and numerous novellas and short stories since she was first published by Simon & Schuster's Gallery Books imprint in 2011.

Michelle was born in London and currently lives in Australia with her husband and children.

You can contact Michelle through her website or sign up to receive notification when she has a new book out on her New Release Notification page.

Connect with Michelle
www.michellediener.com

acknowledgments

Once again, thanks to Creative Paramita for the wonderful cover. Massive thanks as always to Claire and Jo, I am always so grateful for your suggestions. Thanks also to Sheila R., Sandra B., Barbara E., & James McR of my ARC team for their eagle eyes.